SING
ALL THE
WAY

BOOKS BY KAREN KING

Snowy Nights at the Lonely Hearts Hotel
The Year of Starting Over

Karen King

SINGLE
ALL THE
WAY

bookouture

Published by Bookouture in 2019

An imprint of StoryFire Ltd.
Carmelite House
50 Victoria Embankment
London EC4Y 0DZ

www.bookouture.com

ISBN: 978-1-83888-073-6
eBook ISBN: 978-1-83888-072-9

To Ann, fellow author and friend. Memories of our joint author visits still make me chuckle.

Chapter One

Sunday, 14 December

Meg

How could Oliver be so cruel? Meg Preston wiped the tears from her cheeks with the back of her hand, sat up and hugged her knees, trying to process everything that had happened. She loved Oliver so much, thought they would be together forever, and now… now she didn't see how they could be. Not after the bombshell Oliver had dropped. He should be apologising, grovelling, explaining himself, not storming out as if *she* were the one to blame, the one who had lied. He knew how important this was to her; how could he deliberately deceive her? She was the one who should have stormed out! How bloody dare he put this on her?

She glanced at the clock: just after ten. Oliver had been gone over two hours now, leaving Meg sobbing on the bed, her world crashing around her ears. She couldn't believe he could be so heartless. Some Christmas this was going to be. And she'd been hoping they'd be starting the new year with something to celebrate. Oliver had made it very clear that there was no chance of that. Well, she'd had enough of him calling the shots. She wasn't waiting for him to return, for an apology and an explanation that she obviously wasn't going to get. She needed to get away, to give herself time to think about it all, to decide if she wanted to be with Oliver now she knew how he really felt. And right now, the answer was no.

Where could she go? She cast her mind over their various friends; they were all happily coupled and didn't need her turning up with her suitcase at this time of night any more than she needed to see their togetherness right now. She didn't fancy going to her parents' house either; her mum would fuss and her dad would lecture, telling her that she and Oliver had made vows and should stick to them. As far as her parents were concerned, marriage was for life. Well, she had thought that too until the horrible events of this evening.

So a hotel room was the best option, at least for tonight, until she was clear about what she wanted to do. Meg grabbed her mobile, did a quick search on nearby room vacancies and booked one in a small hotel about a quarter of an hour away. Right, now she needed to move fast; she wanted to be gone when Oliver came back. Let him be the one sitting at home wondering what *she* was doing! She pulled her case from the top of the wardrobe, heaved it onto the bed and opened it up. What should she take with her when she didn't know how long she'd be gone? She grabbed jeans, jumpers, underwear, pyjamas, her make-up and a hair dryer and placed them in the case, then added a couple of dresses too – she might decide not to come back and would need more than jeans if she was staying at a hotel over Christmas. She wished she could take Laurel and Hardy, their cute mini-lop rabbits, with her; they would be such a comfort and she hated to leave them behind, but what choice did she have? *As soon as I've sorted out what I'm going to do, I'll come back for them*, she promised herself, adding a couple of pairs of shoes, her boots and her laptop and charger to the case then closing it up.

She lugged her case downstairs and left it in the hall while she went into the kitchen to give the bunnies a cuddle. Laurel scampered over to Meg as soon as she entered the room, but Hardy was too busy tucking into a mound of fresh kale. Meg smiled as she watched them. It had been Oliver's suggestion to call them Laurel and Hardy, and she had agreed even though one of the bunnies was male and the other female. After all, Laurel was a female name and suited the tiny, honey-coloured bunny, who always wanted to please, whereas Hardy suited the bigger, fatter, lazier and greedier – but just as gorgeous – white bunny. She loved them both so much and would miss them like crazy. She bent down and scooped up Laurel, who was making her 'happy' noise and flicking her ears. The little bunny licked Meg's hand and snuggled into her. Hardy looked up then went back to nibbling the kale.

'I'm sorry I have to go, but I'll be back soon.' Meg kissed Laurel on the forehead then put her back in the pen and stroked Hardy, who was still eating. 'Be good and don't squash Laurel,' she told him. Hardy loved to lie on top of Laurel, and Meg and Oliver often joked that the white bunny would get so fat that one day he'd flatten his companion. She closed the pen sadly. She didn't want to leave her pets behind, didn't want to leave her home either. But she couldn't bear to be here when Oliver returned. He had deceived her and ruined the future they had always planned. She didn't see how she could ever forgive him for that. She took her notebook out of her handbag, ripped out a page and scribbled a note to Oliver:

You've really hurt me. I can't believe that you've lied to me over something as important as this. I've gone away to think about whether I want to be with you now I know how you really feel.
Meg

No kisses. She placed the note by the sugar bowl, went back into the hall, grabbed her case and walked out.

She'd unpacked at the hotel and had a bath before her phone rang. She looked at the screen. Oliver. And it was almost midnight. She'd answer it. Maybe now he'd thought about it, and come back to find Meg gone, he might want to apologise, to tell her that he hadn't meant it.

'I can't believe you've walked out just because of what I said. Is that all I mean to you?' Oliver shouted down the phone. No apology, then.

Meg took a deep breath. 'Well, I obviously don't mean much to you as you've deceived me for years!' she retorted.

'You're making this more than it is—'

'Really?' She pressed her fingers to her temple as a dull ache began to form. 'Have you any idea how much you've hurt me? I don't want to talk to you, let alone be with you right now. I need some space to think.'

'I didn't deceive you. You're the one who pushed me into a corner, wanting a decision right now. And just because I don't give you the one you want, you walk out! I thought you loved me. That our relationship meant more than that to you.'

'And I thought you loved me, but obviously you don't, otherwise you would have told me the truth sooner.'

'You're being unreasonable, Meg—'

'How bloody dare you call *me* unreasonable?' she yelled then ended the call and turned her phone to silent. She didn't want to talk to Oliver any more tonight.

*

It took her a long time to fall asleep, and then it was a restless one. She woke early and reached for her phone, hoping to find a message from Oliver saying he was sorry and hadn't meant what he'd said, begging her to come home.

No messages, no missed calls, no voicemails.

Well, that showed how much he cared, didn't it? Shaking her head sadly, she realised she couldn't go back. Nothing would ever be the same between them.

It's nearly Christmas, Meg. You can't split up at Christmas.

Oliver had left her with no choice. There was no way she could spend Christmas Day smiling and being jolly at her parents' house, with Dan and Katya and little Tom, pretending that everything was okay when it wasn't. Her whole world had been blown apart and Oliver didn't seem to understand how devastated she was.

She wasn't even sure her parents would understand. Their marriage was rock-solid, and they believed in working through their differences – not that she could remember many arguments between them when she and Dan were growing up; it was mainly a quiet, peaceful household. 'You should respect each other's opinions,' her father had always said when she and her brother, Dan, had argued. Well, she respected Oliver's opinion and his right to keep some things private, but this was something he should have told her about when they first got together, and definitely before they'd got married. She loved him so much but didn't see how their marriage could continue when it was built on such an enormous lie which had a massive impact on their marriage.

I'll go away for Christmas, she decided. *I'll spend it quietly by myself, give myself time to come to terms with things.*

She picked up her phone and sent Oliver a message.

I don't see how we can get past this, Oliver. I really don't. I'm going away for Christmas, to give me time to think about it. I want you to think about it too, to make sure that really is your final decision.

A message shot back.

Fine. If that's all I mean to you, go ahead. And yes, it's my final decision.

Meg read it, shocked and hurt at the brief contents and the speed of the reply. Obviously he wasn't even prepared to discuss this. She typed back:

Then we're over. I'll be in touch for my things in a couple of weeks and to collect Laurel and Hardy.

Then another message followed.

The bunnies are staying with me.

She'd half-expected – hoped – that he might try to talk her out of leaving, to try and salvage their marriage, but obviously he didn't care. Fuming, she shot a message back.

You're not having the bloody bunnies.

She'd have to let her parents know that she and Oliver wouldn't be coming to them for Christmas. Then she'd book herself in somewhere for a week or so, until she sorted herself out. Heartbroken, she called her mum. It went straight to answerphone.

'I'm sorry, Mum, but me and Oliver have split up. We won't be coming over on Christmas Day,' she gabbled. 'I'm really sorry to let you all down but I need to get away for a bit.'

She sat up on the bed, her head resting on her bent knees, her phone still in her hand. What should she do? Where could she go? She could maybe stay at this hotel over Christmas; it didn't seem that busy but it was a bit close to home. She wanted to put more than a quarter of an hour's distance between her and Oliver, to get right away from Exeter. Maybe she could rent a little cottage? But then she would be completely on her own. Is that what she really wanted? She might be better off in a hotel where she could mix with other people if she wanted to. She started to do an Internet search on Christmas holiday breaks.

She caught her breath as her phone rang, feeling a pang of disappointment as her mum's name and image appeared on the screen. She'd hoped it was Oliver, begging her not to leave him. Did he really care so little about her?

She wasn't sure she was up to talking to her mum. She would have a dozen questions and Dad would probably be shouting in the background, telling Meg to talk it through, that they had made vows, that if they loved each other they could sort it out. The ringing stopped. Then it started again. Mum was determined to talk to her, so she might as well get it over with.

'Oh, Meg, sweetheart, what's happened?'

The sound of her mum's concerned voice brought a lump to Meg's throat. 'I don't want to talk about it, Mum, it's too upsetting, and I don't think we can fix it.' Her voice broke. 'I need to get away for Christmas, think things over.'

'Then come with me, we can spend Christmas together. I've… I've actually just rented a cottage near Boscastle, down in Cornwall, until the second of January. There's plenty of room for you too and it's a lovely area.'

'Are you going with Dad?' Meg was confused. She'd thought the family Christmas at home was all planned, same as every year. When had they decided to go away? And why? She couldn't remember the last time her parents had gone away together. Dad was a homebody, preferring familiar surroundings.

'Not with your father, no,' her mum replied. 'I don't know exactly how to tell you this. Especially right now.' She paused. 'I'm leaving, Meg. I'm leaving your dad.'

'W-what?' Meg stammered. Her parents were splitting up? She couldn't take it in. She had thought they were happy together. How could they be splitting up after all this time? 'Why?' she asked. 'What's happened, Mum?'

'I… Look, it's complicated. I don't want to talk about it on the phone, let's both talk when we're at the cottage – if you want to, that is. Please say you'll come, Meg,' her mother said. 'It's only about a ninety-minute drive. I'm setting off later this morning and I'll send you the location so you can drive down when you're ready. It's probably best if we each go in our own car in case one of us wants to go home at any point.'

Her parents lived less than half an hour's drive away so they could easily have shared a ride, but Meg guessed Mum was right. She might not want to stay until January. They might drive each other mad! She and her mum got on fairly well, but even so, over two weeks with just the two of them in a cottage could be difficult, especially as they were both bound to be emotional. She still couldn't get her head around the fact that her mother had walked out. What on earth had happened? She might as well go for Christmas though. It was better than spending it alone. And she had to find out what had happened with her mum and dad. Maybe she could get them back together again. 'Okay. I'll come. Thanks, Mum,' she agreed.

'You will? I'm so pleased. I've got to go now. See you later, love.'

A few seconds later a message zinged in, showing an image of a pretty terraced cottage in a place called Goolan Bay.

Meg stared at it, still stunned from the phone call. Why was her mum leaving her dad, and why go to Goolan Bay of all places? She had never known her parents to go to Cornwall. Why had Mum chosen to spend Christmas there?

Chapter Two

Sally

As soon as she'd sent the message, Sally Carter sat down, shaking. She couldn't believe she'd actually told Meg that she was leaving Ted. She hadn't even told Ted yet! In fact, she'd only just made the decision. Yes, the idea had been playing around in her mind for a long time now. It had gotten stronger just lately but she had been shelving it until after Christmas. Then she'd received Meg's answerphone message, and although it had shocked her – she'd thought Meg and Oliver were happy together – she'd realised that it must be something important for Meg to take such a step. Meg adored Oliver. She would never split up with him, especially just before Christmas, if it wasn't something serious. It was a brave step not to put up with whatever it was until at least the holidays were over.

It had given Sally the courage to finally take that step too. She didn't *want* to act all merry on Christmas Day, cook dinner, make small talk with the family, pretend everything was all hunky-dory. She didn't want to settle for spending the rest of her life on autopilot with Ted. She wanted to get away. Why wait until after Christmas?

Where could she go at such short notice, though? She didn't want to tell any of their friends yet, especially Frances and Martin – thank goodness they were off on that cruise tomorrow; Frances would be all questions and then gossip about it to everyone they knew. And a hotel was so… busy. She wanted somewhere she could completely get away from it all. Give her a chance to think, to be sure she was making the right decision to leave Ted. She was so miserable and didn't think he was happy either, but they'd been together so long…

Then it had come to her: Smuggler's Haunt, the little fisherman's cottage near Boscastle that held so many happy memories for her. She just hoped that it wasn't booked up. She did a quick Internet search, saw to her relief that the cottage was free until 2 January, and immediately booked it with her credit card. Then she'd phoned Meg.

She felt a mixture of trepidation and freedom: she really wanted this, had wanted it for so long, but now she had to break it to Ted. Not a prospect she was relishing. She'd pack a case first then go out into the garden where Ted was busy, as usual, and tell him.

She went up to their bedroom and started packing some things into a suitcase. She was almost done when the bedroom door opened and Ted walked in, dressed in his usual gardening gear of faded navy corduroy trousers, red and blue checked shirt, and navy quilted body warmer. He'd put on some weight since he'd retired, despite the hours he spent in the garden, and his cheeks were always ruddy – probably the fresh air, and the tipple of Scotch he liked to have every night before bed. He glanced at the case, a puzzled frown creasing his forehead. 'Where are you going now? You never mentioned you were going away.' She could hear the mix of resentment and annoyance in his voice.

'Meg and Oliver have split up. I'm going to spend a couple of days with her.'

'What? Why?' Astonished, he sat down on the edge of the bed. 'I thought they were both happy together.'

'I don't know why but it sounds serious.'

'Where are you both going?'

'Cornwall. Meg needs my support.' She carried on folding her clothes into the case, then closed it.

'Cornwall?' he repeated, puzzled. 'How long for? And what about Christmas? Meg's still coming for Christmas, isn't she?'

Is that all he could think about? His traditional Christmas? 'Oliver and Meg have *split up*, Ted. I should think Christmas is the last thing on her mind.' She paused. 'And it's the last thing on my mind too, right now. I'm not sure when I'll be back.' She took a deep breath. 'Or if I'll be back.'

He stared at her uncomprehendingly. 'What do you mean?'

'Isn't it time we stopped pretending? Meg's marriage isn't the only one in trouble. Our marriage hasn't been working for a long time, Ted. We both want different things in life. I think… I think we'd be better off apart,' she stammered.

She saw his confusion turn to hurt. 'You mean you're leaving me? At Christmas?' He ran a hand over his almost bald head. 'Is this because I don't want to go gallivanting around the world on a perishing cruise with Frances and Martin?'

That was typical Ted. He never listened to her, never tried to understand. 'No, Ted, I'm not leaving you because you don't want to go on the cruise. I'm leaving you because you don't want to do *anything* or go anywhere with me.' She stuffed another pair of leggings into the case and slammed the lid shut. 'I don't even think you actually want to be with me, you've just got used to me being here.' She looked over at him, silently begging him to understand. To say something that made her feel like he cared. 'There's so much I want to do with my life, Ted, whereas you don't seem to want to do anything except be out in the garden or play bowls.'

Ted snorted. 'What's this? Some kind of old-age crisis?' He stood up and pointed a finger at her. 'I never stop you doing anything. You can live your life how you want. And you do.'

If only. 'That's not true, and you know it. When I go anywhere you sulk about it even though you refuse to do anything with me. Don't you see we live separate lives, Ted? We're not a couple any more; we're just like friends who share the same house.'

Ted glared at her. 'And what's wrong with being friends? Life isn't all about soppy stuff, you know. It's about getting along. We're too old to be bothering about all that romantic nonsense.'

'That's just it, we aren't too old for romance, Ted. You're never too old for romance.' She sighed. 'We don't share any interests or do anything together any more. I'm sorry, but – especially with what's going on with Meg and Oliver – I can't face pretending we're happy together just for the sake of a family Christmas. I'm sure Dan and Katya will invite you to their house; it won't hurt them to cook the dinner for a change. I'm going away with Meg and I don't know if I'm coming back.'

'Well, you have your "singletons" Christmas then, see if I care. Of course you'll be back. And when you do, I hope you'll have changed your attitude and learnt to appreciate what you've got. There's plenty of women who would love to have a steady, reliable husband like me,' retorted Ted, and he walked out of the room.

He's treating it like I'm going on a holiday, Sally thought crossly, *and he's only miffed because it has left him in the lurch at Christmas. Typical Ted to pooh-pooh my feelings and just carry on with life as normal.*

When she went downstairs with her case, he was back in the garden.

'I'm off now. I'll keep in touch,' she told him.

He looked up, his face stony. 'Do what you want. You always do.'

Which is wrong, she thought. She hardly ever did what she wanted. But starting from now, she was going to.

Chapter Three

Meg

Meg checked out of the hotel and drove down to Goolan Bay in a mixture of disbelief and shock as she tried to get her head around the fact that her parents had split up. Something major must have happened for her mum to walk out after all these years – it was their fortieth anniversary in a few months – and right before Christmas too.

Surely her dad hadn't had an affair? Meg shook her head. He wouldn't. Dad had never been the sort to go off with another woman; he was solid, reliable. Had Mum found someone else, then? Surely not. Although she did still turn heads, even in her sixties. Mum looked years younger than her age and was so outgoing and popular. No, she wouldn't cheat on Dad. It had to be something else. But what? And why had Mum chosen Cornwall for her escape? The announcement had certainly taken Meg's mind away from her own troubles for a while.

She turned off the motorway and drove down isolated country lanes, flanked by bare-branched trees silhouetted in the dusk. It looked so eerie; she was a little spooked and wished she'd been able to set off earlier and arrive before it got dark. Still, according to Google Maps she would be there in ten minutes. The app led her down another long country lane which wriggled through a small village of whitewashed houses, the roads so narrow that she was thankful she was driving her Volkswagen Golf, not the van they used for their party planning business. Her mother had said there was no parking at the cottage itself but plenty of road parking nearby at this time of year.

She glanced around for an empty spot and was relieved when she drove around a corner and found one, noticing her mother's silver Corsa already parked a few spaces away. Meg's phone buzzed as she pulled on the handbrake. *Oliver?*

She took her phone out of her bag and was pierced by a prick of disappointment when she saw her best friend Helen's name flashing on the screen. Her first instinct was to ignore it but then curiosity got the better of her. Helen normally texted, and if she did call, it was on a Friday or Saturday evening when they'd both finished work.

'Are you okay, babe?' Helen asked as soon as Meg answered the call. 'Oliver was in Mersey's last night, totally off his head, telling everyone you had dumped him.'

Anger surged through her. How could he go out drinking as soon as she had left, as if he was celebrating being single, and then announce their private business to everyone? She'd thought Oliver was better than that. They had both agreed to never talk about private stuff to anyone, and she had kept to that promise. Always. That's why she hadn't told Helen that she'd left. Obviously, Oliver had decided to announce it to the world and make her sound like the bad guy.

'The utter bastard!' She then demanded furiously, 'What else did he say?'

'He was a bit too drunk to make much sense, to be honest,' Helen told her. 'I was surprised though. I thought you two were perfect for each other. What's happened?'

'It's personal. I don't want to talk about it right now.' Meg could hear the wobble in her own voice. 'I've come down to Cornwall to spend a few days with Mum. She and Dad have split up too.'

'What! Wow! That must have been a shock.' Helen sounded incredulous.

'It was. Please don't tell anyone.'

'Cross my heart.' There was a pause. 'I'm so sorry, babe. You must be devastated.'

'I am. Look, I've got to go now, Helen. Mum's waiting for me. I'll catch up with you in a couple of days.'

'Okay, babe. Take care. And remember, I'm here if you ever want to talk.'

'Thanks.' Meg slipped her phone into her bag as she got out of the car, pulled on her coat, then grabbed her case out of the boot and made her way along the thankfully well-lit street and around the corner. A row of quaint former fishermen's cottages lined the cobbled street. She checked the names on the doors for Smuggler's Haunt – the name of the cottage Mum had said she was staying at. There it was, half a dozen houses down.

She knocked on the door, and a few seconds later it opened to reveal her mother, clad in black leggings and a long red jumper, her arms outstretched in welcome. 'Meg, darling!'

'Hello, Mum.' She anxiously scanned her mother's face, noticing that her eyes were red as if she'd been crying, but she was wearing make-up and was smiling, as usual. For the first time in her life, Meg wondered what her mother hid behind that perfectly made-up face and permanent smile.

'I'm so sorry about you and Oliver, love,' her mum said as she stepped aside for Meg to pass into the hall. 'Can you patch things up, do you think?'

'I don't see how.' Meg put her case against the wall as her mother closed the door. 'But never mind me and Oliver, what about you and Dad? I can't believe that you've split up! What's happened? He hasn't… he hasn't had an affair, has he?'

Her mum looked surprised. 'Goodness me, no. It's nothing like that.' Her eyes narrowed as she scrutinised Meg's face. 'What about Oliver? Is that why you two have split up?'

Meg shook her head vehemently. 'No, of course not.' Oliver would never cheat on her; she was sure of that.

'Well, now we've got that out of the way, why don't you take off your coat and boots and go and sit in the lounge – first door on the left. I've got a fire burning. I'll bring you a hot drink – coffee and brandy okay? – and we'll talk about things then.'

Coffee and brandy sounded perfect – she had no intention of driving anywhere else today – but before she could reply, her mum had already disappeared into the kitchen to put the kettle on. Meg slipped her coat off and hung it on the coat hanger in the hall, put her boots underneath and headed to the half-open door on the left. As she pushed it open, the warmth from the log fire in the centre of the room hit her. She looked around: the room was small but comfy, with a faded cream-and-blue floral sofa and two matching chairs, the thick seat cushions inviting you to sit down and sink into them, and the big blue scatter cushions just right for resting your head on. She chose one of the chairs which were placed each side of the roaring fire. A beige patterned carpet covered most of the floor, the gap around the edges revealing varnished floorboards. The walls were painted white, with low dark-wood beams, and various nautical pictures and objects hung here and there. Very cosy.

The door opened and her mother came in carrying two steaming mugs. 'Here you are, this will warm you up.' She placed a mug on the coffee table next to Meg then curled up on the other chair cradling the second mug, her legs tucked under her. 'Now do you want to talk about it?' she asked. 'I don't mind if you prefer not to. Although I admit I'm surprised. I like Oliver a lot and always thought you two were perfect for each other.'

Meg didn't want to talk about her and Oliver; she wanted to talk about her parents. To find out why, after almost forty years of marriage, her mother had walked out. Her mind couldn't take it in. Her parents' marriage had seemed rock-solid. She'd thought they were devoted to each other. They were never openly affectionate, that wasn't their way – Dad didn't like public displays of affection – but they always seemed to get on well. Never in a million years had she expected them to split up. 'I will in a bit but first I'd like to know why you've left Dad. What's he done?'

Her mother sighed and gazed at the fire for a few seconds before she answered. 'I don't know how to explain it, Meg. We've drifted apart. All your dad is interested in is his garden and playing bowls. He never wants to go out, go away, do anything with me.'

Meg stared at her, bewildered. Had Mum really walked out just because Dad was a bit of a homebody? 'I know Dad is a bit set in his ways, and that must get you down, but surely that isn't enough to split up over, is it? Besides, you have lots of friends to go out and on holiday with. And Dad loves you and you love him. Don't you?'

Her mum's face crumpled, and she tugged a tissue from the sleeve of her jumper, dabbing her eyes with it. 'That's the trouble, Meg. I don't think we do love each other. On the surface we're jogging along, but we're just tolerating each other, really, and I can't live like that any more. I want more out of life. I want to live. To experience things.' She paused then gushed out, 'I know you might think this sounds silly at my age, but if I'm with a man, I want it to be because he loves me and wants to spend time with me, not because we've been together for years. The thought of living the rest of my life with your dad fills me with dread. There's no… affection between us.' Her cheeks reddened at this admission. 'I can't do it any longer, Meg. I really can't.'

God, this was awful. She hadn't realised her mum felt like this. Poor Dad probably hadn't either. He must be sitting at home, upset and bewildered, wondering what had happened. She'd give him a ring as soon as she had the chance, see if she could get more out of him. She had to get her parents back together for Christmas.

Chapter Four

Sally

The cottage brought back so many memories, as she knew it would. Images of them so in love, so happy. They couldn't get enough of each other, always touching, kissing, holding hands. Curling up on the sofa in the evenings, arms around each other as they watched the little portable TV that had now been replaced by a sleek, modern one, lying in each other's arms in the morning, his wavy chocolate-brown hair half over his eyes, smiling down at her, pulling her towards him for another kiss, hug or more. The cottage had changed, of course, had been modernised, the furniture updated, the metal-framed bed they had shared – the springs squeaking so much when they made love that they had both giggled, hoping the sound didn't carry to the house next door – replaced by a huge divan, but essentially it was the same. She had taken their old room for herself, leaving the other slightly smaller one for Meg, because it didn't seem right for Meg to sleep in the room where they had been so happy, where they would stand every morning, his arm around her shoulders, gazing over the rooftops at the ribbon of shimmering sea beyond. She wondered if the seagulls still pitter-pattered over the roof early in the morning, if they would wake her up with their loud squawks. Probably not as it was winter.

'Mum?'

Meg's voice dragged her out of her thoughts. 'Sorry, were you saying something?'

'I asked you what made you come here. I can't remember us ever coming to Cornwall for our holidays when we were young. I remember going to Weymouth a couple of times, and Woolacombe, but not Cornwall.'

Meg was right. Sally and Ted had never taken Meg and Dan to Goolan Bay. Sally hadn't wanted to. She'd wanted to keep it their special place.

'I came here once a long time ago,' she said slowly. 'I loved it and it seemed like a good place to spend Christmas.'

Meg was staring at her. 'Who did you come with?' She paused. 'It wasn't an old boyfriend, was it?'

'What's with all the questions? Can't we have a relaxing evening and not question each other? Just let each other talk when we're ready?' Sally said, with a note of aggravation in her voice, then she instantly regretted it when she saw the hurt look on Meg's face. 'Sorry, I didn't mean to snap.'

'Why did you? It was an innocent enough question.' Suspicious, Meg narrowed her eyes. '*You're* not having an affair, are you?'

Sally glared at her. 'Of course I'm not! What a question to ask!'

Meg shrugged. 'Well, it would explain why you're being so secretive.'

'It's personal, Meg. I haven't asked you why you've left Oliver, have I? I know you well enough to realise that it isn't a decision you have taken lightly, and that's good enough for me. Just because we are your parents it doesn't mean we aren't entitled to our privacy.'

Meg looked a bit taken aback but then she nodded. 'Okay, I didn't mean to pry. I'm shocked, that's all. You've been together so long. Dad must be devastated.'

'So am I. I didn't want to leave, you know. You've no idea how much I've hung on, tried to make it work…' Sally swallowed the lump in her throat and got up out of the chair. 'Look, I'm going for a stroll – do you want to join me? It's still quite early and the harbour is just down the hill. It'll look so beautiful this time of the evening.'

Meg nodded. 'I'll get my coat.' She was up and out of the room in a flash.

I guess she doesn't want to talk about things any more than I do, Sally thought. When she'd invited Meg to join her, she hadn't thought any further than her daughter needing somewhere to spend Christmas, and that they could keep each other company. It was only natural that Meg would take the break-up hard; she was sure Dan would too. She couldn't bring herself to phone her son and tell him yet; she was dreading his reaction.

As she got up to follow Meg into the hall, Sally wondered why she had left Oliver. *She'll tell me in her own good time*, she thought. *Don't interfere.* But her daughter's pale face and dark eyes worried her. Whatever the reason was, Meg looked completely heartbroken.

Wrapped up in their boots and winter coats – a berry-coloured parka for Meg and a dark blue duffel coat for Sally – they walked down the hill towards the harbour. Sparkling Christmas lights, adorning many of the windows and strung across the streets, twinkled merrily in the darkness while gaily decorated Christmas trees shone out from windows, porches and even a few front gardens.

Sally remembered the narrow street as if it were yesterday, but it had been summer when she'd been here before: the sun had been shining and colourful pots of flowers had covered windowsills and hung in baskets by the doors of the cottages. The picturesque buildings ran right down to the sea, and at the bottom of the hill, set back from the harbour, was the little café where they used to have breakfast. She wondered if it was still there.

She smiled as Meg linked an arm through hers and exclaimed, 'It's so pretty and festive! I wonder if there are any Christmas lights down by the harbour.'

When they reached the bottom of the hill, Meg gasped and looked up at the strings of colourful decorations, their reflections shimmering in the calm, black, velvet sea. 'It's so beautiful.'

But Sally wasn't looking at the lights; she was looking for the café set back a little way from the beach. Her heart flipped when she saw that it was still there. Tears pricked her eyes as the bittersweet memories flooded back. Why had she thought coming here was such a good idea? It had only made things worse.

Chapter Five

Meg

As they walked along the harbour, chatting more easily now, Meg felt herself relaxing. She was ready to talk, she decided; it would be good to get her mother's advice. And she also desperately wanted to find out what had gone wrong in her parents' marriage. *I guess I'll have to start it off*, she thought. Her mother seemed very reluctant to confide. She could understand that in a way; parents were used to keeping their problems from their children, and she guessed that habit continued even when the children were grown up.

'Shall I make us a hot chocolate, then we can talk?' she suggested when they returned home.

'That would be lovely.' Sally tugged off her boots and hung up her coat. 'I'll just pop to the loo.'

As Meg made her way into the kitchen, her mind flipped back to the previous evening, when her life had been blown apart. It had started out so well; she and Oliver had organised and run another children's party and it had been a big success.

*

Meg looked around at all the happy, beaming faces. This was what she loved most about her job as a party planner: seeing the pleasure on the children's faces. Amazing Anna, with her bright red curly hair, flamboyant rainbow-coloured cloak and matching hat, was a brilliant magician and had held them all enthralled with her skilful tricks. The last one, making a row of feathers change colour simply by passing her hand over them, had made the children gasp with amazement. She'd been right to give Anna a chance, although Oliver hadn't been sure she was experienced enough – she'd admitted this was only her second party, but Meg was always one for giving people chances.

She glanced over at Oliver, who was setting up the music for the games, his dark hair flopped over his face. The same colour hair as Meg's, although, like today, Meg often wore her hair up in a messy bun whereas Oliver's curled wildly beneath his ears. Sometimes, when they lay in bed together, their hair spread out on the pillow, it was hard to tell whose hair was whose. She often teased him about it, and he would laugh, threatening to put it up in a man bun so they could look like twins.

As if he felt her gaze, Oliver looked up, his rich brown eyes meeting hers, his face breaking into a grin as he put up his thumb, acknowledging that he agreed with her choice. For a moment their eyes locked and an intense surge of love gushed through her. Seven years they'd been together, five of them married, and she loved him more each day. He looked the same now as the day they'd met, handsome in a dreamy, romantic kind of way, his thick dark eyebrows and dark stubble enhancing the faraway look that never left his eyes, as if his mind was somewhere else. If she hadn't known, she'd have thought he was an artist or musician, but he was actually a landscape gardener, and the baggy T-shirts he wore hid a fit body, toned from the hours of working outside – although she later found out that he played the guitar well and had once been in a band. Oliver had come to help her dad, Ted, redesign the garden, and Meg had popped in for a cuppa just as Oliver was digging the flower beds. She had fallen in love with him at first sight, and he said he had fallen for her right away too. She'd taken him a mug of coffee – black, one sugar. Their eyes had met as she'd passed him the mug and neither of them had been able to tear their gaze away until her dad had coughed rather awkwardly and broken the spell. Her mother had spotted it, taking a break from complaining about the hours her dad spent in the garden to comment that they'd make a nice couple. When Meg had gone out to retrieve the empty mug, Oliver had asked her out for a drink and they had been inseparable ever since.

Party MO had been Meg's idea – MO standing for Meg and Oliver. She had previously worked for a promotions company and had wanted to run her own party-planning business for some time. Then a couple of years after she and Oliver had got married, Meg was made redundant so she had decided to take the plunge, supplementing party planning with a bit of freelance PR and social media work. She'd persuaded Oliver to come on board, working around his gardening jobs, and they made a good team. Meg loved kids, and Oliver had a natural rapport with them too. He would make a great dad and Meg couldn't wait until they had their own family.

Oliver was playing his guitar now, the children sitting around him, singing along to 'Old MacDonald Had a Farm' as the party was drawing to a close. Parents were already milling in the hall, many of them pausing to listen to Oliver. He always had that effect on people: women fancied him, men wanted to be him, some men fancied him too – she remembered one guy when they'd been visiting Oliver's mum, Faye, in Portugal...

A loud round of applause broke through her thoughts; the song was finished. She smiled and went forward to greet the parents, and to hand out party bags and say goodbye to the children. Several of the parents wanted to enquire about booking a party for their child, so Meg made a note of their names and the birthday dates, promising to email them with information. She'd placed a Party MO card in each party bag too, knowing it might drum up future business.

'Thank you, both. Emily has really enjoyed herself. And it's so nice to not have to organise any of it myself!' Alisha, the mum who had booked the party, said. 'I'll definitely be writing you a nice review on your Facebook page and recommending you to my local mum-friends.'

'We'd appreciate that,' Oliver told her in the rich, deep voice that always made Meg's heart skip a beat. She was sure it had that effect on other women too but had never for one second doubted Oliver's love and loyalty.

'I bet you really push the boat out for your own children's parties,' Alisha said. 'Or do you get someone else to do it so you can enjoy the occasion?'

'We don't have any children yet, but when we do I'm sure we'll go completely over the top organising their parties, won't we, Oliver?' Meg replied, grinning. It was something she was really looking forward to.

'Knowing you, yes!' Oliver nodded.

Alisha smiled. 'Well, enjoy the years before you do have kids. Because once you do, I promise life will never be the same again.' She reached out to grab her toddler before she ran off.

'We are,' Oliver assured her.

It's what Oliver had said right from the beginning when they'd realised how serious they were about each other and the subject of having a family had come up. 'Let's enjoy a few years together first, go out, travel, do things as a couple before we get tied down with kids. Life isn't the same when you have a family.'

'You do want kids though, don't you?' Meg had asked. She'd always wanted a family. She'd grown up in a happy family and wanted the same for herself. Her brother Dan was two years older and already had a little son, Tom. She'd told Oliver as soon as they'd started to get serious that having children was important to her, and if he didn't feel the same he needed to tell her right now, before they got in too deep.

'Of course I do,' he'd said, kissing her forehead. 'Just not yet. We've got plenty of time.'

She hadn't wanted them in those early days either. When they had met she was only twenty-seven and felt, like Oliver, that she needed to have a few years doing what she wanted with her life first. However, over the last couple of years, the longing to have children had grown stronger. She'd broached the subject with Oliver a few times but he'd suggested they leave it a little longer, until he'd finished redecorating their house, getting the garden straight, had another couple of holidays abroad, got Party MO up and running, and she'd agreed it made sense to wait. Only time was running out now: Meg would be thirty-five in two months' time and was very aware that the longer they left it, the harder it might be to have a baby. Besides, she felt ready now. She wanted to be still young enough to do things when the children had grown up. Her mother had been twenty-five when she'd had Dan, twenty-seven when she'd had Meg, and had always been a buzz of energy; still was. She was frequently out with her friends, especially since she'd retired from her teaching job three years ago, the same time as her dad, a civil servant. Meg wanted to have children while she was still young enough to run around with them, take them swimming, to theme parks. And Oliver was three years older than her. He'd be almost forty by the time their baby was born even if she fell pregnant right away. She'd talk to Oliver tonight. She smiled at the thought of a mini-Meg or mini-Oliver. Maybe both, in time. She'd like two children ideally.

She looked up as a little boy ran back and held his hand up to Oliver, who knelt down and high-fived him. He would make a brilliant dad. It was Christmas in just under two weeks' time. Wouldn't it be lovely if they decided it was finally time to try for a family in the new year? They could have a baby by next Christmas. How amazing would that be?

*

I was so happy then, Meg thought as she took the milk out of the fridge and poured it into a saucepan to warm up. She spooned the cocoa powder into two mugs and her mind drifted back to later that day, as they packed the party equipment away, when it had all gone wrong.

*

'The party went well, didn't it?' Meg said as they cleared the hall, piling all their party equipment into the bright yellow van with balloons painted all over it and 'Party MO' written across the sides in rainbow colours. Oliver had been hesitant about painting the van yellow at first, but Meg had persuaded him that they wanted it to look bright and jolly and to stand out. She'd designed business cards, flyers and a website in the same design. Working in promotion, she knew how important branding was and wanted to give the image that Party MO were fun, professional and unique. They specialised solely in parties for children at the moment because they wanted to build a reputation in one field, but later they planned to branch out into parties for adults too, celebrating all sorts of occasions. They had big plans, she and Oliver.

'It was great, and we've had three more bookings from parents already. Christmas is quiet though – thank goodness, because we need to put the van in for a service,' Oliver said when everything had been put into the back of the van. He closed the doors. 'Fancy a drink at the pub to celebrate?' They often did this, popping into the local pub to unwind after a party.

'Why don't we get a bottle of wine and celebrate at home instead?' she suggested. 'We could get a takeaway too?' Home was cosier and more intimate, much more suitable for raising the subject of starting a family. Tonight seemed the perfect time for it: Oliver had enjoyed himself so much with the kids – he always did – and the work was coming in. How brilliant it would be to tell her parents on Christmas Day that they were planning a family.

'Chinese?' Oliver grinned.

'Perfect.' She grinned back.

They stopped for the Chinese and bottle of wine on the way home. As soon as they opened the front door, they heard Laurel and Hardy, chattering loudly.

'Happy to see us, are you?' Meg called as she carried the Chinese takeaway into the kitchen while Oliver, his guitar slung over his shoulder, carried the wine. Meg put the takeaway down on the table and made straight for the big pen pushed against the kitchen wall. Oliver carefully laid the guitar against the wall, then took two plates out of the cupboard and started dishing up their food.

'Have you two been good, then?' Meg cooed as she opened the door of the pen that was the bunnies' home when Meg and Oliver were both out. Although both rabbits were house-trained, and the electrical wires were all covered up, she still worried about leaving them to roam if she and Oliver were out for more than an hour or so. Hardy dashed

out first, dancing around her feet, followed by Laurel. The two little
rabbits leapt around Meg and Oliver, making the soft purring noise
that indicated they were happy.

Meg took a bag of rabbit treats out of the cupboard under the
sink and gave one to each bunny, kneeling down to fuss them. 'You're
such a pair of cuties, aren't you?' she said softly. They'd bought the two
adorable rabbits for their first wedding anniversary, both wanting pets
but knowing they were out so much it wouldn't be fair on a dog, and
Oliver wasn't really a cat-lover. His mum had had a cat when he was
younger, and it kept bringing home dead mice and birds, which Oliver
had found upsetting. Meg had suggested having house bunnies as she'd
had a rabbit as a child and had loved those precious moments when
she'd been allowed to bring Benji inside and cuddle him on her lap.

Oliver grinned over at her. 'The food's ready. Do you want to eat
at the table in here or on a tray in the lounge?'

'Let's eat here and let the bunnies run around for a bit, then we can
finish off the wine in the lounge,' she suggested.

They sat chatting as they tucked into their meal – sweet-and-sour
chicken with egg-fried rice for Meg, chow mein for Oliver – talking
about their week at work, how the day had gone, their plans for Party
MO. Then they opened a second bottle of wine and headed into the
lounge, each carrying a sleepy rabbit.

Meg sat with Hardy on her lap while Oliver stroked Laurel. It had
been such a good idea to get them, she thought as she often did; they
were so adorable and hardly any work at all.

'Will you play me your new song?' she asked. Oliver had been
working on a song the last couple of weeks and she was eager to hear
it, but he would never let anyone hear or read his songs until they
were finished.

He looked a bit doubtful. 'It's still not quite ready. I need to work on the lyrics a bit more.'

She lifted her hand and touched his cheek. 'Please. It might help you tweak it if you sing it aloud.' She loved to hear Oliver sing; his voice was so rich and tender, it often brought tears to her eyes. Ballads and slow love songs were his favourite.

His face broke into a smile and he placed his hand on top of hers, caressing it gently. 'Okay.' He passed Laurel to Meg then eased himself off the sofa and padded barefooted across the carpet to the kitchen, coming back a few minutes later with his guitar. Sitting cross-legged on the floor in front of Meg, who was now stroking both sleeping bunnies, he strummed the strings for a little while, getting the tune, then, satisfied, he started to sing:

> *Love makes you walk over mountains,*
> *Through roaring flames and raging seas.*
> *Love sees you through when times are tough,*
> *But sometimes love isn't enough.*

As he sang she thought how much she loved him, and wanted a family with him. Their life was wonderful as it was but becoming a family would make it even more perfect. Love was definitely enough for them.

'That's amazing,' she told him, clapping enthusiastically. The bunnies were awake again now and both jumped down onto the floor, scurrying over to the tartan basket they shared. Meg picked up the half-empty wine bottle. 'Shall we finish this off?'

'Go for it.' Oliver put his guitar down and sat beside Meg, taking the glass of red wine that she handed him. She picked up her own glass and snuggled into him, sighing with contentment as he put his arm around her shoulder and pulled her closer, kissing her forehead tenderly. 'Love you,' he said softly.

'Love you too,' she whispered back, turning to look up at him. She was so lucky to have found this wonderful man. They were both lucky. 'Olly…' She paused, trying to form the words in her head.

He smiled at her. 'Ooh, I know that look. What's up?'

'Nothing's wrong,' she reassured him. 'Quite the opposite. The party-planning business is doing well, we both have plenty of other work, we're in a really good place…'

He squeezed her shoulder tighter, his eyes deepening as his smile widened. 'We are. Things are really looking up.'

'So…' She paused again. *What the hell, Meg, just say it.* 'Don't you think this would be the perfect time to start our family?' She saw his forehead crease into a frown and she straightened up to look at him as she quickly added, 'I know it would mean a drop in income for a little while, but it would only be for a few months. I can still do the parties almost until the baby is born, and we can take him or her along with us afterwards.'

Oliver reached out for her hand and held it in his, his expression earnest. 'I don't think it's a good idea yet, Meg. We've just started expanding, and a baby will take up a lot of our time. I think we should focus on building up the business a bit more first.' He licked his lips and she wondered why he suddenly looked so nervous. 'Let's leave it for another couple of years, give ourselves time to be more financially stable.'

'Olly, I'm almost thirty-five. If we wait much longer, I might not be able to have children,' she pointed out. 'I know it's a bit scary to take the step, I'm a little nervous about it too, but we can do it. We'd make great parents. I know we would.' She reached out her hand and tenderly stroked his cheek. 'Just think, a little OllyMeg. How cute would that be?' She imagined planning for the baby, decorating the spare room, buying baby clothes, a pram, a cot, her body blossoming into a big bump, feeling their baby kick inside her tummy. She glossed over the actual birth – something she definitely didn't want to think about – to the moment when they saw their baby for the first time, both staring down proudly at their new son or daughter.

Oliver leant forward, caressing her hand. 'I know you really want a baby, Meg, but I'm not ready yet...'

She stiffened. 'What do you mean, *I* really want a baby? I thought *you* did too? That we both wanted a family...' She drew back and searched his face. 'You do want children, don't you, Olly?'

There was a flash of hesitation on his face and panic filled the pit of her stomach. 'Olly, do you want a family?'

'Yes, of course, but not yet...' He was avoiding her eyes.

'Oliver.' Her tone was sharp, forcing him to look at her. 'Please tell me the truth. Do you want a family or not?'

'I don't know,' he admitted, flushed.

'You. Don't. Know,' she repeated, her voice rising slightly.

'I mean...' He rubbed the stubble on his chin. 'Look, Meg, a baby is a big responsibility, never mind the financial side of things and the fact that we won't be able to work like we do now. What if we don't get it right? If we're rubbish parents?'

'Why should we be? People are having babies every day and they cope. Why shouldn't we? Yes, of course we might find it difficult at first, but we'll soon get used to it.' She placed her other hand over his, clasping it reassuringly, and looked him straight in the eyes. 'We can do this, Olly. I know we can. I'm scared too, but I know we can do it.'

Oliver looked down at their hands joined together, his face downcast, his shoulders slumped. 'I don't think I can do it, Meg. I'm sorry.'

She released his hands and sat back. 'What do you mean?'

For a moment he didn't move, then he lifted his head slowly and his face was like a stony mask. 'I don't want children. Not now. Not ever. I'm sorry.'

She recoiled as if he'd slapped her across the face. 'Y-You don't mean that,' she stammered.

It was as if a shutter came over his eyes. 'I do. I'm sorry but I mean it, I don't want a family.' He reached out for her hand but she snatched it away; shocked and hurt, she jumped to her feet. *How could he do this to me?*

'I love you, Meg. And you love me. We don't need a child to make our love complete. We have each other – that's enough, isn't it?'

She shook her head, her mind a whirl of hurt, anger, heartbreak. 'We talked about this. I told you right at the beginning, when we first got together, that I wanted a family at some point. We talked about it again when we got engaged. And you agreed. You said you wanted a family too. And we can't wait much longer, I probably only have a few fertile years left,' she pointed out.

Oliver was on his feet now too. They were standing at opposite sides of the coffee table, facing each other, the low, black, smoked-glass table a poignant symbol of the divide between them. 'I did. Well, I thought I did, when it was years away. Now you're saying it's got to be now and I can't do it.'

'Do you need more time?' She asked the words calmly, forced herself to unclench her fists. She had to focus, to listen, to make sure she understood what he was saying. This was too important to mess up.

Oliver shook his head, ran his hand through his thick hair. 'I can't do it, Meg. I don't want to be a father. It's too much responsibility.'

She recoiled at the determination in his voice. 'We're happy as we are, aren't we? We don't need a child.'

'I want a *child*. I've always wanted children. And you have always known that. Now you're trying to back out of our plans.'

'And you're acting like all you want me for is my bloody sperm!' he yelled at her.

Meg gasped, her hand going to her mouth, tears springing to her eyes. 'That's a terrible thing to say!'

'And so is trying to force me to have a baby I don't want. I do have a say in this, you know. It would be my child too.'

'I can't believe you conned me into marrying you, knowing that I wanted children. Knowing you didn't. That you've deliberately robbed me of my prime, child-bearing years.' Tears pouring down her face, she ran out of the lounge and into the bathroom, slamming the door shut behind her.

A few minutes later she heard the front door close. Oliver had gone out.

They often rowed but never seriously, and never for long. One of them would say they were sorry then the other one would say they were sorry too, and they would cuddle and make up. This time she didn't see how they could possibly make up. Oliver had betrayed her. He had lied to her. If he'd been honest with her at the beginning, maybe they could have talked about it, worked something out. How long would he have spun it out? Until she was too old to conceive? How could he be so cruel? And to suggest that she was only with him so he could give her a baby... How dare he?

*

The hiss of the milk boiling over dragged Meg's mind back to the present, and she reached for the handle, lifting it off the hob before more of the contents could spill out.

She poured the milk into the mugs, stirring it quickly, then grabbed a cloth to wipe the spilt milk before it set on the hob.

'How's that hot chocolate coming on?' Sally called from the lounge.

'It's coming right now.' Meg put the two mugs on a tray, with a packet of biscuits she found in the cupboard, and took it into the lounge, where Sally was now sitting in front of the fire.

Meg set the tray down on the coffee table between the two chairs then blurted out, 'Oliver doesn't want any children. Ever. That's why we've split up.'

Chapter Six

Sally

Sally listened as Meg haltingly explained how Oliver had finally confessed yesterday that he never wanted children. 'He's deceived me all these years and he knew how much I wanted a family, Mum.' She sniffed. 'I mean, if we had tried and found out we couldn't have children, that would be different. But to pretend that he did want children and now, when we really need to think about starting a family, to refuse to even consider it…' She took a tissue out of her jeans pocket and wiped her eyes.

Sally's heart went out to her. 'That's terrible, I'm so sorry, darling.' She got out of her chair and gave Meg a hug. 'Do you have any idea why he's suddenly decided he doesn't want children?'

'He hasn't *suddenly* decided. It turns out that he's never wanted them. He just didn't tell me. I think he was hoping he could keep delaying it until I was too old.' Meg dabbed her eyes again. 'I hate him for that. All these years I've been thinking that one day we'd have our own little family, and all the while Oliver…' She gulped.

'It's horribly cruel of him, I know, Meg. But Oliver is so good with children, you can see that he loves them. He must have a reason. Can't you talk this through?' Sally asked softly.

Meg jumped to her feet. 'Can't we talk it through? Seriously, Mum? I've split up with Oliver over something really important and you want me to talk it through? You, who seem to have walked out on Dad because he's boring and…' She searched for a suitable word. 'Undemonstrative. How about you talk things through with him instead of tearing our family apart?'

Sally recoiled as if Meg had slapped her across the face and watched sadly as her daughter stormed out of the room. She had known Meg would be hurt. Dan would no doubt be too. How could she explain it to them both? It was hard to say exactly what had made her go. She'd been unhappy for so long but had tried to ignore it. Somehow it had all come to a head yesterday. Her mind went back to the events that had finally caused her to walk out on her marriage and her home.

*

'What do you think?' Frances came out of the changing room and gave a little twirl, the pleated skirt of the navy and white dress swishing around her legs.

'Very smart,' Sally told her. 'Does everyone dress up on the cruise?'

'Oh yes, especially for the meals. Last year we sat at the captain's table, you know.' Frances studied her reflection in the mirror. 'I wonder if I should buy navy or white shoes.'

'Navy,' Sally said firmly. 'They'll look much smarter.'

Frances nodded. 'Yes, I think you're right.' She studied her reflection again, looking satisfied. 'I do wish you and Ted were coming; it would be such fun.'

Frances and her husband Martin had asked Sally and Ted to join them on their Caribbean cruise this year, but Ted had refused right away, saying he and Sally preferred to spend Christmas at home with the family.

'Actually, Ted, maybe it would make a nice change to go away?' Sally had suggested, but Ted had looked horrified.

'Christmas is for family,' he'd said firmly.

Which was all very well for him to say when it was Sally who did all the preparing, cleaning, present-buying and cooking. Ted thought making cups of tea, carving the turkey, refilling the glasses of wine and loading the dishwasher was more than pulling his weight. Sally loved her family, but it would have been nice to have just one Christmas away, to go somewhere different, be waited on and entertained.

Ted had never been one for socialising, which hadn't bothered her so much when the children were little. In fact, Sally had been pleased that Ted wasn't down at the pub a few evenings a week like some of her friends' husbands. And babysitters had been an expense they could ill afford in the early years, so they'd had separate nights out, Ted taking up bowling and Sally going to the cinema and the theatre with Frances and their old school friend, Sylvia.

As Dan and Meg had got older, Sally and Ted had sometimes gone out with friends to see a show, or for a meal, but once a month was more than enough for Ted, and that had lessened as he got older. When Dan and Meg were young and there hardly seemed to be time for each other, Sally and Ted had made so many plans for their retirement: they were going to travel, see a bit of the world, take up hobbies, enjoy their life. However, instead of bringing them closer, retirement seemed to have driven them further apart. Sally had sadly come to the realisation that they had virtually nothing in common any more. She and Ted had grown into different people; the whirl of bringing up two children and the bustle of going to work every day had masked that, but now,

now they were both at home, together for hours, she realised that they were like friends sharing a house. They rarely argued, they were polite, friendly, rubbed along smooth enough on the surface providing neither of them scratched too deep, but there was no togetherness, no sparkle. They wanted different things out of life, and Sally felt like a butterfly trapped in a cage who longed to break free and fly off and spread her wings. She had a list of things she wanted to do, places she wanted to see while she was still fit enough to get about and do it.

'Maybe I can persuade Ted to come next year,' she said to Frances, although she didn't have much hope that she could.

'I hope you can,' Frances shouted from inside the cubicle where she'd retreated to take off her dress. 'He's a bit of a stick in the mud, your Ted. He needs to get out more.' Frances and Martin were out all the time, at one social event or another. They were in so many clubs, and they went abroad on holiday at least four times a year. Sylvia and Graham were the same. Sally couldn't help envying them all. If only Ted had a bit more get up and go.

I guess I should be grateful that Ted isn't a drunk, a gambler, a womaniser... She kept reminding herself of this every time Ted irritated her, which seemed to be constantly at the moment, although she tried very hard to keep a lid on it. She liked a peaceful life; they both did. Arguments and shouting had never been their style. Outside they lived a content, calm existence, but inside her wilting spirit was beating at her ribcage, begging to be let out and soar free.

She bought herself a new dress for Christmas Day in an effort to cheer herself up, then she set off home. Ted would be waiting for his Sunday dinner. Lucky Frances was meeting Martin for lunch at a new brasserie in town. Sylvia and Graham were joining them too.

Ted was in the garden, weeding. It amazed – and irritated – her how he could find so much to do out there, even in the winter. How could he enjoy messing with dirt in the bitter cold?

He glanced up as she came out the back. 'Have you had a good time?'

She wanted to shout, *No!* A good time was going to a West End show, or a holiday abroad soaking in the culture, things she desperately wanted her and Ted to do, not just shopping with Frances and listening to her talking excitedly about the cruise she and Ted could have gone on too, if only he wasn't so set in his ways. She tried to keep the resentment out of her voice as she said, 'Frances was shopping for clothes for the cruise. It sounds so much fun. Perhaps we could go another time.'

Ted leant on his spade. 'You know I don't like the idea of being on water. Maybe you and Frances could go on a cruise together in the summer?'

That was Ted's answer whenever she asked him to go somewhere. 'Go with your friends.'

She didn't want to go with her friends. She wanted to go with her *husband*. She wanted them to do all the things they had said they'd do when they retired, before Ted had decided he no longer wanted to do them. She remembered on their honeymoon how they'd sat in bed talking about all the things they were going to do, the places they would go, the dreams they had. Then Dan had come along, followed by Meg a couple of years later, and their dreams had been postponed as paying the mortgage and looking after their precious family had taken priority. They'd do it all when the children had grown up, they'd promised each other. Somewhere along the years, Ted had wanted to do those things less and less.

'What time will dinner be?' Ted asked. 'I'm a bit peckish.'

She bit back the retort that he could have put the meat in while she was out. 'I'll get the beef in now. Fancy a cuppa and a piece of cake to tide you over?' she asked, hoping he would stop his gardening for a bit and come and sit down, talk to her. They rarely actually had a conversation. And as for making love or any other kind of affection, that had gone out of the window years ago. Ted considered they were too old for all that 'lovey-dovey' stuff.

'Love one.' Ted nodded. 'Bring it out, will you? There's still a bit to be done on the garden yet.'

There always is, she thought, annoyed. It's a wonder Ted didn't put a camp bed in his shed and live in the perishing garden!

She put the oven on and took Ted's favourite blue-and-white striped mug out of the cupboard. Ted was a creature of habit, he liked routine, normality, his own mug, builder's tea with two sugars with every meal, cosy evenings in front of the fire. For years it hadn't bothered her too much, but now, since they had retired and spent most days together, it really irritated her. How she wished she could persuade Ted to step out of his comfort zone and do something different now and again. It would be lovely to spontaneously go out for an hour or so this evening instead of spending it yet again in front of the TV. She didn't want to exist; she wanted to *live*.

She made two mugs of tea and took Ted's tea and a slice of fruit cake out to him, came back and put the beef in the oven to roast, then sat down at the kitchen table with her drink to check the Christmas list. There was a week and half to go. She ticked the items off one by one: turkey ordered, Christmas cake iced, most of the presents bought, just a bit more Christmas food to get in and mince pies to make. She'd already brought the tree down from the attic and decorated it – silver and blue baubles this year. Ted had been aghast; they always had red and gold. 'It's a family tradition,' he'd said, but Sally had been desperate for something to be different even if it was only the tree!

Oh, if only we were going on the cruise like Frances and Martin. She sighed as she nibbled the end of her pen.

To be honest, it wasn't even the cruise that specifically appealed to her; and good friends that they were, Frances and Martin could be trying company to spend two weeks with, especially as Martin tended to be a bit pompous. It was the idea of doing something new. Of breaking away from the traditional Christmas lunch with Dan, his wife and little Tom, Meg and Oliver. She loved seeing them all but after a few hours catching up, swapping presents, playing a couple of board games, they would all go home, leaving just her and Ted. Ted would fall asleep in front of the TV, as usual, then they'd go to bed, where he'd immediately fall asleep again. Then that would be it, Christmas over.

Next Christmas has to be different. I'll make sure of it, she thought determinedly.

*

She hadn't realised then how different this Christmas would be. Giving the dwindling fire a stoke, she decided it wasn't worth putting another log on now. She doubted if Meg would be down again this evening, which gave Sally a bit longer before she had to tell her 'why I walked out' story. She sat back in her chair, her mind going back to the argument that had caused her to leave.

*

It was a couple of hours before the door opened and Ted came in, minus the wellies he'd left by the back door, his empty mug in his hand. 'Is dinner almost ready?'

'It'll be about ten minutes. There's just enough time for you to get cleaned up,' Sally told him, getting the plates out of the cupboard. Honestly, it was dark now. What did Ted find to do in the garden when he couldn't see properly, despite the lights he had set up?

She watched resentfully as her husband padded across the kitchen floor in his thick gardening socks and disappeared into the downstairs washroom to get cleaned up. She flicked the switch of the kettle back down and washed up his mug so she could make him another cup of tea.

'Beef and Yorkshire pud, is it?' Ted asked as he walked back in, crossed the kitchen and sat down at the kitchen table, where Sally had just put his mug of tea.

Of course it was beef and Yorkshire pudding. They always had beef and Yorkshire pudding on a Sunday. Ted liked traditional food: steak and kidney pie with chips, stew and dumplings, roast chicken and potatoes with two greens. Sally had tried to broaden his tastes a few times over the years, serving up curry, paella, lasagne. Ted had frowned, disappointedly picked at the food and asked her if they could have a proper meal next time. In the end she'd given up trying to change his tastes.

She dished out the food, poured herself a glass of water, and sat down opposite him.

'I've been thinking, I might get myself a new shed for next year. That one's chock-a-block. Maybe we could get a summer-house style; you might enjoy sitting out in it, reading a book and chatting to me while I work.' He cut up a roast potato and bit into it.

She couldn't think of anything worse. She didn't want to spend the summer sitting in a glammed-up shed reading or watching Ted gardening. She wanted to be paddling in the Mediterranean Sea, sunbathing on a far-flung beach in an exotic location, riding a camel across the desert. She wanted to see the world. If only she could persuade Ted to see the world with her.

'I've been thinking too,' she said. 'Why don't we go out for the day tomorrow? We could have a drive out and have a bit of lunch – it'll make a nice change.' *Please say yes*, she thought.

'I've got quite a bit to do in the garden: the sprouts still need picking and the cabbages need weeding.'

There was always an excuse. But she wasn't going to give up this time, not like she usually did. Things *had* to change.

'How about we go away for a week right after Christmas, then? Somewhere warm? It would be a lovely start to the new year.'

Ted shook his head. 'January's a busy time in the garden. I can't go away then.'

'February, then, or March?' Her voice sounded desperate even to her own ears.

Ted chewed on a piece of beef before answering. 'I don't really like going away…'

'You don't like doing *anything*,' Sally snapped, then seeing the hurt look cross his face, she checked her tone. She didn't want to argue; Ted would only go off in a huff and sulk all evening. *Oh, if only he wasn't such a stick in the mud.* 'I really want to go on holiday, Ted. I want to finally do all the things we planned on doing when the kids grew up. Remember?' she said, her voice softer now. 'We said we'd go out and explore the world, take short city breaks, cruises, spend a couple of weeks soaking up the sun and the culture whenever we could.'

Ted pursed his lips the way he did when he was getting annoyed. 'We were younger then, Sal. Things change. We've got a good life, no money worries, mortgage paid off, time to spare. Why can't you be happy with that instead of always wanting something else?'

It was a long speech for Ted and the resentment in his voice annoyed her. She wasn't asking much, for goodness' sake! 'There's more to life than these four walls and the garden,' she snapped. 'I want to get out and about, to enjoy myself while I still can. You don't seem to want to do anything or go anywhere.'

Ted thumped his mug down on the table, his face growing red with anger. 'That's because I'm content, Sal. I'm happy with my life as it is. We're nearly pensioners, for God's sake, not teenagers. It's enough for me for us to grow old together, in this house, seeing the family regularly, ambling along. It's not enough for you though, is it? You think it's boring, I'm boring. You want to be like Frances and Martin – but they're not happy. Everyone knows Martin has a wandering eye but Frances ignores it because she likes their lifestyle. Is that what you want our life to be like?'

This was typical Ted: any time she hinted that she wanted to change their life in any way, he went on the defensive, knowing she would back down to keep the peace. Well, this time she wasn't going to. She was only asking for the occasional holiday and night out, things that most couples did as a matter of course.

She took a sip of her water and calmly put the glass down again. 'I'm not saying that at all, and you very well know it, so stop getting all grumpy. I don't think it's a lot to suggest we go for a holiday abroad. Surely you can manage one week away from the garden and your precious bowls? Or doesn't what I want matter?'

Ted stood up. 'All I ever hear is what you want. Well, I don't always want the same things as you. And while I would never stop you doing anything, I don't think you should try and force me into doing something I don't want to do either.' He took his mug and plate over to the sink, then put them in the dishwasher. 'Now I'm back off to the shed for a bit.'

Sally watched, anger surging inside her, as Ted walked out of the back door, pulled on his wellingtons and went down the garden path. As far as Ted was concerned, that was it, subject closed. If Sally wanted to go on holiday or for an evening out, she usually had to go without him. Then put up with his sulking for a couple of weeks before she went, and for a few days when she came back.

Obviously her happiness, her dreams, meant nothing to him.

Maybe *she* didn't mean anything to him, not in the way she wanted to. They had individual friends, interests, lives. There was no intimacy between them and hadn't been for years. And Ted was happy for it to remain that way.

Well, she wasn't. Being with Ted was killing her spirit. She felt like she was withering away inside, just going through the motions each day, yearning for a better life.

She could leave him.

The thought had been going through her mind a lot for a while now. At first it had shocked her and she'd pushed it away quickly, but then it had interested her and she'd mulled it over, imagining a life of doing exactly what she wanted. A life of not feeling guilty because she wanted different things from Ted.

But it would be a life *without* Ted.

How could she do that? Next year they would be celebrating their fortieth wedding anniversary. It was such a milestone. But it felt more like a millstone. Hanging around her neck.

Ted would be devastated. And what would Meg and Dan say? And their friends? Everyone seemed to think that Sally and Ted would be together forever. At one time she had thought that too, but now the thought of spending the rest of her years with Ted horrified her. She felt like she was being suffocated.

I need to get away, to think. Maybe after Christmas I will go away by myself, think about what to do. I've just got to get through Christmas.

*

Little had she realised that the very next day she would leave Ted, Meg would leave Oliver, and they would both be planning to spend their Christmas together in Smuggler's Haunt.

There's still over a week until Christmas, she reminded herself. *Perhaps Meg and Oliver will make up.* She hoped so. She very much doubted if she and Ted would though. She wasn't even sure she wanted to. For the first time in years she felt like she could breathe, like she could be herself. And that was a good feeling, even if it was mingled with sadness.

Chapter Seven

Tuesday, 16 December

Meg

Meg slept restlessly and was up early the next morning, only to find when she'd showered, dressed and gone downstairs that her mother had been up long before her. 'Gone to the shop for some bread and more milk. Back soon,' read the note propped up by the kettle. She guessed that Mum hadn't slept very well either. And they never had got around to fully discussing why she had left Dad. Instead her mum had been too busy lecturing her about leaving Oliver.

God, Mum was insufferable sometimes. It was bad enough that Meg's own marriage was falling apart without having to cope with her parents' break-up as well!

Meg used the last drop of milk to make herself a cup of coffee while she checked her phone: still no word from Oliver. She walked over to the window, looking out into the garden as she sipped the warm liquid. This was the first Christmas she and Oliver had spent apart for seven years. And the only time she could remember her parents being separated at Christmas. What a Christmas and new year this was going to be.

She blinked back the tears from her eyes and glanced at the clock. Ten past nine. Dad would be up now – he was always up at seven thirty on the dot – and was probably already out in the garden. She'd give him a ring while her mum was out, check if he was okay and see if she could talk him into phoning her mum and trying to sort things out. She selected a video call so she could see how he was.

'Hello, pet, how are you?' her father asked in his just-woken-up voice.

'Sorry, Dad, were you sleeping?' she apologised, surprised to see him still in bed.

'Had a bit of a late night after the bowls game,' he told her as he sat up, plumping the pillow behind him.

God, he was as bad as Oliver. 'Dad! Mum's left you and you're out playing bowls,' she scolded. 'How could you?'

'She's not left me. She's gone away for a couple of days to spend time with you. She'll be back soon. Now how about you and Oliver? I can't believe you've walked out on him so near to Christmas. What's he done, pet?'

Meg drew a breath. She didn't want to talk about her and Oliver right now; she needed to convince her dad that the situation with her mum was serious. 'Dad, what did you fall out about? Mum is adamant that she's had enough and I'm not sure she will come back.'

Dad rubbed his eyes before replying. 'Of course she'll come back. She's just in a sulk because I don't want to go on holiday…'

'It's got to be more than that.'

'Your mum is such hard work sometimes. Many women would be grateful for a bloke like me.' Dad looked annoyed. 'I'm a good husband. I've worked hard and taken care of you all, haven't I? I've never strayed like bloody Saint Martin, Frances's husband, but I'm still not good enough.'

'Mum's worked hard too, and she hasn't strayed either,' Meg reminded him. 'And she's got to be really upset over something to walk out, especially at Christmastime.'

'It's all because she wants to go on a cruise like Frances and Martin and I don't want to. She's bored, that's what. She's been like this ever since she retired, always wanting to do something, go somewhere. I've told her I've got plenty to keep me busy here, and what's the point of me traipsing around the shops with her, or going to the cinema to see a film I'm not interested in, just so we can have some "couple time"? We're not a pair of flipping newlyweds.' He sounded indignant now and Meg couldn't help feeling sorry for him. Had Mum really walked out because she'd got bored with him?

'She'll be back when she's sulked enough. She's not going to leave me, split up our family after all these years. And make sure you come back with her if you and Oliver don't make up. I don't want you spending Christmas alone.' He paused. 'What have you argued about anyway? I like Oliver, he's a nice chap, always helpful and a miracle worker in the garden. Don't tell me he's played away?'

Why did everyone assume that? But then she'd asked her mum the same question, hadn't she? 'No, he hasn't,' she replied emphatically. 'And I don't want to talk about it, Dad. It's personal.' She was still too wounded to tell her father how Oliver had deceived her.

'What made you go down Cornwall, anyway?' Ted asked. 'What area are you?'

That was typical Dad – he hadn't even bothered to ask Mum whereabouts she was going. 'We're in a place called Goolan Bay, Dad. Mum's booked a cottage here. Apparently she's stayed here before, years ago.'

Dad looked surprised but didn't say anything. Maybe she shouldn't have told him about Mum going to the cottage before. She remembered her parents saying that they'd met as teenagers but had split up for a while as they'd felt too young to settle down, then got back together and got engaged. What if Mum had had another boyfriend then and come down to Goolan Bay with him? Dad might not want to be reminded of that, especially if it was those happy memories that had drawn her mum back down here.

She looked over her shoulder as she heard the front door open. Mum was back. 'I've got to go, Dad, but please phone Mum and talk to her. Soon. Or your marriage might really be over.' Then she ended the call before her dad could reply.

I hope I've said enough to convince him the situation is serious, she thought, getting up to fill the kettle. He was treating it as if Mum was taking a little holiday.

'Want a coffee?' she asked as the kitchen door opened and her mum came in.

'Please.' Sally put her bag down on the table and glanced at Meg. 'I thought I heard you talking to someone when I came in. Was it Oliver?'

She might as well confess. 'It was Dad. I wanted to see how he was.' Keeping her back to her mum, she took a mug out of the cupboard and spooned coffee into it. 'He seems to think you'll be home in a day or two, Mum. He even suggested that I go back with you if I don't make up with Oliver.' She added milk and hot water to the coffee, stirred it then turned around. 'He said you walked out because he wouldn't go on a cruise like Frances and Martin.' She tried not to sound accusing. 'I told him there had to be more to it than that but he was adamant that was the reason.'

Sally looked at her steadily. 'Of course there is more to it than that, but I don't think you'll understand. It's hard to explain.'

'Try me,' Meg said. 'After all, I did tell you why Oliver and I split up.' She felt a bit guilty about how she had snapped at her mum last night. 'And I'm sorry I was snappy and stormed out. I didn't mean it.' She handed her the mug of coffee. 'I promise I'll listen and try not to be judgy.'

'Okay,' Sally agreed. She pulled out a chair and sat down at the table.

Meg pulled out the chair opposite and sat down too. She waited expectantly as her mother nursed her cup of coffee, seeming to stare into space, probably trying to find the words, Meg guessed, to explain why she had walked out on her dad.

'Look, I know this is difficult for you, Meg. I'm sure you love us both and I'm not expecting you to take my side or trying to turn you against your dad. I'm just trying to explain.' She paused. 'Dad is right in that him not wanting to go on the cruise was the catalyst for me leaving, but to be honest, Meg, I've felt trapped in a loveless, boring marriage for years.'

Meg stared at her incredulously. *How could Mum say that?* Her parents were happy together; they'd hardly ever rowed like some of her friends' parents. 'That can't be true. Dad loves you. You both get on so well. I've hardly ever heard you argue.'

'Because we're not the sort of people who argue if we can help it. We jog along, put up with each other, do our own thing. Think about it though, Meg. When do we ever do anything together?'

Meg had never really given much thought to her parents' relationship; she'd accepted that Dad was steady, reliable, okay a bit boring but that wasn't a crime, and that Mum was outgoing, a doer, always off somewhere. 'I thought you liked going out and on holiday with your friends, and Dad always seemed okay with that. I thought you both liked doing your own thing.'

'Your dad isn't okay with that. He sulks like crazy for a good week before I go on holiday and another week when I come back. But he refuses to come with me. How do you think that makes me feel?' Sally rubbed her finger around the rim of her mug. 'I want to go out with my *husband*, I want us to go away together – but I know if we do, your dad will only grumble and ruin the holiday for me anyway.'

Meg could see her point. She'd hate it if Oliver never went anywhere with her. They did most things together out of work hours. *He just doesn't want a baby with you.* She pushed the thought away. She needed to concentrate on fixing things between her parents. 'Can't you tell Dad how you feel? I'll tell him if you like,' she offered. 'I'll try and make him understand. You can't split up over something like this, Mum. You can fix this, I know you can.'

'I've told him and he doesn't care. Do you really think I've walked away without seeing if I can fix it?' Sally snapped. 'I'm hurt that you think I'm that selfish.'

'Of course not. That's not what I'm saying.' She hadn't meant to upset her mum. She lowered her voice. 'Dad will be devastated if you break up. I don't know how he'll cope without you. And surely you'll miss him too?' She put her mug down on the table and leant forward, convinced that her mum was acting on impulse and hadn't thought this through. 'You don't really want to start again at your age, do you? Where will you live? What will you do?'

Sally sighed. 'Forget for a moment that we're your parents, Meg. Can you do that?'

Surprised, Meg looked at her and nodded slowly.

'Now imagine being married to someone who not only never goes anywhere with you but never shows you any affection apart from the odd kiss on the cheek, who never wants to cuddle you, make love to you, and hasn't wanted to for years…'

Meg felt her cheeks burn. She really didn't want to know about her parents' sex life, or lack of it. 'Oh, Mum, don't get too personal…'

'Believe me, I don't want to tell you anything personal, but I do want you to understand why I've left your father, and why I don't want to go back. You might not agree with my reasons, but please at least acknowledge them.'

Meg saw tears well up in her mother's eyes and immediately felt bad for being so harsh. 'I'm sorry, Mum. I didn't mean to upset you. I do know that Dad is a bit set in his ways, and a bit… reserved. But—'

'But you think I shouldn't bother about things like that at my age and should put up with it?' Sally demanded.

'No, of course not,' Meg floundered.

Sally leant forward, her hands clasped together, elbows on the table. 'I assure you, Meg, that I haven't made this decision lightly. I've really thought about it. That's why I decided to come to this cottage. It has such happy memories for me.'

Please don't let Mum tell me that she came here with another boyfriend, someone she was really happy with and wished she'd married instead of Dad, Meg thought desperately.

Sally's voice broke through her thoughts. 'The truth is that your dad and I came here for our honeymoon. We were so happy here. So in love.'

'Oh, Mum…'

'I came here to remind myself how much we had loved each other, to ask myself if I was doing the right thing, if I could put up with our marriage as it is now.' Sally gazed at her, and Meg saw the pain in her eyes. 'The problem is the more I remember the love we had, how we couldn't keep our hands off each other, wanted to be together as much as we could, relished each other's company, the more I realise that I can't settle for the empty marriage we have now.'

'Oh, Mum!' Meg got up and put her arms around her mother. 'I'm so sorry.' She didn't know what else to say. It was evident that her mum was really upset about how things were with her dad, although personally, Meg still didn't think it was major enough to throw away a long marriage. Not like the situation with her and Oliver.

Chapter Eight

Sally

Meg had some promotion work to do for a client, so Sally left her working on her laptop at the kitchen table and went for a walk back down the hill to the harbour. It was as if she couldn't get enough of it, as if her soul was soaking up the happy memories, willing them back. Memories of her and Ted freshly married, deeply in love. They'd been mad about each other then, happy to spend the days hand in hand, wandering around the small Cornish village or on the beach. They'd been blessed with glorious weather – it was June – as if the sun was shining down on their marriage. How she'd loved Ted, and he her. They would sit out in the little back garden, talking about their plans for the future, the family they would eventually have, the things they would do. So young and in love. Sally had returned to teaching as soon as Meg had started school, and they'd then been able to buy their own house, have a caravan in Devon, the occasional seaside holiday. Life had been busy, but she and Ted had jogged along comfortably, sharing the load. Sally wasn't sure when she'd started to feel restless, that something was missing. It wasn't a sudden feeling, but one that had grown over the years.

She pulled her hood up against the wind and looked out at the sea. They had loved each other so much once; where had it gone? They didn't even make love any more, not since Ted had started having difficulty performing a few years ago. She'd tried talking about it, telling him it was common with older men, but Ted had shut down, refusing to discuss it, and rebuffed her attempts to instigate making love, so that was it: sex life over because Ted said so. Even a kiss and cuddle were off the agenda because Ted seemed scared she'd want to go further. *It's a wonder he doesn't buy me a vibrator and tell me to do that myself, like he tells me to do everything else myself*, she thought crossly. That was Ted's answer to everything she wanted to do and he didn't: 'You do it. I never stop you from doing anything.' But he did, because she was married to him, and if the person you were married to didn't want to do something, then that rubbed off on you too. You either didn't do it or went ahead and did it but felt guilty, like you should be with them. Especially when they sulked as much as Ted did.

She remembered when she first met Ted at the local disco; she had just finished school and Ted was at college. She'd been attracted to him right away. With his longish dark hair and motorbike, he'd seemed so grown up compared to the other lads, and so certain of his future. They'd dated for a while then broke up when she was at teacher training college and Ted at work in his first job, neither of them wanting to be tied down. Then Ted had contacted her again, said he'd missed her, and she had missed him too. They'd got back together, fallen madly in love and got engaged. When she'd said her marriage vows, she had meant them, really believed that she and Ted would be together forever. She was sure that Ted believed it too.

People change; you were so young and now you're different people, she reminded herself. Breaking up the family was the last thing she had wanted to do. She could see that Meg was upset about it, and she knew that Dan would have something to say when he found – after seeing

Meg's reaction she hadn't been able to face telling Dan yet. It was bad timing so close to Christmas, but she didn't feel like she could take any more. Surely she was entitled to be happy?

The question was, was she unhappy enough to end their marriage for good?

Chapter Nine

Meg

Helen phoned Meg again later that morning.

'I had to phone and check on you, Meg. You sounded so upset. Are you okay? Any news from Oliver?'

'Not a peep. He's probably glad to have his freedom.'

'Don't be daft, Meg. He adores you. He looked really upset on Sunday night.'

'Didn't stop him going out for a drink, did it?' *And not upset enough to phone me.*

'I'm so shocked. I thought you two were forever. I was expecting you to announce that you were pregnant any day.'

That stung. 'No chance of that. Oliver doesn't want children. Not ever,' she retorted, trying hard to keep the tremble out of her voice. 'That's why we've split up.'

'Wow! That's heavy. I'm so sorry, Meg.' There was a pause then Helen continued reassuringly, 'He's probably just having a wobble. I'm sure he'll come round. Miles was a bit shocked when we found out we were having Kyle, but as soon as Kyle was born he fell in love with him. He's a great dad now and we're even planning on having another baby soon.'

'Oliver won't come round. He's adamant that he never wants kids.'

'Take no notice of that,' Helen pooh-poohed. 'A lot of men are scared of being fathers, worried about the expense and all that. Just go ahead and have a baby if you want one. Just "forget" to take the pill. I never told you because I thought you might disapprove but... well, that's what I did. And you know how much Miles adores Kyle.'

Meg was astonished to discover that Helen had tricked her partner into being a father. But was that really so wrong? Miles was a fantastic dad and it was clear he adored his son just like she was sure Oliver would love their child if they had one. She shook her head; she couldn't do that. If she and Oliver had a child, she wanted her pregnancy to be a happy event, for Oliver to be as delighted as she would be, for their child to be loved and longed for. It was a deceitful thing to do – there was no way she'd be taking Helen's advice. If Oliver didn't want a child with her, she wasn't going to force one on him.

'He does mean it. He's made that perfectly clear. Now I have to decide if I love him enough to give up my desire for a family. So I've come away for a bit to think things over.'

'It's such a shame, Meg. At Christmastime too. Maybe Oliver will come round to the idea and decide that he does want a family after all.'

How she wished that were true, but Oliver had seemed very sure of his feelings. And she really didn't want to talk about it; it was too upsetting. 'I doubt it. Sorry, Helen, but I've got to go now. I'll catch up with you later in the week.'

'Okay, babe. Take care. I hope it all works out.'

Meg went down into the kitchen and popped on the kettle, then opened the loaf her mum had just bought and made herself some toast. She ate it, standing at the kitchen window, looking outside, trying to imagine her parents as newlyweds, staying here. That revelation had surprised her. *Maybe I'm being a bit harsh on Mum,* she thought as she nibbled her toast. *She must still love Dad to come down here, where they spent their honeymoon.* Maybe Mum wanted Dad to come after her, show that he cared? Did Dad even remember that Goolan Bay was the place he and Mum had spent their honeymoon? Knowing him, he'd probably forgotten. She'd ring him again in a bit, remind him of that and let him know that Mum had booked Smuggler's Haunt, the same cottage they had stayed in, so she must care about him. Maybe that would persuade him to come down. With a bit of luck, her parents would be together again for Christmas, and then she could concentrate on her own break-up.

She frowned as a ball whizzed over the wooden fence and landed in one of the plant pots lining the garden, then a young blond-haired boy peered over the fence. *There must be a family staying next door – or living there; probably not all the houses are rented out,* she thought. She stuffed the last piece of toast in her mouth, slipped on her shoes and went outside.

'Can I have my ball back, please?' the boy asked as soon as he spotted her.

'Sure.'

As she crossed the garden to get it, she heard a man's deep voice say, 'I've told you to watch where you're kicking that ball, Sam.'

The boy turned to face the direction of the voice. 'What else am I supposed to do? You've been working on your laptop all morning. I'm bored.'

Meg scooped up the ball and walked over to the fence, where a fair-haired man dressed in tracksuit bottoms was now standing next to the boy. 'Thank you, I'll take that. Sorry that Sam has been a bother to you.' He grabbed the ball and directed a stern look at his son.

'That's not fair. Now I'll have nothing to play with. You've already taken my iPad off me. I hate it here. I wish I could spend Christmas with Mum.'

She didn't catch the man's reply as they both disappeared into the house.

As she went back inside, the front door opened: her mum was back.

'It's a bit windy out there,' Mum said, hanging up her coat.

Meg looked at her in her jeans, jumper and trainers and thought how young she looked – and acted – compared to her dad. Perhaps it was no wonder she felt stifled in their marriage. She had been a bit harsh on her, she thought, with a pang of guilt.

'I know. Are you okay?' she asked.

'I will be,' Mum said with a determined smile. 'And so will you. We're made of strong stuff.' She slipped off her trainers.

'Sorry if I sounded a bit… unsympathetic,' Meg told her. 'But I still think you should talk to Dad, get him to understand what's he's doing – or not doing – that's upsetting you. Give him a chance to put it right.'

Sally sighed. 'I've tried, Meg. And if your dad cared, he would be phoning and asking me, wouldn't he?'

'I'm sure he will soon.' She was still hoping that once her dad had mulled over their call, he would phone. If he didn't soon, she'd be phoning him again.

Sally narrowed her eyes. 'I'm guessing you tried to persuade him to when you called him earlier?'

'Well, yes,' confessed Meg. 'I told you he didn't realise you'd left him – he's expecting you back.'

Sally sighed. 'Well, if he does ring, I'll listen to what he has to say, but you have to let me handle this my way, Meg. I know we're your parents but this is our marriage, our business.' She reached out and touched Meg's hand. 'Now I don't suppose you've heard from Oliver?'

'No. He's probably glad I've gone; now he's let off the hook and doesn't have to pretend any longer.' She blinked the tears from her eyes. She couldn't believe that Oliver cared so little about her. She had thought they were rock-solid. How wrong she was.

'Right, well, we're not going to sit here and be miserable. Let's have something to eat and take a walk around the village. I'm dying to show it to you, and to see how much it's changed.'

'I'd love to have a look around,' Meg told her. It would be good to get out in the fresh air. She didn't want to stay inside, moping all day.

So, after a cup of coffee, and a slice of toast for Sally, they both set off.

As they walked along, her mother chatted away, saying how she and Ted had walked to the harbour every day and had breakfast in the little café on the seafront. Meg imagined her parents walking along these very streets on their honeymoon, happily in love. What had happened? How had it died out? Had Mum been simmering with frustration and resentment all these years?

'Here we are, and oh gosh, the café is actually open!' Sally almost squealed in delight. 'We must have a cup of tea there, Meg.'

Meg gazed at the sleepy harbour and the deserted beach, imagining it in the summer with the sun shining, the fishermen on their boats, the holidaymakers sprawled on the sand or paddling in the sea. She looked to the right and saw a small café with the words 'Harbour Café' painted on it. In the summer there would probably be tables and chairs outside, she thought, imagining her mum and dad sitting there, all those years ago, holding hands, talking about their future plans.

Like she and Oliver had done on their honeymoon in Mexico. They'd had a room overlooking the beach, and on the first morning,

Oliver had gone down early to draw a big heart in the sand and write 'I love you' in the middle of it. Then they'd sat out on the balcony to eat breakfast, gazing out at the golden sand and brilliant blue sea, talking about all the things they would do, and the places they would go. 'Maybe we'll bring our children here one day,' Meg had said, and Oliver had smiled and kissed her. She'd had no idea then that Oliver never intended them to have children.

Mum was already walking into the café, so Meg followed, and the woman behind the counter greeted them. 'Welcome to Goolan Bay.'

'Thank you. Can we have a pot of tea for two please?' Mum asked.

'We don't get many visitors this time of year,' the woman said as she started making them a pot of tea. She looked about the same age as Sally but wasn't as slender. She seemed a motherly, no-nonsense sort of woman, Meg thought.

'I wanted to show my daughter where her father and I went on our honeymoon,' Mum told her. 'A lovely couple ran the café then. I can't remember their names but they were so friendly. It was almost forty years ago now though.'

'That would be my parents.' The woman smiled. 'They retired years ago. I'm Rose, and I've run the place ever since. Though actually I won't be here much longer either. My daughter and her husband are taking over in the spring. Take a seat and I'll bring this over.' Sally and Meg sat down at the nearest table. A couple of minutes later the woman placed a tray, two pretty china cups and saucers, a sugar bowl and a milk jug onto the table. 'I love this village but there's a wider world out there and I want to see it. So I'm handing over to Jenny and I'm off to see the world.'

'Good for you. I'd love to do that too,' said Mum as she poured tea into one of the cups and handed it to Meg. 'Are you travelling with friends or your partner?' Then she added, 'I'm Sally, by the way, and this is my daughter, Meg.'

'Pleased to meet you both.' Rose's eyes glistened a bit as she continued. 'I'm travelling alone. Me and my Glenn, we always planned on travelling together, but he died of cancer a couple of years ago. God rest his soul.' She paused for a moment to compose herself. 'When he knew he was dying, Glenn made me promise I'd still travel, that I'd see the world and make the memories for both of us. And now I've worked through my grief I'm ready to do it.'

'That's very brave of you,' Sally told her. 'My husband and I always planned on travelling too when we retired, but now he's changed his mind.'

'That's a shame. It must be nice for you both to come back here again though, where you spent your honeymoon. Are you staying long?' Rose asked.

'We're not both here,' Sally confessed. 'I'm afraid that sadly we've just split up. Meg has split up from her husband too so we're spending Christmas together.'

'Oh dear, I am sorry to hear that. What a sad thing to happen, especially at this time of year, but it must be some comfort that you have each other for company.' Rose looked genuinely sorry.

'It is. At least we can spend Christmas together,' Sally agreed.

'Well, I hope you both enjoy your stay here.' Rose made as if to turn away then turned back. 'Look, if you have a few hours to spare on Saturday, you might like to come to our Christmas Fayre in the village hall? We're raising money to buy presents for the children in the local hospital. Don't worry if you have other plans though.'

'I think that sounds fun, and it's for a good cause. How do you feel about it, Meg?' asked Sally.

Saturday, so that was four days away. Would they still be here by then? She didn't want to make promises they wouldn't keep. *Face it: you and Oliver are finished and Mum isn't in a rush to go back to Dad*, she told herself.

'Sure.' She nodded. 'What time does it start?'

Rose's face broke into a big smile. 'One o'clock and it finishes about three. Pop over and say hi if you come. I'll be on the cake stall.'

'We'd love to. And let me know if you need any more cakes made. I'd be happy to help out,' Sally offered as she handed over a five-pound note to pay for the teas.

'I will, thank you.' Rose rummaged in the bag around her waist and handed over the change.

Meg and Sally chatted for a while as they sipped their tea, reminiscing about the Christmas fayres they had helped out at in the past. 'Remember when you roped me into doing some face painting and I painted that little boy's face as a panda instead of a tiger? He was so upset,' Meg said. 'It took me ages to clean it off and repaint it.'

Sally chuckled. 'And then when you'd finished he decided he preferred being a panda after all!'

Their tea finished, they placed the cups on the tray and took it over to the counter.

'Thank you, dears,' Rose said. 'Hope to see you on Saturday! Oh, and we switch on the lights of the big Christmas tree in the square on Christmas Eve if you'd like to come along. There's a carol service too. It starts at six.'

'Thank you. We will probably do that,' Sally told her.

'What a friendly woman,' she said to Meg when they were outside again. 'Her parents were just the same. They made me and your dad feel really welcome. Often slipped us a free cuppa too.'

Rose was friendly, thought Meg, and she could see that she and her mum had already formed a bit of a connection. Her mum had such an ability to make everyone she met like her.

They continued with their walk around the village. There were a few more shops – a small supermarket, a unisex hairdresser's, a doctor's and dentist, a hardware store. Meg wondered what it would be like to live here permanently. It was a pretty village, but she was used to living on the outskirts of a busy town. As was Mum. No wonder Rose wanted to get away and see the world. Just like her mum did. They seemed similar ages too, and she guessed they were both grabbing at the chance to do things while they could.

They were approaching the square now, where a huge Christmas tree stood. It was adorned with baubles and unlit lights. 'That must be the tree that Rose was on about,' Sally said. 'I'd like to come to the switching-on ceremony – would you?'

Meg gazed at the tree. 'If we're still here.' She was hoping that Mum and Dad would have made up by then.

As if on cue, Sally's phone rang. She reached inside her bag and glanced at the screen. 'It's your dad,' she said, hesitating.

Thank goodness! 'I'll take a walk back to the harbour and leave you to talk,' Meg told her. 'I'll wait for you on that bench overlooking the sea.'

As she strolled down the hill, Meg hoped desperately that her parents could sort things out and get back together. It was horrible to think of them splitting up.

If only Oliver would phone me too, she thought, sitting down on the bench. Even though she was still sad and angry, she couldn't help but long to hear his voice again.

Chapter Ten

Sally

'When are you and Meg coming home?' Ted demanded as soon as Sally answered the phone.

'I don't know when I am, Ted,' Sally replied. 'I don't think there's any point in me coming back. And Meg and Oliver haven't sorted things out either.'

'Then bring Meg back here with you. You have a home here, both of you. What's the use of staying down there?' He sounded cross. 'Running off doesn't solve anything. Couples need to talk about things.'

'Sometimes talking about things doesn't solve anything either,' Sally pointed out. 'I've tried talking but you don't listen. We want different things out of life, Ted, and I think we're better off apart.'

'That's ridiculous! Why do we have to want the same things? You can go off on holiday if you want to. Why do I have to come too?'

'Because we're a couple, and anyway you sulk when I go away.' She tried to explain but it was to no avail. Ted reminded Sally that he accepted her as she was and didn't ask her to change, so why should she ask him to? She bit back the retort that just being with him changed her, because she couldn't do the things she wanted, be the person she really was.

'Are you really going to be so selfish as to throw away our marriage just because I don't want to go abroad?' he demanded.

That was just like Ted to make her sound petty and selfish when he knew it was more than that. 'I don't love you any more, Ted, and I don't think you love me either. Not in the way a husband and wife should. You might be content to plod on with things how they are but I'm not. I want more out of my life.'

'Hark at you, you sound like you're having a mid-life crisis. You're almost a pensioner, for goodness' sake! Grow up and be grateful for what you've got instead of being so bloody selfish and breaking up the family.' He abruptly cut off the call.

Am I being selfish? Sally wondered, going over the conversation again as she walked down the hill to catch up with Meg, who looked a solitary figure clad in her berry-coloured parka and matching beanie hat, sitting on the bench staring out at the wintry sea.

She was worried about Meg: she looked so pale and her eyes were dark. It was evident she wasn't sleeping well and was devastated by the break-up with Oliver. If only Oliver would phone her, but no, typical man, he was being stubborn. To be honest, though, she couldn't see a solution to this disagreement. Like her and Ted, Meg and Oliver wanted different things. Even if Oliver compromised and agreed to have a child for Meg's sake, it would always be between them that he had only agreed because he'd wanted to save their marriage. Meg would probably always feel that she had trapped him and that he didn't love their child as much as she did. And Oliver might resent the child, especially because children could be very demanding. Some fathers found it hard to cope with being pushed to what they considered 'second place' because the mothers had to devote so much time to looking after the baby. She wondered if Ted had ever felt this way; if he had, he'd never shown it. But life had been so busy back then – with them both working and two children to look after – there had been little time to think of their own needs and feelings. They'd just pulled together and got on with it.

Meg turned her head as Sally approached, her face pinched and pensive. 'How're things with Dad?' she asked as Sally sat down beside her.

'Same. I'm being selfish and why should he change?'

'Looks like we're going to definitely be here over Christmas, then, doesn't it?' Meg turned back and gazed at the sea.

'Yes, I think we'll both be here for Christmas, so we have to make the best of it,' Sally told her. 'How about we go shopping for a Christmas tree and some decorations and get ourselves in the festive mood? What do you say? No point pining for men who don't care about how we feel, is there? We can have a good time without them.'

Meg nodded slowly. 'Okay.'

So they walked back for Meg's car – her boot was bigger – then set off to the large shopping centre in Launceston. They picked up an assortment of sparkling baubles and then went for a late lunch at a nearby café before going to buy a tree – they'd both decided on a real tree. As they sat down at the table with their turkey, brie and cranberry sandwiches, a deep voice said, 'Hello again.'

Meg glanced across and smiled. 'Hello, are you Christmas shopping too?'

Sally turned around to see a good-looking man, about forty-ish, and a sulky-looking young lad sitting at the table behind them, tucking into burgers and chips. 'It looks like you've been doing the same as us, buying baubles for the tree,' the man said. 'Not that I can get Sam interested in it.'

Sally looked questioningly from Meg to the man. 'Are you going to introduce us, Meg?'

'Mum, this is our neighbour and his son. We met this morning,' explained Meg.

'Leo.' The man nodded. 'Pleased to meet you, Meg's mum. And this is Sam.'

'Hello, Leo and Sam. I'm Sally. Do you both live next door full-time or are you just here for Christmas, like us?' Sally asked.

'I live there. Although I only moved back to Cornwall a couple of months ago – I grew up here but moved away when I went to university and never came back,' he added. 'Sam's mum and I are divorced but she's away for the next two weeks so he's staying with me over Christmas. It's a bit of a drive to his school but they break up on Friday so it's not for long.'

'How lovely that you're spending Christmas with your dad,' Meg told Sam.

'No, it isn't! I'd rather be in Jamaica with my mum. But she doesn't want me along now she's got married again,' Sam replied with a scowl.

'She's gone on honeymoon not holiday, Sam, so of course she doesn't want you along. A honeymoon is just a couples' holiday. Your mum looks after you all year, she's allowed a bit of time alone with her new husband.' He glanced awkwardly at Meg then Sally. 'Sorry about Sam. As you can see he isn't very happy about spending Christmas here instead of sunny Jamaica with his mum and stepdad.'

'Cornwall's lovely,' Sally said. 'There's lots to do here.'

'Yeah, in the summer maybe, but not in the winter. It's boring.' Sam pulled a face as he speared a tomato-ketchup-covered chip.

'How old is he?' Meg mouthed to Leo.

'Nine,' he mouthed back.

She smiled in sympathy. 'I guess you'll just have to make the most of it like me and my mum, Sam. We hadn't planned on spending Christmas in Cornwall either but here we are. We're going to the Christmas Fayre on Saturday, and to the "switching on the lights" carol service on Christmas Eve. Maybe you can come too.'

'We're helping out at the Fayre as it happens. My mum's organising it and has got me and Sam running a games table,' said Leo.

'It's going to be so boring,' Sam said as he speared another chip.

'It might be fun, Sam, and it's for a good cause. Imagine if you had to spend Christmas in hospital – you'd be glad of some presents, wouldn't you?' Leo asked him.

Sam shrugged. 'Suppose so.'

'Is Rose, the lady from the café at the harbour, your mother?' Sally asked. 'She invited us to the Fayre.'

Leo nodded. 'Mum always organises the Fayre but I think this will be her last year as she's off travelling in the spring. My sister Jenny and her husband Grant are taking over the café.'

'Yes, Rose mentioned it when we were having a cuppa in the café earlier. We'll look out for your stall on Saturday and make sure we play some of the games,' Sally said.

Meg gave Sam a sympathetic look. 'And cheer up, you might actually enjoy yourself.'

Sam shrugged his shoulders.

'We're off to see Mum and Uncle Rory – her brother – later. That'll cheer him up. He loves his gran, and Uncle Rory always has a few tricks up his sleeve to try out on him.'

'Have a good day then,' Meg said.

'You too,' Leo said. Then they all returned to eating their food.

'Fancy Rose's son living next door to us,' Sally whispered to Meg. 'What a small world.'

They continued with their shopping, stopping off to buy a luscious real Christmas tree that luckily fitted into the back of Meg's car.

'We'll decorate it as soon as we get home; that will cheer us both up,' Sally said.

'I don't feel like anything will cheer me up,' Meg told her miserably. 'My life's fallen apart. At least Dad's phoned you and let you know he wants you back. I haven't even had a text from Oliver, which shows how much he cares about me.'

'He's probably hurting, love, like you are. And he doesn't want to contact you because he hasn't changed his mind about having a child, so maybe he doesn't know what to say.' She squeezed Meg's arm. 'You could phone him.'

Meg shook her head. 'I'm not making the first move. He's the one who's in the wrong.'

Sally looked at her sadly. This was going to be a tough Christmas for both of them. But she was determined to make it a good one too.

Chapter Eleven

Meg

Meg unpacked the boxes of baubles with a heavy heart. How could she celebrate Christmas when her heart was broken and the happy future she thought she'd had with Oliver gone? If only she could have brought Laurel and Hardy with her, they would have cheered her up. It would be such a comfort to sit one of the bunnies on her lap now and stroke it, or to watch them both run about and play. She knew it would be cruel to separate them though; they adored each other and would pine terribly. Stuff Oliver! He wasn't depriving her of her pets as well as a family.

The future felt so daunting. She would have to find somewhere else to live unless she could persuade Oliver to move out. They'd probably need to sell the house, split whatever little profit there was left and both find new homes. She didn't think Oliver would want to go – he loved the house. And maybe he would say she was the one who'd walked out so it would be down to her to find somewhere. If only Meg could move in with her parents while she and Oliver sorted things, but there was no way she could do that now; even if her mum and dad made up and got back together, they would need some space, some time on their own to repair their relationship. And if they didn't get back together, well, she couldn't move in with either of them otherwise it would look like she was taking sides. She felt a bit like that now, being down here with her mum. No, she'd have to go it alone. The idea of starting again filled her with dread but she shook it off. She was young, she could do it.

Not that young if she wanted children though. Maybe she would never find anyone else she loved enough to want children with. She couldn't imagine loving anyone else as much as she loved Oliver. Maybe her chance of having a family was gone forever… which made her even more angry at his deceit. How could he be so cruel as to do this to her?

She could do this! She needed to pull herself together and stop wallowing. She was going to survive this; she'd had a life before Oliver and she'd have a life after him. A good life.

I'd prefer one with him though. The thought flashed unwanted into her mind. Oh God, how she missed him! She shut her eyes as the memories flooded in, Oliver holding her in his arms, his dark hair pushed back off his face, his soulful brown eyes gazing at her, his mouth lowering towards hers…

'Are you all right, Meg? I can do this if you don't feel like it.'

She opened her eyes to see her mum looking at her worriedly. 'Yes, I'm fine. I was just wondering how the bunnies were,' she said, not wanting to admit that she was missing Oliver.

'Oliver will look after them and you'll see them again soon. You're going to have to get together with Oliver and sort things out, just like I'll have to with your dad.'

Meg nodded miserably. She didn't want to think about going back to their home and packing up the rest of her things, sorting out who was going to have what. It was all too painful.

'Look, forget all about that for now. Let's just concentrate on making this a good Christmas for the two of us – a Christmas to remember. We don't need men to make us happy.'

Mum was right: there was nothing she could do to change the situation between her and Oliver. She had to get on with her life. And she wasn't going to spend Christmas moping.

'Too true. Let's start with some Christmas music.' She reached out for the CDs and slipped a selection of Christmas carols into the CD player. As 'Jingle Bells' blasted out, Sally smiled and sang loudly 'single all the way' instead of 'jingle all the way'. Meg joined in and they both sang away as they decorated the tree.

'Remember when Dan and I used to help you decorate the tree when we were little?' Meg wound some red tinsel around one of the branches. 'You gave us a selection of baubles and we had to decorate a side each. We were so competitive, we wanted our side to be the best. I even sneaked a couple of Dan's baubles once so that my side would have more on it and be prettier. I don't think he noticed,' she confessed.

'You both loved decorating the tree. And you were so proud when you put the star on the top,' Sally said with a smile. 'Once we had a really big tree and your dad had to lift you up so you could reach the top to put the star on it.'

Putting the star on the tree had always been Meg's job, while Dan had turned on the lights. It had made them both feel important. They'd always had carols playing too, and once the tree had been decorated Mum would bring out a tray of warm home-made mince pies and hot chocolate and they'd all sit around the fire. Remembering those happy family days now made Meg feel sad that the family was breaking up. She glanced at her mum. 'You and Dad were happy then, weren't you?'

'Yes, we were, love. And me and your dad splitting up doesn't erase those happy memories. However, things don't always stay the same no matter how much we want them to.'

I do want them to, though, Meg thought. She wanted her and Oliver to be together with a little baby on the way, and she wanted Mum and Dad to be together, like they had always been. Going back to her parents' house wouldn't be the same without her mum there. It wasn't fair – why did her parents have to break up at the same time as her and Oliver! She had enough to deal with without having to cope with their problems too. What was so bad that Mum couldn't at least wait until after Christmas before she left?

She's got her own life. She's more than my mum, she's a person too, she reminded herself.

Meg and Sally shared family Christmas memories as they finished decorating the tree: some memories that made them laugh and some that were a bit sad, such as when Meg's guinea pig, Fudge, had died on Christmas Eve and they'd put a photo of the beloved pet in a clear bauble and hung it on the tree.

When their tree was finally decorated and twinkling merrily in front of the large bay window, Meg did feel much better. Christmas celebrated a new life, she told herself, and that's what she was going to make for herself. A new life. Without Oliver.

Mum came in with two cups of hot chocolate and some mince pies. She put them down on the coffee table and looked over at the tree. They hadn't chosen any particular colour scheme, choosing the baubles at random simply because they liked them. 'It looks lovely, very cheerful,' she said.

Meg and Oliver had put up their tree earlier that month, an artificial one they'd bought when they were first married and used every year, and there was already a pile of presents underneath it. She wondered if Oliver would go away for Christmas now, perhaps get a flight over to Portugal and visit his mum? Or would he spend Christmas at home with the bunnies? She thought of the Christmas they had planned: getting up a bit later than usual, sitting up in bed to open their presents, with Laurel and Hardy nestled on top of the duvet chewing one of their carrot treats. They'd made a stocking up for each of the bunnies, as they did every Christmas, filling it with little toys and treats. The bunnies would squeal with delight as they opened their presents – with a little help from Meg and Oliver, of course. Later, they'd go to her parents' house for lunch and to spend the afternoon with Dan, Katya and Tom, then back home for a lovely romantic evening together. Now it was all gone.

Chapter Twelve

Wednesday, 17 December

Oliver

Oliver slept restlessly. Meg was in his dreams again. Meg with her dark hair, smiling eyes, inviting lips. Half-awake he'd reached out for her, his hand resting on the empty, cold side of the bed, his mind registering that it had been a dream and Meg was gone. He'd got up then, made himself a coffee and taken it back to bed, sitting up to sip it as he and Meg used to do on holidays and weekends, talking about the week's events, laughing, making love. They had talked so much but not about this, this Important Thing that had driven them apart. Meg had tried to, he had to admit that, but he'd always flitted over it, letting her think that it would happen someday, and changed the subject. He'd thought that they had plenty of time, that he didn't have to worry about it now. How wrong he'd been.

How had this happened? Sunday had been so full of promise: the children's party had gone well and he and Meg had both been excited for the future with bookings coming in. Then Meg had ruined it by bringing up the subject of having a child. Or was it him who had ruined it by telling her he didn't want one? Not now. Not ever. When had he actually decided that? When had his nervousness of becoming a dad grown to this suffocating fear?

He got out of bed, padded across to the window, pulled aside the curtains and looked out at their neat garden, mowed lawn, pretty flowering tubs, and imagined a child playing out there. His and Meg's child. Paddling in an inflatable pool in the summer, chasing bubbles, kicking a ball about, watching the two bunnies play in their outdoor run. All the things he had done with his mum because his dad had never been there. His dad hadn't wanted a child, had tried to talk his mum into having an abortion, and had walked out not long after Oliver was born. Oliver had found this out when he'd overheard his parents arguing on one of his father's infrequent visits. Well, it seemed like he had his father's genes because he didn't want a child either. And he certainly wasn't going to bring one into the world just to walk out on it, only returning when that child was older because he needed money or a place to rest his head for the night, like his dad did. All his dad ever thought about was himself. Oliver wasn't, and had never been, important to him.

He never really talked about his childhood, not even to Meg. It hadn't been a good one but his mum had done her best for him and he'd always known that she loved him and 'had his back', as she would often say, although he was also aware of the sacrifice she had made, a teenage mum giving up her youth for him, struggling alone. As soon as he'd been old enough, he'd tried to take responsibility for himself, getting a paper round, then a Saturday job, working to see himself through college. He wanted his mum to be free, to be happy.

Oliver hadn't told his mum that Meg had left him yet because he knew that she would try to talk him into spending Christmas with her and Adrian, her latest boyfriend, in Portugal. He didn't want to do that; he'd feel in the way, and while he accepted the various men in his mother's life, always had, he didn't really want to be on 'best buddy' terms with them.

He wondered what she'd say if he told her why he and Meg had split up. Would she blame herself, as she always did? She'd blamed herself when he was growing up and they had no money for electricity so had to sit huddled together with a blanket over them and had to boil a kettle on the gas stove to wash; she'd blamed herself when he had holes in his shoes and she had to cut cardboard insoles from a cereal box to put inside; she'd blamed herself when she couldn't afford to buy him a winter coat, or throw a birthday party for him like his friends'. It wasn't her fault though: she'd worked as hard as she could but it had been difficult for her to hold down a full-time job while she had him to look after. It was his dad's fault. It takes two to have a baby and two to look after it but his dad had walked out and left it all to his eighteen-year-old mum. His mum who had been brought up in care and had never been parented herself. She'd loved him, though, and done her best.

Sometimes he'd thought he'd like to be a dad. Especially since he'd met Meg. Meg was fun, gorgeous, caring – she would make a great mum. She herself had brilliant parents: they adored her and her brother Dan, and were like substitute parents to him. Ted was far more of a father to him than his own father, Markus, had ever been.

'You'll make a great father,' Meg had told him. 'You're so good with children.' Yes, he was – with other people's children who weren't his sole responsibility. Children who he only spent a couple of hours with, who then went home with their parents; children he didn't have to love and provide for, who didn't rely on him for a roof over their head, food in their belly and guidance. He had no idea how to be a dad and he'd rather not be a dad at all than be a rubbish one. Like his dad.

And if not taking that risk meant losing Meg, then that was a price he would have to pay.

Chapter Thirteen

Meg

Meg turned to see Leo jogging towards her. Sam was obviously at school but she wondered why Leo wasn't working. *Don't be so nosy; he might be thinking the same about you,* she chided herself. Meg had been working on her laptop all morning so Mum had left her in peace and gone out. After a spot of lunch, Meg had decided to go for a walk along the beach.

'A bit wild today, isn't it?'

'I don't mind. I like the sea no matter what the weather. It's good to get out in the fresh air after a few hours at my desk.'

'You work from home?' she asked.

'Mostly. I'm an accountant, which isn't as boring as it sounds, honest.' He stopped jogging and stood next to her. 'How about you? What do you do?'

'I'm a PR and social media manager – and a party organiser – so I work at home a lot too. I've been working on some online promo stuff for a make-up company and, like you, decided I needed some fresh air.'

Leo gazed out at the white-tipped waves crashing against the shore. 'I always find that walking – or jogging – along the beach helps me unwind.'

'Me too,' she agreed. 'My parents came here for their honeymoon, you know. It was summer then, though.' She wasn't sure why she'd told him that.

'A nice place to spend a honeymoon. Is that why you and your mum are here? Is your dad…?'

He didn't finish but she guessed what he was going to say. She shook her head. 'No, Mum's left him. I've left my husband too. We both walked out at the weekend, so Mum suggested we come down here to… think things over, I guess. It's a big decision to end a marriage.' As soon as the words were out of her mouth, she wished she could snatch them back as obviously Leo was divorced. Had it been his decision to end the marriage? And why was she telling him all this anyway? She couldn't seem to stop gabbling.

'I know. I wish I'd thought about it a bit more.' He looked thoughtful, as if he was casting his mind back. 'I walked out on Nicky when Sam was five, although the spark had gone out of our marriage years before. As soon as Sam was born, to be honest. Nicky had always wanted a child; now she had one and her life was complete. It was like she didn't need me apart from the income I brought in.'

Is that why Oliver doesn't want children? Meg wondered. *Is he scared he'll become second best?* That seemed a bit selfish – surely a man could understand that children took up a lot of your time without feeling that they were being neglected? Her expression must have given her thoughts away because Leo quickly added, 'I know how that sounds but I promise I wasn't some needy, petulant father. I adore Sam but once he was born it was like I became invisible. Nicky was obsessed with Sam, to the extent that she wouldn't let me do anything for him; she was convinced that only she knew what to do.' He paused. 'Looking back, I don't think she meant to be so obsessed. I probably should have tried harder to make it work,' he confessed. 'We've sorted things out since. It took a while for Nicky to trust me alone with Sam. She was terrified I wouldn't look after him properly, but gradually we worked it out and now we share custody.'

He bent down, picked up a couple of pebbles and threw them into the sea, gazing at the ripples they made on the water as if deep in thought.

'It must be hard going. Do you ever wish you hadn't walked out?'

'Sometimes. I don't love Nicky and regret my part in the break-up, but we're all in a good place now. Even if Sam is upset he hasn't gone to Jamaica!'

'Did you plan to have a baby? Sorry, that's a rude question.'

He looked at her curiously. 'Yes, we did. Nicky had always wanted to be a mother. Why are you asking? Since we're going for oversharing, I'm thinking maybe this has something to do with your marriage break-up?'

The wind was bracing now, blowing her hair all over her face into a tangled mess. She swept it back. 'I want a family and it turns out Oliver doesn't, although he's only just decided to tell me that and we've been married five years,' she said flatly.

'That's a tough one,' Leo said sympathetically. 'Nicky was desperate for kids; I wasn't against it so I agreed. I don't regret having Sam. He's the best thing in my life and I'll never let him down again.' Leo turned away from the sea. 'Anyway, I'd better be off. I'll have to go and collect Sam soon.' He waved and jogged off.

He's clearly got his hands full with Sam, thought Meg. She'd seen how much Sam resented his mum going off to Jamaica without him and how he was determined to make things difficult for his dad. Relationships were so complicated. Perhaps she should be grateful that she and Oliver had split up now, before they had children. At least there were no custody battles to fight, no sharing of children to consider. Working out who was going to look after the bunnies was difficult enough. Parents splitting up usually had an effect on children – she felt devastated about her own parents' split even though she was an adult.

Meg remained on the beach for a while, watching the foamy waves churning back and forth. At least Dad had phoned Mum, and had made it clear that he didn't want their marriage to end. She hadn't heard a peep from Oliver since that morning in the hotel. Did that mean he accepted their marriage was over? That he didn't want them to sort things out? Could they even sort things out? It hurt so much that Oliver didn't even care enough to try and put things right.

She was almost back at the cottage when a message pinged. She took her phone out of her pocket to read it.

I miss you. Please can we talk? x

Oliver. Finally. She almost cried with relief.

She immediately went to press the call button then hesitated. She longed to hear his voice, to see him again, to feel his arms around her and his lips on hers – but how could that ever be? How could they solve this?

Then the phone rang, jolting her out of her thoughts. Oliver had clearly seen she'd read the message and had decided to chance it and call her. Her mind wondered whether to answer but her finger had already swiped to accept the call. Realising it was a video call, she quickly switched off her camera, not wanting him to see her yet.

'Meg.' Oliver's face flashed onto the screen. He looked tired and vulnerable, dark hair tousled, eyes heavy. She longed to reach out and touch him. She closed her eyes as the word flowed through her. Just the sound of his voice made her want to see him again, to tell him that she was coming back home, that all she wanted was him.

'Meg. I miss you so much.' His voice was husky, faltering, as if he wasn't sure what to say.

'I miss you too,' she confessed.

'Then come home. Let's talk this through. I don't want to spend Christmas without you.'

She closed her eyes again. Oh God, how she wanted to go back.

'Meg, put the camera on. Please. I want to see you. I miss you.'

She opened her eyes and stared at his image on the screen. Oliver. The love of her life. She hit the video button and a thumbnail image of her appeared in the bottom left corner. She looked tired too, her hair tangled by the wind, her eyes dark and puffy, the wintry sea just visible behind her.

'Where are you? Are you on a beach?' he asked, surprised.

'I'm in Goolan Bay, near Boscastle, with my mum.' She paused, suddenly feeling a wave of sadness. 'She and Dad have split up and she's rented a cottage down here for Christmas.'

'What? When? I didn't know they had split up! I'm so sorry.' He sounded genuinely upset.

'So am I. I was shocked when I rang Mum to... tell her what happened between us and she said Christmas was cancelled anyway as she'd split up with Dad and was going to Cornwall. She asked me to join her so I did.'

'That's a bit of a coincidence Is that why you're not coming home? You prefer to go on holiday to Cornwall with your mum?'

His voice was loud now, angry. How could he even think that?

'Of course not. That's a horrible thing to say.'

'It doesn't exactly sound like you're missing me.' He looked hurt.

'And you miss me so much it's taken you three days to phone, and the night I left you went clubbing with your mates,' she reminded him. 'And don't deny it, Helen saw you.'

'Okay, so I went out. It's not a crime, is it? You were the one who walked out.' He sounded aggrieved.

'Yes, because I had just found out that you lied to me for our entire relationship.'

'It wasn't a lie. I wasn't sure how I felt. Look, please can we meet and talk about this properly?' He ran his hand through his hair, pushing it back off his face. 'We can work this out, surely.'

'I don't see how we can work it out, Oliver. You don't want children. Or have you changed your mind about that?'

There was a long pause and as she saw the conflicting emotions on Oliver's face, Meg felt her heart sink.

'Then you've given me my answer, Oliver,' she said sadly.

'And you've chosen having a baby over me. Well, who are you intending to have the baby with? Is that why you've gone away, to find a suitable father?'

'That's a disgusting thing to say!'

'And it's a disgusting reason to split up. If you really love me, I should be enough for you. We came together as two people, not three or four, and *our* relationship should be the most important thing to you. It is to me but obviously you don't share my feelings.'

How dare he twist it like that! But before she could find the words to retort, Oliver ended the call.

Chapter Fourteen

Sally

She was glad Meg had some work to do today; she needed this time alone. Sally strolled around the village that had changed so much since her honeymoon yet was still achingly familiar. Especially the Harbour Café. It was as if her feet led her there, her head full of the happy memories of her and Ted so madly in love. Could she get that back? Had she given up too easily?

'Hello, Sally. Pot of tea, is it? And how about one of my freshly made scones too?' Rose called from behind the counter.

'That'd be perfect, thank you.' Sally walked over to the counter to be served but Rose shooed her away. 'Go and sit yourself down. I'll bring them over to you.'

What a nice woman, Sally thought, deciding to sit at the table by the window.

She wasn't sure it had been a good idea to ask Meg to join her in Goolan Bay; she might have been better coming alone. Her daughter obviously thought that she didn't have a good enough reason to break up with Ted, not like she did with Oliver. And maybe Meg was right. Sally could understand why Meg had walked out: it was terrible for Oliver to lead her on like that then drop the bombshell when Meg only had a few child-bearing years ahead of her. She didn't think he'd done it on purpose though. Oliver adored Meg, anyone could see that. He was probably panicking at the thought of being a father. He never talked about his childhood but Meg had mentioned that Oliver had been brought up by his mother, rarely saw his father, and they had no close family. Sally was sure they could both sort it out if only they would talk it through. There was no telling Meg, though. She had always been stubborn.

Just like me. Sally smiled, acknowledging how alike they were. Once she and Meg had decided on something, that was that.

Was she being stubborn now? Should she settle for the life she had with Ted, accept him how he was and make do with going away with her friends now and again even if he did sulk?

'There you are, love. Sorry I took so long. I had a panicky phone call about the Fayre.' Rose's voice broke through Sally's thoughts.

She glanced up, noticing that the other woman seemed a bit flustered. 'Problems?'

'Can't be helped – time of the year, isn't it? Two of the ladies have come down with the flu, which means I've got to run the cake stall by myself and we're a craft table short too.' She put the tray down on the table. 'I don't suppose you have a couple of hours to spare to help, do you? I hope that doesn't sound cheeky – feel free to refuse,' she added.

It was just what she needed, something to keep her busy. She was driving herself mad going over and over things. She wasn't sure if Meg would want to help though; better ask her first.

'I'd love to. Do you want me to help you out on the cake stall? I can make a couple of cakes if you want. And I'll ask Meg if she wants to help out with a stall. She's working on a couple of projects though, so I'm not sure if she has time.'

'I would really appreciate that, Sally – if you're sure? I feel a bit cheeky. You're on holiday, after all.'

'Not exactly a holiday. I've come to think things over,' Sally told her then hesitated. She didn't want to share too much with a stranger, although she and Meg had already told Rose that they'd both left their husbands.

'I'm happy to lend an ear if you want to offload, but I don't want to intrude if you prefer to keep it private,' Rose offered.

She *did* want to offload, and she had no one to talk to except Meg, who clearly didn't understand. So Sally found herself telling Rose, who had now pulled out a chair and was sitting next to her, all about how unhappy she was with Ted.

'It sounds so petty, I know. Lots of people have bigger issues to deal with in their marriages, but I feel at the end of my tether,' she confessed.

Rose patted her on the hand. 'It's not petty at all. You've got a life to live and it seems your husband is making you pretty miserable. The important question is, will you be happier with him or without him?'

'Without him, I'm pretty certain of that. But should I choose my happiness over everyone else's?' Sally poured herself a cup of tea and added milk. 'Meg is upset, and my son Dan will be too when he finds out. And so is Ted. He doesn't want us to break up.'

'Only you can answer that, love. Remember, though, you don't have to be a martyr to keep everyone else happy. They're all adults. You aren't responsible for any of them, nor are you required to make anyone happy.'

The door opened, bringing in a waft of cold air and another customer, a woman with a child. 'I'd better get back to work,' Rose said, getting to her feet and leaving Sally staring thoughtfully into her tea. Would she really be happier without Ted? Starting all over again at her age? Where would she live? What would she do?

Meg was back from her walk and was sitting in the lounge reading a magazine when Sally got home. She looked up as Sally walked in. 'Have you been to your favourite café again?'

'How did you guess?' Sally asked with a smile. She told Meg about Rose needing help at the Fayre. 'I've promised to make some cakes and help out with the cake stall. But she needs someone to run another stall. I don't know if you fancy it?' She looked questioningly at Meg.

Meg closed the magazine. 'I wouldn't mind. I could make some balloon animals if you like. The kids love those. We could sell them for a couple of pounds each. Luckily I've got my kit in the car.' Making balloon animals was one of Meg's specialities and they were always a big success at the children's parties she and Oliver ran. When the children had finished running around playing games, Meg would sit them down to make some balloon animals, giving them a chance to calm down before their parents arrived and something to take home with them. Sally had been to a couple of the parties and seen how much the children loved it.

'That's fantastic. I'll let Rose know. She gave me her number in case we had any questions.'

'I'll start making them tomorrow,' Meg said.

At that moment, Sally's phone rang. She picked it up off the coffee table, where she'd placed it when she'd come in, and looked at the screen. Dan. Her heart sank. Ted must have told him that she'd walked out, and she could guess what their son would have to say.

Meg raised an eyebrow questioningly.

'It's Dan,' Sally mouthed as she answered the call.

'What the hell are you playing at, Mum?' Dan's voice boomed out. 'I've just been talking to Dad and he's really cut up. He said you've walked out because he won't go on holiday with you and your cronies…'

Sally held the phone a little away from her ear. 'Look, Dan, you don't understand—'

'Understand! I understand that Dad has worked hard all his life to provide for us.'

'I've worked too,' Sally reminded him.

'And he's a decent bloke, hardly goes out for a drink, doesn't gamble or womanise, lets you go out or on holiday with your friends—'

'Lets me? You think I need his permission, do you? And I only go with my friends because your father won't go with me.'

'For goodness' sake, you should be settling down to old age together, not splitting up!' Dan roared. 'You can't do this to him, Mum. You can't split the family up.'

Sally's chin wobbled and she bit her lip, her eyes brimming with tears as she tried to find the words to explain her decision to Dan.

Suddenly Meg snatched the phone out of Sally's hand. 'You've no right to talk to Mum like that, Dan. She's really unhappy and upset. Who do you think you are telling her what to do and assuming that she's the one in the wrong?' Meg demanded furiously. 'You have no idea how much she's tried to make things work with Dad.'

Sally listened, astonished and pleased that Meg was sticking up for her. She heard Dan catch his breath.

'I might have known you women would stick together. What's Dad done that's so terrible?'

'That's between Mum and Dad, Dan. It's none of our business. We have to leave them to sort it out between themselves.'

'And what about you and Oliver? Dad said you've split up too. What's the *matter* with the women in this family?' Sally heard him demand.

'I don't want to talk about me and Oliver. Our marriage is none of your business either,' retorted Meg.

'It's bloody Christmas, Meg. Can't you and Mum at least put up with things until after Christmas? Goodwill to all men and all that? You both couldn't have chosen a worse time to walk out. Dad is devastated. Mum can't leave him on his own over Christmas.'

'If you're really so worried about Dad, then you do Christmas at your house for a change. You and Katya cook the dinner and invite Dad over,' Meg told him firmly.

'There's no talking to you. You're both bloody selfish.' Dan snorted and ended the call.

'Thank you.' Sally dabbed her eyes with a screwed-up tissue. Dan had really upset her. 'I feel like I should go back home, just for Christmas. But if I do, how can I ever leave again? And although I'm really sorry that your dad is hurt, I don't want to go back, Meg. I feel trapped.'

'You've got to do what's best for you, Mum,' Meg said, hugging her. 'I'm sorry that I was a bit off with you about it at first. It's hard when your parents split up. But like I told Dan, it's none of our business. This is between you and Dad, no one else.'

Chapter Fifteen

Thursday, 18 December

Meg

The next day was mild with a low wind, so when her mum suggested taking a picnic up to the Cragg, Meg was happy to go along.

'Your Dad and I spent many a happy afternoon here when we were on our honeymoon,' she told her as they sat at the top of the Cragg, tucking into ham sandwiches, scones and strawberries and cream – the food Mum had brought with them today and always made for a picnic. Meg guessed the tradition had started way back then. She asked the question as she squeezed tomato ketchup onto her ham.

Her mum nodded. 'Yep, the first time we decided to go on a picnic it was on impulse; we'd seen the Cragg a few times and said we wanted to go to the top, so one day we decided to have a picnic up here. We only had ham in the fridge, and we bought strawberries, scones and cream on the way.'

Meg bit into the sandwich and chewed it thoughtfully as her mum continued. 'It was a lovely day. We sat up here for hours, just talking.' A wistful look came over her eyes. 'We never talk like that now. In fact, we hardly talk at all unless it's about you and Dan, what we're having for tea or the latest darn plant that's springing up in the garden.'

We talk all the time, Meg thought, remembering the Sunday mornings she and Oliver had sat up in bed, drinking coffee and talking about their week; the conversations as they'd eaten breakfast in the week that had often seen one of them stopping mid-sentence and saying, 'God, I'm late,' giving the other a quick kiss and dashing out of the door, coat half on; the evenings they'd sat down to watch a film and missed half of it because they'd been chatting about their day. It seemed that Mum and Dad used to be like that too. If she and Oliver decided to get back together and have a child, maybe they'd be like her parents as they grew older. Only Oliver would probably be the resentful one, the one who thought he'd missed out on life because Meg had blackmailed him into having a child and then he hadn't been able to do the things he'd wanted to do. Because it was emotional blackmail in a way, wasn't it? *Have a child or we'll split up.* She hadn't looked at it like that before.

It isn't so much that he doesn't want a child but that he didn't tell me until now, she reminded herself. If only he'd been honest in the beginning… then what? Would she have still married him? Meg thought this over and she honestly didn't know. Yet she loved Oliver so much. Should he be enough for her, as he had said? What if she was the one who didn't want a child, but Oliver did? *I would have told him right away*, she thought, *and set him free to find someone he could have a family with, and be happy with, if that's what he wanted.*

Was it what she wanted?

'Penny for them,' Mum said softly.

Meg briefly relayed her thoughts. 'Oliver said that if I loved him, he should be enough for me. That we came together as two people, not three or four, and our relationship should be the most important thing.' She raised her knees and wrapped her arms around them. 'Am I being selfish?'

Mum picked up the thermos flask and poured some hot coffee into a mug, handed it to Meg, then poured herself one. 'It's not as simple as one of you being selfish, Meg. You both want different things out of life, so one of you is going to have to compromise to make the other one happy. That's what I feel like I've been doing all my life, and maybe your dad feels like that too. For one person to be happy the other one sometimes has to make sacrifices. You have to ask yourself if your relationship is worth those sacrifices.'

'Oliver obviously doesn't think it is. And, actually, I don't want him to make a sacrifice. I don't want to make a sacrifice either. If he doesn't want a baby, I don't want him to pretend he does, or to have one just for me. I think it's best if we set each other free to live our lives how we want to. Although I wish we didn't have to,' she added sadly.

'Which is exactly how I feel about your dad. I don't want to change him. I just want to be me.' Mum raised her cup. 'To being us!'

Meg raised her cup and they clicked them together. 'To us.'

Talking to her mum had made Meg's mind clearer. It definitely was best for her and Oliver to part. There was no going back from this. Okay, maybe she would never have a child anyway – she certainly wasn't in a rush to get into a relationship with someone else and start a family – but that wasn't the point.

'It'll be all right, you'll see. We'll get through this,' Sally said, squeezing Meg's hand.

Yes, we will, Meg thought, because like her mum, she wanted to live her life not waste it.

She looked out to sea and saw a boat bobbing about it.

'We should go for a boat ride,' she said impulsively. 'Do you think we'll be able to hire one out in the winter?'

'We'll ask Rose – she'll know,' Mum said. 'I'll phone her.'

Rose did know. Her younger brother had a boat and took people across the bay in it during the summer months. She was sure that he was more than willing to take them out for half an hour for a very reasonable fee. She said she'd message him and arrange it then replied ten minutes later to say that Rory would be waiting at the harbour for them in an hour; she attached a photo of Rory standing by a blue and white motorboat. 'The boat's called *Seaspray*,' she told them.

When they'd finished their picnic, Meg and Sally made their way back down the Cragg to meet Rory. He was sitting on the deck of his boat and stood up when he saw them. A tall, sturdy man with a thick mop of salt-and-pepper hair, a full beard and moustache, he looked every inch a fisherman.

'Hello, are you Rory?' Sally asked. 'Rose said you would take me and Meg, my daughter, for a ride across the bay in your motorboat.'

'I certainly will.' His face broke into a huge smile that reached right up to his eyes. 'I must say though that most people want to go for a boat ride in the summer rather than mid-winter.' His eyes flitted from one to the other. 'You're wrapped up well, mind, and it's a mild day. Is it half an hour you're wanting?'

'Just across the bay and back,' Sally told him.

'Half an hour then.' He took two orange life vests out of the boat and handed one to Sally and one to Meg. 'Put these on and we'll be off.'

'You forgot to mention the price,' Sally said.

'Oh, a tenner will do it,' Rory told her. 'Here, let me fasten that.' Sally had gotten in a bit of a tangle with the strings of her life vest. He sorted it out for her then turned to Meg, who had already tied hers. 'I can see we've got an expert here,' he said with a nod. 'Let's be going then.'

As they crossed the bay in Rory's motorboat, the wind gently blowing their hair, listening to Rory pointing out various landmarks and sights, and answering Mum's constant questions, Meg felt calm, peaceful. *I'll get over Oliver*, she realised, *and I'll be happy again.*

Chapter Sixteen

Friday, 19 December

Meg

Meg spent most of Friday finishing off the big promo event she'd been dealing with while Sally had gone off shopping and to see Rose about the Christmas Fayre the next day.

'I'm officially finished with work now until the second of January,' she said when her mum returned.

'That's great.' Sally carried the shopping bags into the kitchen and put them on the table. 'I've asked Rose and Rory to join us for mince pies and mulled wine this evening. They share a cottage so I didn't want to leave Rory out. I hope you don't mind?'

'Of course not,' Meg told her, going over to help unpack the shopping.

'I thought you wouldn't.' Mum smiled and held up a bag of flour. 'Want to help me make the mince pies? Or the cakes for tomorrow?'

Meg screwed up her nose. She wasn't really into baking. 'I'll lick out the bowl,' she offered.

Sally laughed. 'You and Dan always argued over that, didn't you? I had to give you a spoon each and tell you both to keep to one side of the bowl.'

'Yes, and Dan always sneaked a spoonful from my side.' Meg chuckled. 'We must have driven you mad, the things we used to argue over.'

'Sometimes. But I wouldn't swap either of you. Even if Dan can be bossy and shouted at me down the phone on Wednesday.' Sally took a big bag of flour out of the shopping bag. 'I'll get started now, if that's okay with you? Then it'll all be cleared away in time for dinner.'

'Good idea,' Meg told her. 'I'll fetch my balloon kit out of the car and make up some animals for tomorrow. I'll make a few different designs so that people have plenty to choose from.'

As she walked back from the car, she bumped into Leo and Sam – dressed in his school uniform – just about to go into their house. Leo had obviously just picked him up from school.

'How are you doing?' Leo asked cheerily. 'Mum said you're both helping out at the Fayre tomorrow.'

'Yep. Mum's about to bake cakes as we speak, and I'm going to be making balloon animals to sell.' She indicated the kit in her hands.

'Really?' Sam's eyes were like saucers. 'We saw a man making balloon animals when we were on holiday in Newquay last year, didn't we, Dad? He made a dragon and a dinosaur. What can you make?' he asked Meg.

'Lots of things. Poodles, unicorns, dinosaurs and dragons, of course, snakes, monkeys. And I'll do some Santas and reindeer seeing as it's Christmas.'

'Cool! Can I help?'

Meg glanced at Leo, trying to gauge how he felt. He was probably planning on Sam helping him with the games. She didn't want him to be upset that Sam might prefer to make balloon animals with her. 'I think your dad might need your help.'

'Please, Dad!' Sam begged.

'It's fine by me if Meg has time…' Leo shot Meg a 'do you mind?' glance and she smiled.

'I'd be glad of the help, if you're sure. Blowing up those balloons isn't easy! Why don't you both come around later? Your mum and uncle are coming too.' She was sure her mum wouldn't mind the extra company.

'That'd be great. We can get your opinion on some of the games we're organising too,' Leo said. 'Shall we make it a couple of hours? Sam needs to get changed and have a bite to eat.'

'Perfect,' Meg agreed.

Mum had already started making the mince pies when Meg returned and didn't mind at all when Meg told her that Leo and Sam would be joining them too. 'I'll make an extra batch of mince pies and leave the cake-baking until tomorrow,' she said.

Meg was looking forward to their guests. It'd be good to have some company. And it might stop her from thinking about Oliver.

It turned out to be a fun evening. Leo and Sam had decided to organise games of Hook the Snowman, Reindeer Hoopla and Santa Skittles and wanted to try them out. There was a lot of laughter as they all played the games, so much that Meg didn't hear the door knock at first. She glanced at the clock – nine thirty. Perhaps it was carol singers. Leaving Mum and Rory competing with each other to win Hook the Snowman, she went to answer the door. And there, on the doorstep, was her dad, a holdall in his hand.

'Dad!' Meg gave him a big hug. 'I didn't know you were coming!'

'Well you told me to talk to your mum so here I am.' He stepped inside and walked into the lounge before she could warn her mum, who was cheering, a snowman dangling from her hook, and half-turned towards Rory, who was laughing too.

Sally spun around at the sound of Ted's voice, the surprise evident on her face. 'Ted! What are you doing here?'

'I came to see if I could talk some sense into you. What are you doing and who's he?' Ted demanded.

'This is Rory and his sister Rose, Dad. We're helping them with the Christmas Fayre tomorrow, and this is Leo and Sam. Leo is Rose's son and he lives next door,' Meg explained quickly.

'Well, you all look very friendly, I must say,' her father remarked, disapproval and suspicion evident on his face.

There was an awkward silence in the room.

'I think we'd better leave you to it,' Rose said.

Rory nodded. 'We'll see you tomorrow at the Fayre.'

'We need to go too.' Leo and Sam started packing the games away.

'Let me just say goodbye to our guests and we'll go into the kitchen to talk, Ted,' Mum said calmly.

'I'll go through and put the kettle on, shall I?' Dad put his holdall on the floor by the sofa and marched into the kitchen.

'Awkward. Sorry,' Mum mouthed at Rose. 'I had no idea he was coming.'

'No problem. He probably wants you both to make up so you can spend Christmas together, and who can blame him?' Rose said sympathetically. 'Let us know if you can't manage to help out at the Fayre tomorrow; it's no problem at all,' she whispered, giving Mum a reassuring hug.

'I *will* be helping out at the Fayre,' Sally said determinedly.

'I'll go for a walk, Mum, give you both a bit of space to talk. Text me and let me know how things are going,' Meg told her, following everyone out so she could get her coat. That had been dead awkward, and Dad had his overnight bag with him, obviously intending to spend the night. Would they manage to sort things out?

'Come with us – we haven't made any balloon animals yet,' Sam begged. 'And I don't have to go to bed early tonight, it's the Christmas holidays.'

Leo nodded. 'You're welcome, if you want to.'

'Thanks, I will,' Meg replied.

'I'm going around to Leo's for a coffee,' she said, popping her head around the kitchen door. Her parents were now standing by the sink, both looking very ill at ease, and Mum was filling up the kettle. How she wished they could both sort it out, make up and go home together. She didn't think that was going to happen though. She'd seen a new side to her mum these past few days and it was obvious that she was happier without her dad. It was such a shame.

At least Dad had made the effort to come down and try to sort things out, which was more than Oliver had done.

Her parents *did* have years of being together to salvage. It must be hard to turn your back on a lifetime of marriage and children, building a home together. She and Oliver didn't have that. And now they never would.

Chapter Seventeen

Sally

'Well, you all look like you're having fun!' Ted said sarcastically as soon as everyone had left.

Sally swallowed down her anger. How dare Ted turn up unexpectedly and show her up like that? 'It's not a crime to enjoy yourself,' she retorted sharply.

'Meaning I don't know how to. I'm boring and that's why you've left me! You certainly seemed to be having fun with your new friends.'

'You should have told me you were coming, Ted.' She thought of the holdall he'd carried. 'Especially as you're obviously intending to stay. It would be nice to be asked.'

'So I have to ask to see my wife now?' Ted demanded. 'And who were those people?'

Sally flicked on the kettle and took two mugs out of the cupboard. 'Do you remember that little café we used to go to on the seafront when we came here on our honeymoon?'

Ted frowned. 'The one overlooking the harbour? Where the woman used to sneak us an extra scone sometimes?'

'Yes.' Sally kept her back to him as she popped a teabag into each mug. 'Well, the older couple that were here are the previous owners' son and daughter, Rory and Rose. Meg and I went to see if the café was still open and we met Rose; she said their parents had retired years ago and that she is retiring herself soon. The younger man, Leo, is Rose's son and lives next door; the little boy is his son, Sam, who is staying with him for Christmas.' She kept her voice even as she poured hot water into each mug. 'We're all helping out at the Christmas Fayre tomorrow, which is why they were here. We were having a meeting about the stalls we are running,' she explained matter-of-factly as she fished out the teabags and added a drop of milk then two sugars for Ted.

'It didn't look like a meeting to me.'

Keep your cool. Sally took a deep breath and handed Ted his tea. 'Well, I'm telling you it was. Now would you like a biscuit or a mince pie?'

He shook his head, seeming momentarily lost for words.

Sally walked over to the kitchen table and pulled out a chair. 'Let's sit down, shall we? Then you can tell me why you're here.'

Ted pulled out the chair next to her and sat down, resting his elbows on the table. 'Look, I don't want to argue.' He sighed wearily. 'I got thinking this afternoon that maybe I am a bit set in my ways – not that it's a crime; not many people want to go off here and there at our age. It's only natural to settle down, take each other for granted a bit, and yes, maybe I am guilty of that. But it's not a good enough reason to throw away all those years of being together, of building our home, our family. We need to fix this, Sally.' He fiddled with his earlobe as he awkwardly met her gaze. 'You came here, where we had our honeymoon – that must mean you still have feelings for me.'

He looked tired and there were dark shadows under his grey-blue eyes. She remembered the first time she'd seen Ted: his hair was jet-black then and his eyes had sparkled, especially when she'd agreed to go out with him.

She realised that he'd stopped talking and was waiting for her to reply. *He really can't understand why I've left him*, she thought, *and I don't know how to explain.*

'I came to Goolan Bay because I wanted to remember how it used to be between us, how in love we were. Do you remember all the things we said we'd do, the places we would go? How full of hope and dreams we were?' she asked softly.

He looked down at his hands, clasped together on the table in front of him. Ted was always uncomfortable talking about his feelings. 'A lot of water has flowed under the bridge since then, Sal. When you're young, the world seems your oyster; you feel like you can do anything you want with your life. When you're older, you're wiser – and have the aches and pains to prove it! You change, settle down, mellow. Well, most of us do,' he said pointedly.

'That's just it, Ted. I don't want to settle down, to take each other for granted, to sleepwalk into old age. I want to feel loved, to have the passion back that we used to have.' She swallowed. How could she make him understand? 'I want to feel alive, to see the world, to experience things.'

'You talk like we're in our forties instead of our sixties!' Ted told her. 'I'm happy as we are, Sal. I'm settled. But I can compromise. We can go out for a meal now and again, a holiday if that's what it takes to make you happy.' He raised his head, his eyes meeting hers. 'I want you to come home, Sal. I was hoping you'd come back with me. We could go to the Bowls Club Christmas dinner together tomorrow night. I don't want to set the tongues wagging, having people talk about us. It's embarrassing.'

So that's why he'd come. It was all about him not losing face. The Bowls Club Christmas dinner was the highlight of Ted's year, the only time he donned his posh suit, a shirt and tie. He'd even been known to actually dance with her. She'd forgotten all about it and certainly wasn't going back just so he could walk in with her on his arm.

'I'm not coming home, Ted. Nothing's changed. The problems are still here, and we'll only end up splitting up again. It's best for both of us if we make a clean break now.'

She hated seeing the stricken look on his face. She didn't want to hurt him, she just wanted to be free.

'I can't believe you're being so bloody selfish!' Sally jolted as Ted thumped his fist on the table. He stood up and went into the lounge, coming back in with his holdall. He rummaged through it and took out the family photo album.

'Take a look through this; think about all the years we've had together. All the memories. We're supposed to be celebrating our ruby wedding anniversary in June. And you're throwing it all away because you're chasing your youth! Grow up, woman!'

Sally watched speechlessly as Ted took out a wrapped Christmas present. 'I've brought your present too, in case you aren't home for Christmas. Not completely selfish, am I?'

Sally knew without opening it what it would be: a bottle of her favourite perfume. Ted bought her the same thing every year. It was expensive, and a generous-sized bottle, but she wished he would buy her something different, something that showed he had really thought about what she would like.

'Thank you. Your present is underneath the tree in the lounge at home.' She stood up. 'Look, Ted, I'm sorry it's ended like this. I've tried. I really have.'

'Not hard enough.' Ted fixed her with a glare. 'I'm done trying to reason with you, Sal. If you aren't back for Christmas, then don't bother to come back at all.'

Sally watched him grab his holdall and walk stiffly out of the kitchen. As soon as she heard the front door close behind him, the tears poured down her face and she crumpled into a sobbing heap at the table, her head resting on her arms. *God. Why does it have to be so hard?*

Chapter Eighteen

Meg

Meg heard the door slam and hurried over to Leo's front door, opening it and peering out into the dark. She could just make out the shadow of her dad walking down the path, carrying his overnight bag. They hadn't made up, then.

'I've got to go,' she called to Leo, grabbing her coat off the hook by the door and dashing outside. 'Dad. Hang on!'

For a moment she thought he was going to ignore her but then he stopped and turned and in the glow of the street lamp she could see tears in his eyes. Her dad was crying. She stood still for a moment, shocked. The only time she had ever seen her dad cry before was when his parents – her grandparents – had died. 'Oh, Dad!' She ran towards him and gave him a big hug. 'I'm so sorry, Dad. What happened?' she asked.

'What do you think? It seems your mum has no intention of coming home any time soon. It's the Bowls Club Christmas dinner tomorrow night and I was hoping she'd come back with me so we could attend it, but no. I don't know what to do, Meg.' His voice was choked. 'Your mum doesn't want me. She said we've grown apart. We're over. Forty years we've been together next June. And now it's all over.'

'Don't go home yet,' Meg begged. He looked exhausted and had already driven for an hour and a half to get here; she didn't want him to drive back without having a rest, especially at this time of night. They had a spare room at the cottage but it wouldn't be right to ask him to stay; she wouldn't like her mum to ask Oliver to stay, would she? 'Maybe you could stay at a B & B and talk to Mum again tomorrow.'

'It's a waste of time. Your mum's enjoying herself down here, so I'll go back home and enjoy myself too. I've told her that if she's not back for Christmas, I don't want her back.'

Mum wouldn't take kindly to that sort of ultimatum. 'I'm sorry, Dad. I know it's hard for you, but Mum is really unhappy. I wish you two could sort it out.' Meg kissed her father on the cheek.

'Don't worry yourself about us. You've got your own troubles to contend with,' he said.

Meg swallowed the lump in her throat as tears threatened to spill out of her own eyes. She felt so sorry for her parents; this was hard for both of them. 'Come to the pub for a while, Dad, we'll talk about things. I don't want you to drive home upset.'

He shook his head. 'There's no point us talking, pet; your mum's made up her mind and that's that.' He blinked back the tears from his eyes. 'Now what about you and Oliver? Can you make up, do you think?'

'No, Dad. I don't think we can.'

'I'm sorry to hear that. I really am.' He wiped his forehead with the back of his hand. 'I'll be in touch, Meg, but right now I need to get home, to be in my own house.'

She gave him a big hug. 'Love you, Dad. Look after yourself. Drive carefully and please message me and let me know you've got home safely.'

'I will,' he promised.

Meg watched her father walk off, shoulders sloped. He looked older since the split, she realised, whereas Mum looked younger.

Sadness weighed heavy in her heart as she returned to the cottage to find her mum sitting at the kitchen table, head on her arms, crying.

'Oh, Mum!' She rushed over and put her arms around her mum's shoulders.

'I don't want to hurt your dad, Meg. I really don't want to. I'm just so miserable when I'm with him, it eats me up inside.'

This is awful, Meg thought as she hugged her mother, when a few minutes ago she had hugged her distraught father. Both her parents were so terribly upset and she had no idea how to help.

This would be me and Oliver in a few years' time, she realised. *Either I'd be angry because I'd sacrificed my dream of having a family for him, and it would eat me up, or he would feel that I'd tied him down, given him the responsibility of having a child when he didn't want one. We'd destroy each other, and our child – or children – would be caught up in the middle of it all. It's better to end it now.*

Not that she had much choice anyway. Oliver hadn't come down to see her, to beg her to go back with him, like Dad had done, had he?

But then Mum and Dad had been together for so long.

Mum's words flashed back across her mind: 'I'm so miserable with him, it eats me up inside.'

Well, it was the opposite with her and Oliver. She was so happy with him she felt a warm glow inside. Being with him lit her up. And now that glow had gone forever.

Then the last line of Oliver's new song came back to her, the soulful ballad he'd been singing to her the night it had all fallen apart.

'Sometimes love isn't enough.'

It hadn't been enough for her and Oliver, had it? It was almost as if he'd been warning her.

Chapter Nineteen

Saturday, 20 December

Meg

Sally spent Saturday morning baking. Rose had told her what cakes the other villagers usually made – she didn't want to step on anyone's toes – so she made something different: a Battenberg, a chocolate and orange gateau and some more mince pies. Baking was one of the things Sally enjoyed; she'd always made Dan's and Meg's birthday cakes and a cake for Sunday tea when they were young.

'That looks lovely, Mum,' Meg said as she came into the kitchen holding a pink balloon poodle.

'So is that,' Sally told her. 'I don't know how you make those things so quickly, and without popping any balloons either!'

'It's quite easy once you've got the hang of it, and they're so popular at parties,' Meg told her. 'I'm going to take a break now. Want a cuppa?'

'Love one – tea please,' Sally said.

They both looked around questioningly as someone knocked on the door. 'That must be either Rose or Leo,' Sally said.

'I'll get it.' Meg headed out into the hall, opening the door to find Leo and Sam standing on the doorstep, holding a big cardboard box.

'We're off to the community centre now and wondered if you needed help taking anything down there?'

'Well, Mum's made enough cake to feed an army, so it'll be a few trips to the car,' Meg told him. 'But you look like you've got your hands full already. Are those all games in there?'

'Yep, we've got Pin the Beard on Santa too, and a fluffy snowman for everyone to guess its name.'

'Pin the Beard on Santa was my idea,' Sam piped up. He looked at the balloon poodle peeping out from under Meg's arm. 'That looks cool.'

'Thanks. Look, we've just put the kettle on – fancy a cuppa before you go? There's over an hour yet before the Fayre starts.'

'That sounds a great idea; we've run out of milk,' Leo told her. 'Someone had two bowls of cereal for breakfast and used it all up.'

Judging by the look on the lad's face, that 'someone' was Sam. 'We've got a bottle you can have. Mum always has plenty,' Meg told them. 'Come on in and put that box down for a bit; it must be heavy.'

They both followed her in, Sam closing the door behind his dad. He didn't look so sulky today, Meg noticed. Getting involved with the Christmas Fayre had kept him occupied, she guessed. He and Leo had looked like they were having fun when they were practising the games yesterday.

'We've got two more for refreshments,' she announced as they walked into the kitchen but Sally had already heard them and was taking a cup and tall glass out of the cupboard. 'Coffee and a chocolate milkshake?' she asked.

'Yes, please!' Sam replied. 'We've got no milk—' He stopped and stared at the chocolate and orange gateau. 'Wow, that looks awesome! Did you make that?'

'I did, and I'll be cutting it up into individual slices to sell at the Fayre. I'll save one for you, if you want?'

'Yes, please!' Sam said again, practically licking his lips.

Leo put the box down in the corner of the kitchen and they all pulled out chairs and sat down at the table to have their drinks.

'What other balloon things have you made?' Sam asked.

'I'll show you.' Meg fetched the box of balloon animals that she'd made up that morning and took them out one by one: there was a crown hat, a teddy, a turtle, a rabbit, a monkey, a giraffe, a unicorn and a dinosaur. Then she took out the last two – a balloon reindeer and a balloon Santa – and held them up proudly.

'They're fantastic!' Sam said, his eyes wide. 'Can you show me how to make them? We can get some of the balloons, can't we, Dad?' he asked.

Leo picked up the Santa admiringly. 'These are pretty spectacular. I don't think we'll be able to do anything like this,' he said. 'How did you learn to make them?'

'And why do you make them?' Sam chipped in. 'Do you sell them?'

'One question at a time,' Meg said with a grin. 'I make them because I organise children's parties with Oliver, my… husband. And I learnt to make them because I saw a man making balloon animals when we went to Blackpool when I was younger, and I was so fascinated that my parents bought me one of the balloon kits he was selling. I practised a lot and now I can make all sorts of things. They're really popular at our parties. Sometimes children ask for something special – a little girl asked for a unicorn once – so I learn how to do it and that's another one added to my list.'

'Can I have a balloon-making kit, please, Dad?' Sam begged.

'Sure, if Meg tells me where she gets them from.' Leo grinned at Meg. 'I think you've just come up with a solution to keep Sam occupied.'

'I'll give you the website later. But right now, we need to drink this up and get to the Fayre,' Meg said. She had a couple of spare packs of balloons in her car; she'd tell Leo later that she'd give Sam one for Christmas. 'I'll show you how to make some of the animals too.'

Sam's eyes sparkled. 'That'll be ace. I want to make one of those poodles for Mum. She loves poodles. We've got two – one black and one white – they're a bit naughty but cute,' he added.

'Thank you,' Leo whispered to Meg as she put the balloon animals back in the box. 'I don't think I've seen him so enthusiastic about anything for months.'

She smiled. 'It's a pleasure.'

She was glad that Sam was coming out of his mood. It must be hard for Leo – he seemed a good dad, and he clearly cared about his son.

Oliver would have made a good dad too, she thought, her mind casting back to how he got the children involved with making up silly songs at the parties, putting a tune to them and playing them on his guitar while the children loudly sang along. It was a shame he didn't want to be one.

It didn't make sense to her. Oliver loved children; he was good with them. Why didn't he want one of their own? Was it because he didn't think their marriage was strong enough, and he didn't want their child to grow up in a broken home, as he had done? Oliver rarely spoke about his dad, Markus, but she knew Markus had walked out when Oliver was a baby then turned up years later and popped in and out of his life whenever he needed anything.

It suddenly occurred to her that she had never stopped to consider *why* Oliver didn't want children. Mum had asked that too, she remembered. Maybe she really should have asked him.

She shook the thought from her head. This wasn't just about Oliver not wanting children. It was about him lying about it. But even if he had told her the truth earlier, would she have been able to accept not having children? Was Oliver enough for her?

Chapter Twenty

Sally

The hall was bustling with activity when they walked in. Tables were laid all around the large room and across the middle, while more were being set up. Sally could see a tombola table with an assortment of interesting goods to win, a Christmas crafts table with some beautiful handmade decorations, and a toy stall. She was so pleased that they'd got involved with this Fayre; it had taken both their minds off their marriage problems and had certainly cheered Sam up. She liked Sam, and Leo – although she was bothered that Leo and Meg were getting a bit close. She just hoped Meg wasn't on the rebound, looking for a bit of attention from someone else. Sally knew that her daughter still loved Oliver and was heartbroken over him. Meg was vulnerable right now, and Sally hoped Leo wouldn't take advantage of that.

'Sally! Meg!' Rose was waving as she walked over to join them.

'I've put you over here, Meg, by Leo,' Rose said, leading them over to the left wall where two empty tables stood side by side. 'I thought you might feel more comfortable being by someone you know. And Sally, the cake stall is the other side of the hall. I hope that's okay?'

'That's perfect,' Sally told her. She enjoyed Rose's company; she was so outgoing and friendly.

'Hello, Granny!' Sam said, looking quite cheerful. 'I'm glad you've put Meg next to us because then I can help both her and Dad.'

'I think he would have deserted me and helped you,' Leo said with a grin. 'Those balloon animals have got him hooked.'

'Ah, but you have the Santa Skittles,' Meg told him. 'I can't wait to see those.'

'I'll leave you to it, then. Leo and Sam will show you the ropes. See you all later.' And with a cheery wave, Sally went off with Rose.

There was already a big selection of cakes laid out on the table: the inevitable mince pies and gingerbread Santas and reindeers, a three-layered Victoria sponge, butterfly cakes, iced cakes, and in the centre of the table, on a silver stand, was a large Christmas cake decorated with holly, mistletoe and a Santa on a sleigh. It was a lovely display.

'Did you make the Christmas cake?' she asked Rose.

'No, my mum did. She's made a Christmas cake for years, and being almost ninety isn't going to stop her.' Rose reached in her handbag and took out a book of raffle tickets. 'We're raffling that cake; it should raise us a few pounds.'

'I'll buy some raffle tickets for it. I've made a Christmas cake but I've left it at home.' Sally's voice faltered. How silly, but thinking about the Christmas cake had suddenly made her think of Ted and all the Christmases they'd spent together. It had always been a family Christmas for them; even when Dan then Meg had left home, they had always come back for Christmas. Now it was a divided Christmas. Her with Meg – thank goodness she still had her darling daughter, although she did wish Meg and Oliver hadn't split up – and hopefully, Dan and Katya would invite Ted over. She realised she hated to think of him spending Christmas alone.

Maybe I shouldn't have walked out like that, she thought. *Maybe I should have left it until the new year.*

What difference would it have made? She still would have left and then Ted would have had the next Christmas on his own. *You can't stay together just for Christmas then up and go.* She took out her purse and paid for a few strips of raffle tickets, then set about putting her own cakes on the table. Luckily, she'd found some pretty, decorated plates in the cottage so had placed the cakes on those.

'Now I fancy a slice of that,' a deep, rumbling voice said as Sally took the chocolate and orange gateau out of the plastic container she'd carefully placed it in. She looked up to see Rory smiling at her.

'Thank you. I'll be cutting it up later so I'll save you a slice, shall I?'

Rory pointed to one of the chocolate flakes decorating the top of the cake. 'Make sure it's a slice with one of those on, will you?'

'I knew you'd turn up soon,' Rose said with a smile. 'He never can resist cake,' she told Sally.

'Are you helping out on a stall or just sampling the cakes?' Sally asked him.

'I'm over on the house signs stall in the corner.' He pointed over to a table where she could see some decorative house signs painted on bark and slate. 'Bit of a hobby of mine; keeps me busy in the winter when there's not many people wanting boat trips.'

'They look unusual – I must pop over and have a look later,' she said. 'Have you been doing it for long?'

'A good few years now. They're nothing fancy, mind. I'm no artist, but folks often like something a bit different.'

'They look good to me,' she told him. One of them had already caught her eye: a highly polished piece of bark with some flowers around it and the words 'The Beeches' written in a lovely calligraphic script in the middle. It surprised her that Rory wrote in calligraphy; he seemed such an 'outdoor' sort of man, but he obviously also had a softer, more creative side. She'd always wanted a name for their house but Ted thought it was a bit pretentious. 'A number is enough,' he'd said.

Maybe she could buy a sign for her new house? She had no idea where she'd be living though. She hadn't thought beyond coming down here for Christmas.

Rory went off to his table as people started to pour into the hall. It was quite a crowd. *I hope we raise a lot of money*, Sally thought. *Enough to buy presents for all the children in hospital.* Obviously, the children would have presents from their parents and families too but it would be nice to cheer them all up with a few more. It was such a shame to be in hospital over Christmastime.

Quite a crowd had gathered around the cake table, so Sally and Rose were busy serving for the next half hour or so. When finally there was chance to get away, Sally offered to fetch a much-needed cup of coffee for herself and Rose. As she walked back with the drinks she spotted Oliver standing at the entrance, watching Meg.

Chapter Twenty-One

Meg

Meg felt something, she wasn't sure what. A feeling of being watched? She glanced over at the door and her heart skipped a beat. 'Oliver!'

His eyes met hers then he smiled and walked over, and her heart did a giddy little leap. He'd come to see her. Did he want to talk? To apologise? God knew she wanted to talk to him.

She turned to Leo, who was supervising an extremely loud game of Reindeer Hoopla. 'Would you watch my stall for a moment please? Oliver's just arrived.'

Leo nodded. 'Of course.'

Meg started walking towards Oliver, her eyes on his. Closer and closer they got until suddenly he was standing in front of her and she longed to wrap her arms around him and kiss him. Instead they stood feet apart, but their eyes locked so intensely she knew he still loved her just like she still loved him. Knew it for certain. For a moment they stood in silence, staring at each other as if there was no one else in the room but them. Oliver's deep voice broke the spell. 'Hello, Meg.'

'Hello, Oliver.' She had no idea how she managed to keep her voice steady, how she stopped herself from flinging herself at him. 'How did you know I was here? Did Dad tell you?'

'Yes, he phoned me last night,' he admitted, adding quickly, 'I was thinking of phoning him but wasn't sure if I should, what with him and your mum splitting up too. He's pretty cut up about it, Meg.'

'I know, so is Mum. I'm not sure they can work it out though.'

Oliver looked over at the stall where Leo was now selling someone a balloon dinosaur. 'You seem to have settled in well down here.'

'We're just helping out. The villagers are raising funds for Christmas presents for the children in the local hospital,' Meg told him.

'Meg, can we talk?' he asked softly.

She nodded, although looking at him – his dark hair tousled, his eyes gazing at her intently – talking was the last thing on her mind. She wanted to wrap her arms around him, trace her finger over his lips then kiss them slowly. 'I'm tied up here for another hour or so though; I can't just abandon my stall.'

'Then I'll help you,' he offered. As they walked over towards the stall together, she longed to reach out and wrap her hand in his. They always used to hold hands when they walked along, sit as close as they could on the sofa, always within reach of each other. The thought that they would never hold hands again filled her with sadness.

'Leo, this is Oliver, my… husband,' she said as they reached the stall.

Leo held out his hand. 'Hi, I'm Leo. Sam – my son here – and I are in charge of the games.'

'It looks like you're all having fun,' Oliver said easily as he shook Leo's hand.

'We are, but it's manic. Give me a shout if you need me to cover again, Meg,' Leo said as he shifted over to his own stall, which Sam had been proudly manning alone.

Meg and Oliver slipped behind Meg's table. Oliver looked admiringly at the assortment of animals Meg had made with the balloons. 'This is a fantastic display.'

'Thank you.' It felt so strange, so awkward, almost as if they were strangers. She wanted to cry for the love and closeness they'd once had.

A young girl approached the stall, clutching her mum's hand. 'Can I have a unicorn balloon, please?'

'What colour do you want, sweetheart?' Meg asked. 'I have white or pink.'

The girl pondered for a moment then decided. 'Pink, please.'

Meg passed her the pink unicorn, took the money the little girl handed her and put it into a box under the table.

The table was a magnet for children, and Meg and Oliver were both busy serving them for the next hour or so. Leo and Sam's table was busy too, and laughter often exploded from the children participating in the games. Now and again Sam shouted something to Meg and she laughed, glad to see that he and Leo were getting on so well. Her own takings box was brimming, and when she'd glanced over at the cake stall, she'd seen a crowd of people around that too. In fact, all the stalls were busy. It looked like the Christmas Fayre was going to be a success.

And Oliver was standing beside her, helping her. He'd come to see her. He wanted her back. And she wanted him back too, so desperately, she admitted to herself. Seeing him again had brought everything rushing back, made her realise how much she loved him.

But Oliver had made a future together impossible. Even if Oliver said he'd changed his mind, she would always wonder if he'd just been saying it to please her.

The hall was emptying now, most of the stalls bare of their goods, including Meg's. All she had left was a balloon dinosaur and a pink poodle. *I wonder how much we've collected*, she thought as she turned to Sam and handed him the two remaining balloon animals.

'Would you like these for helping me?' she asked. He really had been a big help today, transforming into a smiling, helpful lad. He and Leo had been joking about with each other and she'd caught a glimpse of an easy bond between them. Meg wondered if Sam's mother knew how unhappy he was about her going away without him. But then, she had a right to her happiness too, didn't she? You couldn't expect her to take Sam on her honeymoon, especially when he had a loving father he could stay with.

'Yes, please!' Sam eagerly held his hands out for the balloon animals.

'Looks like it's been a success,' Oliver said. It had been so good to be with him again. 'When will you know how much you've raised?'

'We're meeting up later. Then Rose will go and buy the presents on Monday. I think her brother is going with her too,' Meg told him, closing up her balloon kit.

'That went really well. Rose is pleased. We've been completely cleared of cakes,' Sally said as she came over to the table. She smiled at Oliver. 'Hello, love.'

'Hello, Sally.'

Mum and Oliver had always got on well. Although Oliver clearly adored his own mum, Faye, she had moved over to Portugal years ago and he hardly saw her, so Sally was like his substitute mother. Oliver didn't have much of a family, actually, she acknowledged. Oliver had told her that neither of his parents had any siblings and he'd hardly ever seen his grandparents on either side. It had been just him and his mum when he was growing up. *You'd think he'd want a family of his own, to fill his life with people who love him.*

'I'm off for a drink with Rose and Rory so the cottage is empty for a few hours if you two want a bit of privacy to talk things over,' Sally said.

'Thanks, Mum.' Meg turned to Oliver. 'Do you want to go for a walk, to the pub or back to the cottage?'

'Can we go for a walk?' he asked.

She'd hoped he'd say that. She wanted some fresh air after spending the afternoon cooped up in the hall. Besides, she found it easier to talk when walking, rather than the intimacy of being close together in a small room. It would be too easy to end up falling into Oliver's arms. And maybe into bed. But the problem would still be there.

'Sure. Shall we walk along the harbour? It's only a few minutes down the hill,' she suggested. 'Where's your car parked?'

'In the car park here. Yours?' he asked.

'Same,' she told him. 'They'll be fine there for another couple of hours, but first let me put my balloon stuff in the car.'

'I'll put it in mine,' Sally told her, taking the box off her. 'You two get yourselves off.'

They walked down the hill side by side, not quite touching. Meg wondered if Oliver had his hands in his pockets because, like her, he was trying to stop himself from reaching out and taking her hand, slipping into the easy familiarity they'd always had. She missed him so much her soul ached.

'It's a pretty village. What made your mum come here?' Oliver asked as they walked past the rows of pastel-coloured terraced houses.

'It's where she and Dad spent their honeymoon. So it's got lots of special memories for Mum. She said that she wanted to come here to think things over, to make sure she was making the right decision.'

'Do you think they'll get back together?'

They were almost at the harbour now; she could smell the sea air, hear the seagulls squawking.

'I don't know. Mum is sad, of course, but she seems so… different… when she's not with Dad – sparkly, happy. Dad is upset, angry, being stubborn… He's told her unless she comes back for Christmas, they're finished. I think they've just grown apart and Dad will settle for that but Mum can't.'

'How do you feel about it? It must be hard for you.' That was typical Oliver, to think about her feelings. That was one of the reasons she loved him so much. Yet he had decided they weren't going to have a family without thinking of her feelings, hadn't he?

'It is. I don't want them to split up. Of course I don't. But Mum deserves to be happy, and Dad… well, he's so set in his ways. I'm sure that he loves Mum but he rarely shows it.'

'I don't want us to split up either,' Oliver said softly.

Meg turned to him, saw his thick hair blowing in the wind, and she longed to reach out and touch his face, run her fingers over the dark stubble on his chin. 'Neither do I,' she admitted.

'Then let's not. We're meant to be together, you and me. We don't have to be apart.' He gazed at her and she felt herself sinking into the soulfulness of his deep brown eyes.

'I want a family and you don't, Olly. And you've only just decided to tell me that, after seven years of being together. That's a big thing to get over.'

He lifted his hand and stroked her cheek gently with his thumb, sending shivers down her spine. 'I handled it clumsily, I know. I'm sorry. That's why I came down. I owe you an explanation because you're right: I knew you wanted babies right at the beginning and I said I did too. I thought I did when it was years away; I thought that in a few years I'd feel ready, but instead I started to feel more and more panicky at the thought of being a father.'

'Panicky?' She stared at him, confused.

'Please can I try and explain?'

She nodded and listened as they walked side by side along the harbour, the sea breeze blowing their hair.

'You know my dad walked out when I was young, what a waster he is?' She could hear the bitterness in Oliver's voice. He'd told her early on in their relationship about how his mother had struggled to bring him up alone, how his dad hadn't wanted to be tied down. Markus hadn't even bothered to come to Meg and Oliver's wedding, and she had only met him a couple of times but had seen immediately how self-centred he was.

She wanted to ask him what this had to do with them. Oliver would never be that kind of father. He was caring, giving, great with children, but she kept quiet, sensing this was important to Oliver, wanting to give him time and space to speak. She felt her resolve to end the marriage wavering. She missed him so much.

'I don't want to be like that, Meg. I think that children deserve two parents who love them, who both take care of them, not one who flits in and out of their lives, who only cares about themselves. It damages them, makes them feel that they're not worthy of being loved.'

So that's what the problem was: Oliver didn't think he would be a good enough father. She turned to face him, reached for his hand to reassure him.

'Oh, Olly, you won't be like that. You're so good with children. You'll be a wonderful father.'

'You don't know that, Meg. Yes, I love kids, but it's one thing being good with other people's children, who you only see now and again, only spend the odd hour or so with, and it's another thing being a good parent. Children completely change your life; they're there twenty-four-seven forever. You never stop being a parent. What if I can't do that? I don't know what it's like to have a father figure in my life so how can I just magically be one? It's different for you – you've got brilliant parents – but me, well, my mum did her best but she was so young and she struggled so much, and my dad simply didn't care. I felt a burden, Meg, like my dad didn't want me and I was making life hard for Mum. If she didn't have me to care for, she'd have been free like my dad.'

She saw the pain in his eyes and her heart bled for the child he had been, growing up so unhappy and lonely. 'I'm sure your mum didn't look on you as a burden, Olly. She wouldn't have swapped having you for anything.'

'Maybe not, but that's how I felt. I don't want a child of mine feeling like that. I'd rather not have any children than inflict that misery on them.'

She should have asked him why he didn't want children instead of walking out. She should have known that Oliver would have a good reason; he was one of the kindest people she had ever met. He just needed reassurance that he would be a good father.

'It wouldn't be like that for our child, Olly. We'll love it and be good parents – well, as good as we can be.'

He reached out, wrapped his arms around her and kissed her. She responded instantly, their bodies melting into each other's. Then he released her. 'I can't risk it, Meg. I am not like you. I don't think it'll just magically be okay.' His voice was husky, raw with emotion. 'I want to be straight with you, like I should have been in the beginning, because I love you so much. But I absolutely don't want to have children. I hope that you love me enough to make up for that, though. That I'll be enough for you. Can you do that?'

Oh God, how can he ask me that? She gulped, blinked back the tears, feeling as if her heart was being torn from her body. How she wanted to say yes, but she knew she couldn't do it. That she would carry on resenting him for it. At every children's party. Or every time a friend had a baby and laughed 'you'll be next'. That even if they got back together now, survived this for a couple of years, they would eventually break up.

She shook her head. 'I can't, Olly. I love you so much but I can't live with you, remain married to you, and agree to never have a family together. It would hurt me too much.'

'But if you loved me—'

'If you loved me, you wouldn't have lied about this. And you'd want a child with me. You're not your father. I'm not your mother. We can make it. We really can.' Tears were spilling down her cheeks, and she could see them in Oliver's eyes too. 'Don't do this, Olly. Don't split us up just because you're scared.'

He wrapped his arms around her, pulled her into a big hug, and she collapsed on his shoulder, crying.

'I love you, Meg. But I can't give you what you want. I hope... you find someone else who can. Goodbye.' His voice was breaking with emotion.

Then he released her, and her heart cracked in two as she watched him walk away.

Chapter Twenty-Two

Sally took one look at Meg's distraught face when she walked in and wrapped her arms around her. Meg sobbed on her shoulder, letting out all her grief.

'You couldn't sort it, then? I had hoped…' she said when Meg had finally stopped crying and was wiping her eyes with a tissue.

'Olly is adamant that he's never having children.' Meg briefly relayed their conversation. 'He thinks that he should be enough for me. I understand how he feels about his dad, but if he loved me, he would want a child with me and be determined to be a better father than his dad was, wouldn't he? I can't believe he's being so selfish.'

'He must have been badly hurt as a child, Meg, to be that terrified of letting down his own child. It's a difficult situation and I'm sure he hasn't made the decision lightly. I'm sure he doesn't want to hurt you.'

'I thought, hoped, he'd come down so we could sort it out but there's no sorting this out.' Meg's voice broke as she dabbed her eyes. 'And the hardest thing is that we love each other so much and Oliver is just as heartbroken as me. But we can't get past this, Mum. We really can't.'

'Sometimes things don't work out no matter how much you want them to. I don't want me and your dad to split up either. I would prefer us to grow old together, to keep our family intact, but I have to face up to the fact that we don't want the same things. And that sometimes staying together can make you unhappier than being apart.'

'I know.' Meg sniffled.

'Right now, we've got each other though, Meg. We'll make this a lovely Christmas and then we'll both start the new year afresh. We don't need men to make us happy. Our lives are in our own hands.'

Meg nodded. Mum was right. She had to accept that things hadn't worked out with Oliver and move on. They still had so much to sort out though: selling the house, splitting the furniture and possessions.

I'll get Christmas over with and then I'll sort it all out, she told herself.

'I don't know if you feel up to it, but Rose is having a bit of a get-together tonight to thank everyone who took part in the Christmas Fayre, and to let us know how much we've raised. I was going to drop in, but if you prefer we can have a quiet evening at home instead.' Sally looked at her questioningly.

Part of Meg wanted to say no, she didn't want to face people, she wanted to stay at home nursing her sorrows, but she resolved she wasn't going to do that. Like Mum said, she still had a life to live and she was going to get on with it. She had managed before she'd met Oliver and would manage now they had split up. Her heart would mend. Eventually. 'I'll come. I don't want to stay in moping,' she decided.

'That's my girl. Leo is going too; he said they'll give us a lift. Rose lives the other side of the harbour so it's a bit of a walk.'

When Leo and Sam came knocking on their door just over an hour later, both Meg and Sally had refreshed their make-up, changed into something a bit dressier and greeted them with a smile on their faces.

If anyone looked closely, they might notice that the smile didn't reach Meg's eyes, but it was there.

'Did you manage to talk things over with your husband?' Leo asked as they walked over to his car.

Meg kept her gaze firmly ahead and willed the tears not to fall. 'We talked. But it can't be sorted. We're over. We've both accepted that.'

'I'm so sorry,' Leo said simply

So am I, she thought sadly. Her heart was breaking but she knew she'd done the right thing. Oliver had no right to deprive her of being a mother just because he was scared of being a father. And if he really loved her, he would fight his fear so they could be together and have the family she longed for.

When they arrived at Rose's, the cottage was packed. Rose was obviously very popular. Rory was there too, warming the mulled wine and serving it up in mugs to the guests.

'An extra big one for you,' he said, winking at Sally.

He fancies my mum, Meg realised. And it was obvious that her mum liked him too. The knowledge stunned her. Rory only looked in his late fifties, which would make him five years younger than her mum, although Sally didn't look or act her age. Not that age should matter.

'Does it bother you that they've hit it off?' Leo asked, obviously reading Meg's expression.

'I don't know,' she admitted. 'It seems too soon. Mum only split up with Dad a few days ago, and I guess I was hoping deep down they'd sort it out.'

'Maybe they will. But I guess it's doing your mum good to have a bit of male attention. When people have been married a long time, they often take each other for granted, forget to listen to each other, pay compliments. My parents were the same at times, though Dad's illness brought them back together again.'

Is that what had happened to her parents? Did Mum feel that Dad took her for granted? She had said she didn't feel that he loved her. Maybe Meg should talk to Dad again, try to explain how Mum felt. It would be good to fix her parents' marriage, even if she couldn't fix her own.

Suddenly, a loud clang made them all turn around. Rory was banging two saucepan lids together to get their attention, and Rose was standing by him smiling, holding a biscuit tin.

'Right, everyone, Rose has an announcement to make,' Rory said once everyone was quiet.

All eyes were now on Rose.

'I've counted the money we've taken this afternoon and I'm delighted to say that we've raised almost a thousand pounds! That will mean lots of presents for the children in the hospital!'

This remark was greeted by loud cheers and clapping. Rose smiled, waiting patiently until the clapping had ceased. 'Thank you, every one of you, for all your hard work. And a special thanks to our newcomers, Sally and Meg, who only came down for Christmas and ended up getting roped in to help.'

Meg felt her cheeks flush as the others turned to face her and Mum, clapping enthusiastically. Mum was grinning from ear to ear, her eyes bright. *She's enjoyed doing this*, Meg thought, *being part of this community. It's like she's found a purpose.*

Perhaps if her parents moved to a little village, Mum might be happier. Then Dad could do his gardening and join the local bowls club and Mum could join the Women's Institute and get involved with village life. No, that wouldn't work. Mum didn't want a quiet life in a village, she wanted the opposite – to be out in the world, living life. Mum was a 'people person', she loved to socialise, whereas Dad was quite happy with his own company. Meg guessed it hadn't really mattered when she and Dan were living at home and the house was bustling with life, or even when her parents were still at work, but now they'd both retired and were spending so much time in each other's company, they could no longer ignore their differences.

'Three cheers for Rose for arranging the Christmas Fayre, as she does every year!' someone shouted.

'Hip hip hooray, Rose saved the day!' someone else added, and soon the room was filled with cheering and laughter.

'That's enough, you lot.' Rose clapped her hands, a big grin on her face. 'As usual, Rory and I will buy the presents for the kiddies – we already have a list of suggestions – and take them to the hospital on Christmas Eve. Now there's mince pies and mulled wine in the kitchen, and of course coffee and tea for those of you who don't want wine. Please help yourselves.'

'Can I go and get a mince pie, Dad?' Sam asked.

The day's events had clearly brought Sam and Leo closer, Meg was pleased to see. She idly wondered if Leo had a girlfriend or partner, but surely not, otherwise she would be here with him, wouldn't she?

'Sure, grab one for me too, will you?' Leo asked.

'He looks a lot happier,' Meg said as Sam went off, chatting away to another lad of a similar age.

'He is, thanks to you and your balloon animals. Thank you for involving him, Meg. He really enjoyed it, and it looks like he's made a couple of friends too, which I reckon means he'll want to come and see me more often.'

'I was glad of his help,' Meg said.

'Well, at least let me buy you a drink tomorrow afternoon to say thank you properly. Your mum too,' Leo said. 'Unless you have other plans, of course.'

No plans at all for the rest of my life. 'I haven't but let me check that Mum doesn't,' she said.

'You and your mum really have a close bond, don't you? You must be a support and company for each other at this difficult time.'

'Yes, we are. We jolly each other along. Well, Mum jollies me along – making me dance around the kitchen to carols or take an impromptu boat ride!' She smiled.

'Christmas must be hard for you both this year. So different to how you usually spend it.'

'It is. Oliver and… We always spend Christmas Day with Mum and Dad. My brother Dan and his wife Katya come over too, and my little nephew, Tom – he's three next year so is just getting to the point where he believes in Santa. I adore him, he's such a little sweetheart.' Tom would always come running to greet Meg and Oliver, loving a cuddle with 'Auntie Meg' and squealing with delight when Oliver would swing him around. She'd miss seeing him this year.

'I'm so sorry.'

'Well, at least Mum and I can keep each other company. When I phoned Mum to say I'd split from Oliver, I was gobsmacked when she said she'd left Dad too, and asked me to meet her down here.'

'That must really have been a shock to you.'

'It was. I mean, no one wants their parents to split up, do they? No matter how old you are, you still want to think that they're happy together. I feel sorry for Dad, and Mum's cut up about it but she's not one to mope – she gets on with life.'

'And you?' Leo asked quietly, his eyes searching hers.

'I'm heartbroken,' she confessed. 'But I'm my mother's daughter and I'm not going to spend my days pining for what could have been.'

'Definitely no going back for you and Oliver, then?'

'Definitely not. We've both agreed that it's best for us to part.' She took a sip of the warm wine and savoured it for a while before swallowing it. 'How about you? No other woman in your life?'

'There was. Until Sam's mum decided to get married again and go on honeymoon to Jamaica over Christmas, which meant I had to change my plans so I could look after him. My girlfriend, Melanie, didn't fancy sharing Christmas with me and my sulky son. Sorry, my *ex*-girlfriend.'

'Your decision or hers?' Why was she even asking? It was none of her business.

'She gave me an ultimatum: her or Sam. She lost.' Leo picked up his glass. 'I've let Sam down once and I'm not going to do it again. Any woman in my life has to realise that we come as a package.'

Chapter Twenty-Three

Sunday, 21 December

Meg

The celebrations at Rose's had gone on late, so Meg had fallen into a heavy sleep the moment her head had hit the pillow. It was the first time she'd crashed out like that since she and Oliver had split. When she finally woke, at just gone eight the next morning, she lay there for a while going over the previous day's events. Oliver coming down to see her had finalised things. They were over. There was no going back.

The knowledge made her feel incredibly sad. They had loved each other so much. Still did. How could it all be gone?

If only Oliver had been honest at the beginning, before she had fallen in love with him, before they'd got married. Yes, it would have hurt, but not as much as this, seven years on.

You've got to pull yourself together, Meg. Get on with your life.

A tap on the door dragged her out of her thoughts. 'Want a cuppa?'

'Yes, please,' she replied.

She remembered accepting Leo's invitation for a drink later today and that she was going to ask her mum if she wanted to come too. She didn't want to leave Mum home alone; although she was putting a brave face on things, Meg knew that she was still working through some complicated emotions.

There was another tap on the door a few minutes later and Mum came in carrying a mug of tea. Her eyes were puffy, Meg noticed, and her face pale.

'Did you sleep okay?' her mum asked.

'Like a log.' Meg took the mug from her mum. 'How about you?'

'Tossing and turning. I keep wondering if I'm being selfish, splitting up with your dad like this.' She sat down on the edge of the bed. 'It's so messy, Meg. We'll have to sell the house, split the proceeds, then there's all the personal stuff, the furniture. I feel like I'm going to be turfing your dad out of his home.'

'I know but it's your home too, Mum. You worked and paid the mortgage as well,' Meg reminded her. She took a sip of her tea. 'Oliver and I are going to have to do the same. And I need to get somewhere to live, where I can have the bunnies too. Oliver has to let me have them. We can't split them up, it would be cruel, and I know he loves them too but it was my idea to have them and I can't bear to be parted from them. I miss them terribly.'

'I'm sure you can come to some arrangements, love. As the old song goes, "breaking up is hard to do".'

'You're telling me.' Meg blinked back the tears. *Think positive, Meg. You've got to get on with your life*, she told herself again. It was becoming her mantra.

'Rose asked us both over for lunch today. Do you fancy it?' Mum said. 'Leo and Sam will be there too.'

Why not? It's better than sitting here moping. 'Leo also asked me if he could buy me a drink today at the Anchor, to thank me for cheering Sam up, and to ask you to join us. We're meeting there about four.'

'That would be lovely. We can all go along after lunch. I'm sure Rose and Rory will join us too,' Sally said. 'I can't believe that it's only four more days until Christmas, Meg. I know both our lives have changed drastically but we can still make this a good Christmas.'

Meg wouldn't have known how to get through Christmas as a singleton – for the first time in years – without her mum, and the kind people they had met in Goolan Bay. 'Definitely,' she agreed. 'How about we go for a walk along the coastal path after breakfast? It'll be beautiful scenery along there, I reckon.'

'Good idea, it'll blow the cobwebs away.' Sally got up. 'I'm off to have a shower. I'll leave you to finish your tea.'

'Thanks, Mum, I won't be long.'

Meg sat sipping her tea for a while but she was restless and decided to take it into the lounge while Mum was still in the bathroom. Spread out on the coffee table was the family photo album. Curious, Meg sat down and looked at the page it was open at. Mum and Dad's wedding day. She smiled as she looked at the photo. They were standing outside the registrar's office, Mum holding onto Dad's arm. Mum wore a long, floaty white dress with puffed sleeves and a white hat over her long, blonde hair. Dad wore a burgundy velvet suit, his thick dark hair flopping across his face and almost touching his collar. Very eighties. They looked so young and in love. Meg could see the happiness shining out of their eyes. Dad had always said that he'd known Mum was the one for him as soon as she'd walked into the disco but thought that she was far too pretty to bother with him, and that he had been astonished when Mum had agreed to go out with him. Mum had said she'd admired Dad because he'd been so grown up compared to the other lads. 'I felt I was in safe hands,' she'd said. When had those 'safe hands' got boring, wondered Meg, and when had her dad stopped feeling lucky to be with her mum?

'Your dad brought that with him. He said that he wanted me to look at it and remember all the good times we had, the family we created and that I was breaking apart.' Mum stood in the doorway, clad in jeggings and a baggy jumper, rubbing her damp hair with a towel.

'You look so young in your wedding photo,' Meg said. 'Do you think that's the problem? You got married too young? You never got to have a life, did you?'

Mum sat down beside her, leant over and traced the photo with her fingers. 'We were in our early twenties, love. A lot of people got married younger than that then, often with a baby on the way. We felt very grown up and we wanted to be together – we were so in love.' Her eyes misted over. 'Dan came along, then you a couple of years later, and we were busy rearing you both, but we promised each other that we'd have our life when you were both grown up, that we'd be backpacking pensioners travelling around the world.' She smiled sadly as she turned the pages. 'We couldn't imagine being old then; we had years ahead of us. Now, well, without being morbid, we've got more years behind us than ahead of us, and I want to seize them, to make the most of them.'

They turned over more pages, a few photos of Mum and Dad on their honeymoon – sitting at the café by the harbour, Dad standing by his white Mini. 'He was so proud when he bought that,' Mum said. 'We saved for ages, putting away a bit each week from our pay packets. Your dad didn't agree with debt or borrowing money. I know everyone does it now but back then it was frowned upon.'

More photos followed: both of them standing proudly at the door of their first house, Dad in the garden, Mum obviously pregnant, wearing a loose minidress. Meg and Sally smiled over photos of chubby-faced baby Dan, Mum with her miniskirt and tight polo jumper, hair halfway down her back, holding baby Dan proudly. Then baby Meg in a pram, Dan leaning over, looking at her adorably, Dan and Meg at school, sports day, holidays in Devon. Memories flashed back as they looked through, and one or the other of them would exclaim, 'Do you remember this?' or, 'That's where Dan got lost,' when they came to a photo of a beach in Devon. Meg remembered that day: seven-year-old Dan had wandered off looking for starfish, and her parents had been in a panic until a lady had brought him back saying she'd found him crying by the ice-cream hut.

Mum flicked back to the front of the album. 'This is what your dad looked like when I first met him,' she said, pointing to a picture of a handsome teenager with a mop of dark hair, sitting on a motorbike. 'I loved that bike but your dad got rid of it just before we got married, bought the Mini instead because it was more practical.'

'It's a bit sad looking through the photos, isn't it?' Meg asked. 'We still have lots of lovely memories though.'

Sally closed the album, her face thoughtful. 'Yes, but these photos also make me realise that I'm doing the right thing. I don't know if you can understand that, but when I look at them, I'm happy for those years we spent together. I'm still fond of your father, Meg, and I have no bad feelings towards him, but we are both starting to resent each other. Your dad won't admit it but I think deep down he knows it's true. He seems to have more in common with Paula next door than he does with me. As soon as she gets wind that we've split up, she'll be making him pots of tea and home-made jam.'

'You mean she fancies Dad…?'

'I think she does, yes. She's been extra friendly with him ever since her husband, Jim, died a few years ago. To be fair, your dad seems oblivious to it, he just likes chatting to her about the garden.'

Meg was shocked. Paula, the next-door neighbour, had designs on Dad, and Mum didn't seem worried. 'Doesn't that bother you?'

'It did, but to be honest, Meg, your dad and someone like Paula are probably far better suited than me and him.' She closed the album firmly. 'It's hard, and yes it hurts, but I think it's best for us to break up. If we stay together any longer, we're going to start hating each other; we'll be bitter and the divorce will be messy. I'd rather part now, while I still have fond feelings for your dad, and we can still be friends.'

Bang went Meg's plan to try and get her parents back together, then. If there was already someone waiting in the wings for Dad, and Mum wasn't bothered about it, what chance was there?

Mum stood up. 'I'd better go and dry my hair before it goes haywire.' She went back out, leaving Meg to her thoughts.

How would she feel if Oliver got together with someone else? If someone was comforting Oliver right now, as Paula might be comforting her dad?

She shook the thoughts from her mind. Oliver wouldn't do that. He loved her. The only 'people' comforting him right now would be Laurel and Hardy. She imagined the little bunnies scrambling all over the bed. Were they missing her? They always came to greet her when she walked in and loved snuggling on her lap. How she wished she had one of them to cuddle now.

She took out her phone and typed a message to Oliver.

How are you? And Laurel and Hardy? I miss them so much. Can we talk about how we are going to share them?

A few minutes later a message came through. She opened it up to see a picture of the two bunnies lying on the sofa. A lump formed in her throat as she read the message.

I'm okay. You can have the bunnies. I know how much you love them. I'll move out after Christmas and get a flat until the house is sold. Just let me know when you want to move back and I'll make sure I've gone. It'll be easier for both of us.

She messaged back:

Thank you. Mum's rented this cottage until 2 January so I'll be back then.

New year, new start, she told herself. And a new job too because there was no way they could both still run Party MO and she didn't think she could face running it alone. Her life had changed forever.

Chapter Twenty-Four

Ted

'Is Sally away *again*, Ted? I haven't seen her all week.' Paula popped her head over the fence and smiled at him.

Ted stopped digging the vegetable patch and turned towards her, leaning on his spade. Paula had been their neighbour for years. She and Sally didn't have much in common, although they were always pleasant to each other, but Paula was a fellow gardener and often exchanged seeds and tips with Ted. They'd shared a cuppa over the garden fence a few times when Sal had been off on her holidays, and sometimes Paula had passed him over a slice of pie or a dish of hotpot – Paula was a good cook, as was Sally. 'Yes, she's gone down to Cornwall with Meg,' he replied. He hadn't told anyone yet that Sally had left him. There was no point; he was sure she'd be back for Christmas and he didn't like everyone knowing his business.

'Really?' Paula looked surprised. 'I would think she'd have too much to do at this time of year. You always have Meg and Dan around for Christmas, don't you?'

'We do, but…' Ted paused. He didn't want to tell Paula Meg's business either, but he really wanted to talk to someone and he trusted

Paula; she wasn't one to gossip. 'Meg and Oliver, they've had a bit of a falling out. I'm sure they'll sort it,' he added quickly.

'Oh, so that's why Sally has gone away with her for a few days. These youngsters, they do fall in and out, don't they? Although I must say I think Meg and Oliver make a lovely couple. I'm sure they'll be back together in no time.' She cocked her head to one side as she surveyed the patch Ted had just dug. 'It looks like you've been working out here for a while. Fancy a cuppa? I've just made some scones, nice and hot they are, and I could do with a bit of advice about my cabbages.'

That sounded tempting. He was feeling tired – he hadn't slept properly since Sal had gone, or eaten properly either for that matter. He felt all out of sorts. Sally would be back, he kept telling himself, but remembering how happy she'd looked, chatting and laughing with those people, he was beginning to doubt it. She hadn't exactly been pining for him, had she?

'That's very kind of you, Paula. I could do with taking a break.'

'It's bitter out here; come into my kitchen and warm yourself up a bit,' she told him. 'I'll leave the back door open for you.' Then she was gone before he could reply.

It had been a while since he'd been in Paula's house. When Jim, Paula's husband, was alive, Paula had sometimes invited Ted and Sally over for a cup of coffee, but after a couple of times, Sal had started making some excuse; she wasn't particularly fond of Paula and, besides, she'd been busy working – they both had been. When Jim had died a few years ago and poor Paula had been distraught, Sal had been good to her, inviting her around, checking on her, and Paula had taken over the gardening that had been Jim's domain, so she had often turned to Ted for advice. Ted had been glad to help, especially since he'd been retired and had more time on his hands. They'd always drunk their cuppas in their respective gardens though, leaning on the fence, chatting as they sipped. *Still, it's cold, and what harm is there in going in for a cuppa?* he thought. *Anyway, Sally's walked out.*

So, he took off his wellies, washed his hands, slipped some shoes on and went around next door. The kitchen door was slightly ajar and the waft of fresh scones and flowers greeted him as he walked in. Paula was pouring hot water into a teapot; she turned and smiled at him. 'Make yourself comfy, Ted.'

Paula's kitchen was warm and welcoming, and the tea she poured him was just right: dark but not stewed like Sal's often was, and two sugars. As Ted sat down and sipped the tea, he felt the tension and worry he'd been carrying around with him the past few days evaporate a little.

'Just butter on your scone, Ted, or jam as well? It's home-made.' Paula had cut the scone in half and was now turned to him, smiling.

'Oh, jam too, please,' Ted said. His mum had always made her own jam, and Sal used to years ago, although she didn't do it much now. She was a good cook, mind, but she didn't bother much now Meg and Dan were grown up. It had been a long time since their kitchen had been warm and cosy like this. He watched Paula, her hair tied back, a cheerful apron around her waist, spreading butter and jam thickly onto two scones.

Sal was right: he and her were like chalk and cheese. Should that matter? They'd built a life together, had children, loved each other. Sal had told him that she hadn't felt loved for a long time, though, and wasn't sure that she loved him either. Well, that worked both ways, didn't it? She wasn't exactly the perfect wife for him, but he had made the best of it and they had rubbed along okay. He wouldn't have thrown away all their years together just because they weren't as lovey-dovey as they used to be.

'Are you all right, Ted? You look a bit peaky, if you don't mind me saying so.' Paula sounded concerned as she put the scone on a pretty china plate and placed it on the table in front of him.

Ted stared at it. 'Sal's left me,' he blurted out.

'Oh, Ted.' Paula placed her hand on his shoulder. It was warm and comforting. She pulled out a chair and sat down beside him. 'I'm so sorry. I thought there was something wrong – you seemed so troubled.' She leant forward and asked softly, 'Is there someone else?'

Ted wanted to say no, of course not, then he remembered how Sal had run off down to Cornwall as soon as she had left him, how friendly she had been with that man – Rory. Maybe she hadn't just met him. Maybe all the time she'd said she'd been going abroad with friends, she'd been meeting this Rory instead? He looked a bit younger though, probably late fifties. But then Sal didn't look her age. And she certainly didn't act it.

He shook his head. 'I don't know. She said there's not, but she said we're over. She wants a divorce.' He looked up into Paula's compassionate eyes. 'She said I'm boring, that I never want to do anything.'

Paula pursed her lips. 'Well, really! She should thank her lucky stars that she has such a kind, loyal man for her husband. She's always off gallivanting and you never say a thing.' She patted Ted's hand. 'Now, don't you be sitting at home all miserable by yourself at Christmas. You're very welcome to come and join me and my dad for Christmas dinner. Dad still plays the occasional game of bowls, you know. You'll get on well, you two.'

He'd been wondering what to do about Christmas. Dan and Katya had invited him over to theirs, but he wasn't sure… He always felt like he was in the way when he visited them, and much as he loved Tom, the toddler was a bit of a handful. He just wanted a peaceful life now. It was tempting to accept. Paula always made him welcome and he'd seen her dad a couple of times, a sprightly man in his eighties who had always given him a friendly wave. Why should he sit around waiting for Sal to decide if she wanted to be with him or not? It would serve her right if she did come back for Christmas and he'd made other arrangements. That would show her.

.

Chapter Twenty-Five

Meg

They all ended up in the pub after a huge Sunday lunch, commandeering the whole corner as they sat talking about the presents they would buy with the Christmas Fayre money and who would take them to the hospital – Sam wanted to be involved. Then, once that was sorted, the conversation moved on to the carol service on Christmas Eve, which apparently went on until late in the evening. Rose told them how everyone gathered around the huge Christmas tree on the green for a grand 'switching-on' ceremony, which was followed by a carol service, organised by the local church choir. Sally was enthusiastic about joining in, as was Leo, and even Sam looked interested.

As Meg lay in bed later that evening, she thought what a good idea it had been to come down to Goolan Bay for Christmas. It seemed so natural to be with Rose, Rory, Leo and Sam now, it was as if she'd known them all for ages instead of only a few days. It could have been really melancholy with just her and Mum but meeting the others and getting involved with the Fayre had given them something to focus on. Although seeing the close bond between Sam and Leo – how Leo tried to tease Sam out of his sulky moods, how they jostled along together – only reinforced how much Meg wanted a child of her own.

She realised it might never happen now. She loved Oliver so much that she didn't see how she would ever meet anyone else that she wanted a child with. Right now, she certainly wasn't going looking for anyone, and she couldn't see herself trying to go it alone. But she also knew she couldn't settle for a marriage that was childless by choice. She sighed. Her future that had once felt full of promise now suddenly felt bleak.

Meanwhile, her mum had seemed to come alive. Sally was usually an upbeat person anyway, but Meg realised – although she hadn't consciously noticed before – that her mother hadn't been herself for a while. Now, though, she had a glow about her. This time in Cornwall was like a bit of 'time out' for them both, to allow their broken hearts to heal, to realise that a life without Oliver – and Dad – was possible, and to give them time to sort out what they wanted to do next. Her mum seemed to embrace that, while Meg was still mourning her lost marriage.

She turned over and snuggled into the pillow, her eyes closing wearily in sleep.

She was woken early the next morning by a phone call from a very angry Dan.

Meg rubbed her eyes and blinked at the digital clock on her bedside table – eight thirty! What was Dan doing phoning her so early?

'Meg, you need to do something to get Mum and Dad back together before it's too late,' he blasted down the phone as soon as she answered his call.

'Look, Dan—' she started to say but her brother cut in.

'I've just been speaking to Dad, to ask him if he wanted to stay overnight with us on Christmas Eve then spend Christmas Day with us – I'm in work that morning so could pick him up on the way home – and do you know what he said?' Dan gabbled the words out without even pausing for breath.

Meg sighed. She was guessing Dad had said he didn't want to go to Dan's for Christmas dinner. Dad could be stubborn. Maybe he wanted to spend Christmas by himself to make Mum feel guilty. She should have phoned Dad more, she chided herself; it must be hard for him to have Mum leave him after all these years. It was so difficult being stuck in the middle of them both. 'I'm guessing that he doesn't want to come? I'll give him a call in a little while and see if I can talk him around. He must be missing Mum.'

'He doesn't want to come because he's having Christmas dinner with that woman next door.' Dan could barely contain his fury.

What? Meg sat up and pressed the phone closer to her ear. 'Paula? Are you sure?'

'Of course I'm bloody sure. Dad's just told me. Full of it, he is. I don't know what the hell has got into Mum and Dad lately. They should be settling down to retirement together not splitting up and having affairs.'

'Mum's not having an affair!' Meg retorted, jumping to her mum's defence. 'And Dad isn't either. I'm sure he isn't. It's Christmas, Dan, people do invite other people for dinner at Christmas, especially if they're on their own.'

Dan snorted. 'Well, Dad isn't on his own, he's got us. You need to tell Mum to stop messing about and come home before she loses Dad for good.'

After the phone call had ended, with Meg trying to calm Dan down, reminding him it was only a meal, and promising to talk to Mum, Meg pondered over the conversation. She had to admit that she was seriously worried herself. Mum had mentioned that Paula and Dad were quite friendly, often having a chat over the garden fence. Had Dad decided to go to Paula's for dinner to shake Mum up a bit? Make her realise that if she didn't want him, someone else might? But from what her mum had been saying yesterday, maybe she wasn't bothered.

She heard Sally moving about and knew that she'd be knocking on her door soon with a cup of tea. She had to tell her. If there was any chance of her parents getting back together, this might be it.

Sure enough, a few minutes later there was knock on the door. 'Morning, love, I've brought you a cuppa.'

'Thanks, Mum. Come in.'

She turned to the door as her mum entered, clad in her fluffy white dressing gown, carrying a mug of tea. 'Well, you look like you've been awake for a while,' she remarked as she put the mug down on the bedside table. 'Didn't you sleep well?'

'Dan woke me. He's just called.'

'Still mad about having his Christmas plans messed up, is he? Well, it won't hurt him and Katya to cook Christmas dinner for once, and it will be nice for your dad to get out of the house.' Sally sat down on the side of Meg's bed. 'I'll call Dan a bit later, promise to go and see them in the new year.'

Meg took a breath. 'He's mad because Dad isn't going to spend Christmas with him and Katya. He's…' She faltered, wondering how much this would hurt her mum.

Sally's eyes narrowed. 'He's what?'

Meg took the plunge. 'He's spending it with Paula next door.'

Sally sprang up and paced around the room. 'Well, it didn't take her long to get her claws in, did it?'

'I expect she's only being kind, doesn't want to see Dad on his own.'

'He wouldn't be on his own, he'd be with his son and family,' Sally pointed out. She twisted a lock of her hair around her finger. 'I knew Paula would be there, waiting to pounce.'

'Do you want to go back home? Spend Christmas with Dad? I don't mind.'

Sally shook her head. 'No, I don't. If he wants Paula, he's welcome to her. I didn't expect him to replace me so quickly, that's all.' She nodded to Meg. 'I'll leave you to your tea. I'm going to have a shower.'

Mum had been shocked and upset, Meg could see that. Splitting up was so messy. Her thoughts drifted to Oliver. How quickly would he find someone to replace Meg? Someone who wanted an uncomplicated life without children.

The thought of Oliver with someone else pierced her heart. She couldn't bear to think of another woman lying in his arms, of his lips on hers, of him making up songs for her. Would they be happy songs, she wondered, instead of the sad, melancholy ballads he usually wrote? Did he write those ballads because deep down he was unhappy with Meg? The final lines of his new song ran through her mind again. How did they go? Something about mountains and raging seas. And then… *Sometimes love isn't enough.*

Had he known that their love wasn't enough for her? Because she was the one who had split them up, wasn't she?

Yes, because he lied to me, deceived me, probably ruined my chance of ever having a family, she reminded herself.

Even so, she had walked out, just like Mum had walked out on Dad, so they didn't have a right to complain if Dad or Oliver took up with someone else, did they?

If you're over, you're over. You both have to move on.

Chapter Twenty-Six

Sally

Ted and Paula sharing Christmas dinner. The words kept going through Sally's mind. She'd expected Ted to spend Christmas Day with his family – Dan, Katya and Tom – not the woman next door.

What had Sally expected when she'd walked out? That Ted would be so heartbroken he'd promise to change? Even if he did, he would still be the same person and there would still be no chemistry between them.

It had been her choice to end the marriage, but maybe Ted had been as unhappy as she was but was prepared to soldier on rather than split up their family and home. A home they would presumably have to sell if she went ahead with the divorce. How far would this friendship with Paula go? Would they become a couple? Would Paula move into the house that had been Sally's home? she wondered. Or Ted move in with Paula? Or would they both sell up and buy a new home together?

She was getting ahead of herself now. Paula was just being neighbourly and inviting Ted to Christmas dinner. Except she knew Ted: he wasn't the sort of man who liked being on his own. And Paula clearly didn't like being on her own either. She'd often said she was lost since her husband had died. No one to look after or care for. Paula was one of those women who liked a man to fuss over. And Ted liked to be fussed over. Sally didn't want to fuss over a man.

But did she really want to lose Ted forever?

She sat down on the bench, gazing out at the sea, remembering those early years when she and Ted had strolled along, hand in hand, so in love. How had it all gone so wrong?

It was almost forty years ago. *You outgrew each other*, she reminded herself. *You were different people back then.*

'Hello, Sally, you look deep in thought.'

Sally turned at the sound of Rose's voice.

'Mind if I sit beside you and take a breather?' Rose asked, sitting down before Sally could answer.

'Of course not.' Sally gave her a wan smile. 'I was remembering me and Ted walking along the beach on our honeymoon. We were so happy then. We had some good times down here.'

'Are you missing him, love?' Rose asked gently. 'Is it too late to patch things up?'

Yes, she was missing him. Ted had been a part of her life for so long. He was like an old familiar coat that was faded and worn but you kept because of the memories it held. Did she want to patch it up?

'I don't know,' she said slowly and then found herself telling Rose all about Paula. 'Ted said if I'm not back by Christmas, we're over. And I think Paula will seize on that. I feel like she'll be in with Ted before the new year.'

'Well, if he replaces you that quickly, love, maybe he's as bored with your marriage as you are,' Rose pointed out. She paused for a moment then added, 'The question is, does that bother you? If it does, then surely that means you still have feelings for him and maybe you don't want to split after all.'

That was exactly what Sally was asking herself.

'Look, it's none of my business I know, but you've had a long marriage. If there's any chance you can save it, that you want to save it, then surely you should look into it. Maybe you could invite your husband to spend Christmas with you down here? You'll be in a different environment, one with happy memories for you both. You might rekindle your love.'

Maybe Rose was right. Surely she owed their marriage one last attempt? She didn't want to go back home, but if Ted agreed to come down here for Christmas, maybe it'd show her things could change.

'I think I will ask him. Thank you for listening to me going on about my problems.'

'You're more than welcome. And if it doesn't work out, then I'd be delighted if you and Meg joined me and my lot for Christmas dinner.'

'That's really kind of you, but we wouldn't want to put you to any trouble.'

'It'll be no trouble at all. The turkey's big enough. Rory, Leo and Sam will be there, and my parents. Jenny and Grant, my daughter and son-in-law, are going to Grant's parents for lunch; they came to us last year. Just let me know by Wednesday morning, if you can, so I can make sure I have enough fresh veg.'

'I will, thank you.' Sally had to admit that she much preferred the idea of spending Christmas dinner with Rose and her family than a sulky Ted. *Maybe he won't be sulky*, she told herself. *Give him a chance.* Maybe staying at Smuggler's Haunt again would remind him of the love they'd once had, just like it had her.

'Great, now if we don't bump into each other before, I'll see you at the grand "switching on the lights" ceremony on Christmas Eve? It begins at six.'

'I'll be there,' Sally told her. 'Thank you again, Rose.'

Sally was deep in thought as she walked back to the cottage. How would Meg feel about Ted joining them for Christmas dinner? She and Meg had grown so close over the last few days and had planned on spending a 'singles' Christmas together, and now she was possibly changing it. Although, she was sure that Meg would want her parents to save their marriage if they could.

The question was, could they?

Chapter Twenty-Seven

Oliver

Oliver read the email again. When Frank, one of his old clients, had initially asked him if he was interested in the position of head gardener at Meadow Manor in Cheshire, which included a good wage and working hours, and a two-bedroom cottage, rent-free, Oliver had been flattered but had dismissed it. There had been Meg's work to think about, and their party business, although to be honest it had been tempting – not only would they have been better off financially, they would have had more time to spend together.

Hugh, the owner of Meadow Manor, had then written to him personally, though, asking him to think about it. Hugh was Frank's brother, and he had been so impressed with Frank's recommendation of Oliver, he had promised that the job was Oliver's if he wanted it. Oliver had agreed to think about it over Christmas and give his decision in the new year. He'd been planning on talking to Meg about it although he was sure she wouldn't want to move so far away from her parents. Now, though, it seemed like maybe it could be a good idea. A new start, somewhere to live. Somewhere hundreds of miles from Meg, where he wouldn't risk bumping into her. He missed her so much. The only way he could get over her was to not be near her.

A little squeak at his feet made him look down at the white bundle of fur. 'You miss her too, don't you, Hardy?' He picked up the cuddly rabbit. 'Well, don't worry, you'll be back with her soon.'

He loved the two bunnies and would miss them, but it was kinder to let Meg have them. They had always been her pets more than his.

He stood up and walked over to the window, looking out at the little pots of plants Meg had planted. They'd be in bloom again in a couple of months. The Buddha bench they'd bought from the local garden centre, the two cherubs hugging each other in the centre of the rockery, the bird bath. Meg loved buying statues and plants to pretty up the garden.

He needed move away, make a fresh start, forget all about Meg and the fact she didn't love him enough to stay with him just because he didn't want kids. She was enough for him; why couldn't he be enough for her?

Before he could have second thoughts, he shot off a message to Hugh saying he was happy to accept the position and asked when he could start. A quarter of an hour later he got a reply saying whenever was best for him. The earliest he could start work was 2 January, but if he wanted to move earlier, have a look around and settle down in the cottage before he started work, he could. Hugh attached a map of the location. Oliver replied that he'd be there on 27 December. He didn't see the point of hanging around here any longer. He might as well go, then Meg could move back home. They'd sort out the finances later.

So that was it. He had a new home, new job, new life all sorted out. He just had to get through Christmas.

Word had spread that Meg had left him, and their friends Alex and Natasha had invited him over there for Christmas dinner, but he didn't want to play gooseberry to a happy couple; that would make him feel worse, especially a happy couple who were soon to be parents. They were bound to ask him why he and Meg had split up, and he didn't need three guesses to know whose side they would be on.

He could just stay here, have a solo Christmas drinking and binge-watching TV.

That, he decided, was the most appealing option. He would forget about Christmas – it was one day – and just cook himself a pizza, open a couple of cans, and wait for the day to be over. Then he could start his new life.

Chapter Twenty-Eight

Sally

I'd better phone Ted right away, Sally thought. *I'll need to get something in for Christmas dinner if he does agree to come down.* She went into her bedroom and selected his number on her phone.

'Hello, Sal.' Ted sounded cagey as he answered the phone.

'Hello, Ted. How are you?'

'Fine. Just fine. How about you? Have you decided to come home?' She could hear the hope in his voice.

'No, but I was wondering… Why don't you come down here for Christmas, Ted? I'll cook us a dinner and we can talk about things. It might do us good to be out of our home setting, especially here, a place that holds such special memories for us.'

There was a long silence. Was he thinking about it? And was that someone talking in the background or the radio?

'You've got a nerve, Sal. First you walk out over nothing, then you keep me hanging on all week not knowing if you're coming back or not!' Ted shouted down the phone. 'Now you expect me to drive down there for Christmas Day because you've suddenly decided you want to talk. Well, I've been down there once and I'm not coming down again.'

She winced and put the phone away from her ear as Ted's voice got louder and louder.

'If you want to talk about things, you can come home. But if you're not back by Christmas Eve, I'm going to Paula's for Christmas dinner and that's that.'

Sally pricked up her ears, sure that she heard someone mumble again in the background. 'Is Dan there?' she asked.

There was a long pause. 'Paula's popped in for a cuppa. She worries about me being on my own.'

Paula? In her kitchen? Sally fought down the flood of fury. The cheek of the woman: she'd only been gone a week and here Paula was, sitting in her kitchen, fussing over Ted. 'I see. Well, that didn't take you long, did it? No wonder you always wanted me to go away alone!'

'Now don't you go accusing me of things…'

'Personally, Ted, I don't give a damn if you prefer to spend Christmas with Paula. I hope you both have a lovely time. I certainly will,' she said icily, finishing the call.

She tapped the phone on her chin, trying to calm down and make sense of her feelings. She didn't want Ted back but it galled her that Paula was all over him. Was she already making a move or just being neighbourly? And what about Ted, was he interested in Paula or was he deliberately encouraging her in the hope that it could make Sally jealous enough to come home?

Well, it hadn't worked. In fact, it had only proved how insensitive and uncaring Ted was and made her feel less inclined to go home.

She relayed the conversation back to Meg. 'Well, I tried, but he's not interested so let's leave him to it and concentrate on making a nice Christmas for you and me. Rose has invited us around there if we want to go. Rory, Leo and Sam will be there too, and Rose's parents. It would be lovely to see them again. Or I could get a small turkey crown and we can have dinner here, just the two of us. What do you fancy?'

'I think I'd rather go to Rose's, if that's okay with you? It will make the day pass more quickly if we're with company. If I stay here, I'll be sad, thinking about Oliver, and all the things we usually do,' Meg replied after a moment. 'How about you?'

'I agree. No point us both being stuck at home moping. Let's make this Christmas as good as we can in the circumstances.'

Chapter Twenty-Nine

Tuesday, 23 December

Meg

Meg read Oliver's message over again, stunned.

I've been offered a job working up in Cheshire, with accommodation, so I'm taking it. I'm moving out on Saturday. I'll be gone by midday. I'll leave Laurel and Hardy here for you.

What job? Oliver hadn't mentioned he'd been offered a job, so was this since they had split up? Or before and he hadn't mentioned it because he wasn't interested, but now they'd split up he wanted to get away? She calmed herself down. Perhaps he was going to mention it and didn't get the chance because it had all kicked off about having a baby. She was sure he would have told her. They talked about everything, always made decisions together.

At least she'd thought they did. If Oliver could keep something as important as not wanting a child from her, who knew what else he hadn't told her about? So much for being soulmates.

'Are you okay, Meg?' Mum asked, looking up from the Christmas cards she was writing.

'Oliver's moving away on Saturday. He's got a job in Cheshire,' Meg replied, her voice wobbling a little. She couldn't believe that he was going so far away. Would she ever see him again?

'That's a bit sudden. Do you want to go home, talk to him before he goes?' Sally got up and came over to her. 'I know we've discussed this before but you mustn't let him go if you think there is a chance you can sort this out, Meg.'

Meg thought about it then shook her head. 'There's no way we can mend this.'

Sally rested her hand on Meg's shoulder. 'I know you really want a family, but you and Oliver, you have something special. Do you want to lose him over this?'

'He lied to me, Mum. For years! I can't forgive him for that.'

'People screw up sometimes, love. We all do and say things we wish we hadn't. Maybe Oliver didn't realise he didn't want children until it was time to make that decision. And maybe he'll change his mind in a year or two. You can't always plan things.'

'That's just it, Mum. I can't hang on a year or two.'

'Look, I've got to be honest with you, darling. If you're not with Oliver, surely there's a chance you won't have children anyway? Not unless you meet someone else right away. And I don't see you getting over Oliver that quickly,' Sally pointed out.

'Exactly! That's how much Oliver has messed up my life and why I don't want to stay with him!' Mum was infuriating sometimes. Why couldn't she understand? Why couldn't Oliver understand what a terrible thing he had done? And now he was going away, going to wipe her out of his life as if their marriage had never happened. Well, good, because maybe she didn't want to see him again either.

She would be glad to see the bunnies again. It had been over a week now and she missed them so much, and they would be company and a comfort for her. She was dreading going home though. The house wouldn't be the same without Oliver.

'Will you keep the house, then? Maybe get someone in to rent a room and help with the mortgage?' asked Mum.

Meg had been wondering the same thing. She wasn't sure she would be able to keep living there; it held too many memories of them both. They'd chosen it together. Spent weekends sprucing it up, shopping for furniture, rugs, furnishings.

'I don't know. I wish I could move away, like Oliver. Make a fresh start. There's so much to do.' She bit her lip. 'I guess I'll have to see a solicitor about a divorce. It's so messy.'

'I know, love. I know,' Sally said sadly.

Of course she did. She was going through the same thing.

'I'm going back on Saturday, Mum. I can't leave the rabbits on their own. Do you mind?' She hated to leave her mum here by herself but she needed to get back, to start sorting out her life.

'Of course not, love. You must do what's best for you,' Sally assured her.

Meg typed a message back to Oliver:

Thanks. Take what furniture you want with you for your new place. I'll be back on Saturday afternoon and will arrange putting the house up for sale ASAP.

She'd heard horrible tales from her friends who'd split up, the fights over the house, the furniture, the pets, the children. How their exes had stripped the house of everything; one partner had even taken the fridge-freezer – leaving all the food defrosting on the worktop – the toilet seat, the light fittings. Helen would probably tell her she was mad to tell Oliver to take what he wanted, but she trusted him. And she knew he would trust her to sell the house as quickly as she could. She didn't want to fight, to have a messy divorce. She wanted to get it over with then go away and lick her wounds.

Chapter Thirty

Christmas Eve

Meg

Meg and Sally spent the next day getting last-minute Christmas shopping, some fun presents for each other for Christmas, and some chocolates and bath sets for Rose and her family. The shops were crowded, and by the time they got home it was almost time to go to the Christmas tree lighting ceremony. Meg put the presents in the bottom of the wardrobe, ready to wrap up later, her mind going to her presents for Oliver, wrapped and placed carefully under the tree, alongside his presents for her. And the stockings they'd both made up for Laurel and Hardy, containing bunny treats and toys. She loved helping the bunnies unwrap the presents and watching them play with the paper.

What will Oliver do for Christmas now? she wondered as she changed into skinny black jeans and a thick cream jumper. Would he cook himself a dinner? Go to a friend's house? There was Josh, he always had a big party on Christmas Day – maybe Oliver would go there. Or maybe Alex and Natasha would ask him over. She didn't like to think of him spending Christmas on his own.

Though he'll be living on his own soon, miles away, she reminded herself. Cheshire was at least four hours' drive from Exeter, where they currently lived. Oliver was certainly putting distance between them. Is that why he hadn't told her about the job offer before – because he'd guessed she wouldn't want to move that far away? She considered it. Would she? Their house was in the suburbs, easy commuting distance to the shops and only about half an hour's drive from her parents' house, which meant she could pop in a couple of times a week. Helen didn't live far away, and neither did Josh, Alex and Natasha. Would she want to move so far away from everything and everyone she knew? Well, it didn't matter now; she hadn't been offered the chance. She wasn't really surprised that Oliver had taken the job offer though; now both they and her parents had split up, he had no one he was close to.

She felt sorry for him, not to have the close family that she had. And even though her parents were about to divorce, she was sure she would still see plenty of them. Oliver had always said he didn't mind – he had Meg and that was enough. She was his family.

She would probably never see Oliver again. Once the house was sold, that would be it. She sat down on the edge of her bed as the reality of it hit her. She would miss him so much. Tears welled in her eyes and she blinked them back.

He'd asked her, 'You're enough for me; why aren't I enough for you?'

Was Mum right? Was she being hard on Oliver?

Her phone pinged as a message came in. She picked it up, wishing that she would stop hoping that it was Oliver. It was Natasha.

Are you ok, hun? I didn't like to message before now because I know how hard things must be for you.

Natasha and Alex were good friends of both Meg and Oliver, and their first baby was due in a few weeks. Meg guessed that Helen had told them about her and Oliver breaking up and that Natasha had felt awkward when she'd heard the reason why, guilty that she was having a baby and that she and Alex would soon be the happy family that Meg wanted.

I'm fine, thanks. How are you and Bump? And Alex?

We're good. I'm sorry about you and Oliver. We asked him over for Christmas but he said he wants to spend the day on his own because he's got packing to do?

They exchanged texts for a while, Meg filling Natasha in on what she knew about Oliver's new job, and Natasha obviously trying not to talk too much about her excitement over the new baby.

When they'd finally finished texting, Meg cast her thoughts back to Oliver spending Christmas alone. *He's got the bunnies, and friends if he wants to visit them*, she reminded herself, trying hard to quieten the voice in her head telling her how much she wanted to be with him.

Chapter Thirty-One

Sally

'Okay, everyone, let's start the countdown.' Rory was standing in front of the crowd that had gathered around the tree. 'Five…'

'Four, three, two, one!' everyone shouted together, then there was a loud cheer as the tree was ablaze with flashing coloured lights.

'It looks so pretty!' Meg exclaimed.

Sally looked at Meg's animated face as she gazed at the Christmas tree. Meg had always loved Christmas, especially the lights. She was such a fun but gentle character, enjoying simple things such as family parties, putting up the Christmas tree, family camping holidays. Meg was all about family; she was the one everyone turned to when they needed help or advice. No wonder she so desperately wanted a family of her own. It was such a shame she and Oliver had split up and so cruel of Oliver to string Meg along for so many years, letting her believe that they would have a family together. She felt a flash of anger towards him. Though, she reasoned, she was sure that he hadn't meant to hurt her, and that they had something that could be worth saving, if they weren't both so stubborn. Everything was so black and white with them, Oliver insisting he didn't ever want a child, and Meg refusing to consider a marriage without a family.

Meg turned to Sam and said something to him, and Sam laughed. Meg had really brought Sam out of himself; she'd be a wonderful mother. Leo looked around at Sam's laugh, and he and Meg exchanged a smile. Sally watched them both, their eyes alight, their faces wreathed in smiles, then Meg turned back to the tree where a group of carol singers had now gathered. *Is this the start of something between Meg and Leo?* she wondered. They obviously had a connection. She didn't think that Meg would get over Oliver quickly, but perhaps Leo could help her move on. Life carried on; no matter how in love people were, they found other partners. Look at Ted.

She'd tried not to think about Ted and Paula, to let her mind dwell on whether anything would happen between them when she was away, to ignore the little niggle about just how friendly they had been. Paula seemed to have jumped in so quickly with her offer of cooking Christmas dinner for Ted. It was almost as if she'd been waiting…

Don't be silly. She's being neighbourly so Ted won't be on his own at Christmas.

He doesn't have to be on his own. He could go to Dan and Katya's.

Ted hated the chaos of Dan and Katya's home, though. He liked peace and quiet, a nice dinner then snoozing in front of the TV. She was sure Paula would be happy to provide that, and sympathy. And, who knew? Maybe anything else Ted wanted.

You are the one who left him and you don't want him back, she reminded herself. *It's a waste of time fretting that someone else is interested in him.*

'Good King Wenceslas looked out…' the choir sang tunefully.

Meg, Leo and Sam joined in, singing at the top of their voices.

Sally pushed the niggling thoughts away and joined in the song too. It was Christmas Eve and she was going to make sure she enjoyed it.

They sang 'O Little Town of Bethlehem' next, then 'Silent Night' followed by more modern songs such as 'Rockin' around the Christmas Tree'. Meg was laughing, her eyes sparkling, her foot tapping.

'Enjoying it?' Sally turned to face Rory, who was now standing beside her, his eyes twinkling.

'Very much.' She nodded.

As the carol singers launched into the next song, 'Jingle Bells', Meg turned to her and mouthed 'single all the way', and Sally saw a glint of tears in her daughter's eyes. A knot formed in her throat. She might no longer be in love with Ted but she hadn't imagined herself as being single in her sixties.

'Not easy, a break-up, is it?' Rory asked softly.

Sally remembered that Rose had told her Rory had been married once but his wife had died.

'Nope, but I'm going to make sure it wasn't for nothing,' she said determinedly. 'I'm going to live my life how I want to now. I'm going to travel, experience new things, make the most of every day.'

'That sounds a good plan to me; life's too short to spend it moping.' Rory's eyes met hers. There was the usual twinkle in them, as if he was always suppressing laughter. Sally felt her heart stir a bit.

Chapter Thirty-Two

Oliver

Normally on Christmas Eve, Oliver and Meg would be getting last-minute Christmas presents. Meg enjoyed the hustle and bustle of Christmas Eve shopping, stopping for a hot chocolate and a mince pie, maybe popping into a carol service at the local church. She wasn't particularly religious but had told him that she loved the spirit of Christmas, the hope and joy it brought. He guessed she'd be shopping now, and maybe she would even go to a carol service tonight.

He wished Meg was here, spending Christmas with him. That she'd be waking up with him tomorrow morning, opening the presents that he'd wrapped and placed under the tree. Her presents to him were under the tree too but he doubted if he would open them tomorrow. He didn't want to celebrate Christmas; he simply wanted to get through it. For it to be over. He opened another can of beer and switched channels, hoping to find a film to watch.

It was an hour and two more cans of beer later when someone started hammering on the front door. For a heart-splitting moment, Oliver hoped it might be Meg, arms full of her suitcase and last-minute gifts so not able to get her key out of her handbag, come to tell him that she missed him, that she didn't want to spend Christmas without him.

Oliver hurried to the door and jerked it open, a gasp of disappointment and irritation escaping his lips when he saw his father standing there, a suitcase at his feet.

'Hello, son.'

Oliver looked down at the case then up at his father's face. 'What are you doing here? And what's with the case?'

'I've got nowhere else to go,' Markus announced. 'You and your lass aren't going to see me on the streets at Christmas, are you?'

Oliver fought down the urge to yell at him to go away. When all was said and done, this was his father, and no, he wasn't going to see him on the streets. But he really didn't want him here, not even for one night. 'Why shouldn't I? You never cared if me and Mum were on the streets,' he said as Markus barged past him into the house.

'I sent money when I could. Besides, I knew you'd be okay. Faye is strong and she wouldn't have seen you go without.' Markus placed his case in the hall and headed off into the lounge. Oliver closed the door and followed him, angry that his father thought he could just turn up whenever he liked.

'She struggled to do it by herself – she was only eighteen when she had me, and no parents to fall back on. We often went without; many a night I went to bed hungry. I know Mum did too.'

His dad turned, a self-pitying look on his face. 'It was hard for me too, Olly. I was only nineteen myself, I wanted a life. I didn't want to be tied down with a woman and a child.' He fidgeted with the collar of his shirt. 'You'll understand when you're a dad yourself. It's easy to judge but you don't know what anyone's going through until you're in their shoes.'

'Then I'll never understand because, thanks to you, I'll never be a father,' Olly spat out. The venom in his own voice shook him. He hadn't realised he held so much hate for his father. They were in the lounge now, facing each other.

'What do you mean, thanks to me?' His dad looked worried. 'You aren't infertile, are you? If you are, you can't blame me for that. I've got you, and another couple of kids. There's nothing wrong with me in that department.'

Another couple of kids? Oliver stared at his father in amazement. This was the first he'd heard that he had siblings! *Brothers, sisters or one of each?* he wondered but he didn't ask. Instead he said, 'If you've got other kids, why don't you go to them for Christmas? You've probably seen more of them than you have of me.'

'Because I don't know where they are. Haven't seen them for years.' Markus looked at him questioningly. 'So, go on, why's it my fault you can't have kids?'

'Not can't – won't.' Oliver glared at his dad. 'And I won't because I don't want to be a terrible father to my kids like you've been to me – and my… half-siblings, by the sound of it. I wouldn't bring a child into this world and make them feel worthless, stand by and watch them go without, like you've done.'

Markus fidgeted about from foot to foot. 'I was a kid myself when I had you. I wasn't ready for responsibility. I've always kept in touch with you though, haven't I? I didn't walk away and just forget about you.'

'You might as well have done for all the use you were to me and Mum. When you did show up, all you did was take what little food we had in our cupboard, occupy the sofa for a couple of nights then walk back out again. You never contributed anything. I might as well have had a father who was dead than one like you.'

Resentment filled the air between them like a thick blanket. Then Markus's face crumpled and he sank down onto the sofa.

'I know I haven't done right by you, but I was young and stupid. I regret it all now. If I could turn back the clock and do it all differently, I would.' He leaned back and rested his head on the cushion. 'I might not have shown it enough but I do love you, son. I've never regretted having you. Never.'

'Yes, so you can sponge off me now I'm grown up.' Oliver fought to keep his voice low. 'I bet you regretted it lots of times when I was younger.'

His father shook his head. 'I didn't. Never. I was just too busy, too wrapped up with my life to think about you. I thought you and your mum were coping okay. You always seemed to be doing all right when I came to see you.'

'Because Mum worked hard to give us what she could. But I was a burden to her, Dad. And I was a burden to you. And I'm never going to have a child to make them feel a burden.'

His father raised weary eyes to his. 'Then be better. You don't have to be like me. Be better than me.'

Chapter Thirty-Three

Christmas Day

Meg

'Merry Christmas, Meg.'

Meg opened her eyes sleepily and blinked as her mum came into the room, carrying a mug of tea in one hand and a gift bag in the other. She raised herself up on her elbow.

'Thanks, Mum. Your present is in the chest of drawers. I'll get it.'

'There's no rush, dear. Sit and drink your tea first. I'm plenty old enough to wait for my present.' When Meg was sitting up comfortably, her mum handed her the mug and placed the gift bag on the bed beside her. 'How are you feeling?'

'Probably the same as you. It's weird not being with Olly. We used to sit up in bed and open our Christmas presents together. Then, when we were dressed, we'd go and help Laurel and Hardy open their presents.' She bit her lip. She would not cry. She'd cried enough. She sipped the tea as the memories flooded across her mind.

'I know.' Her mother's voice was barely audible. Meg looked up and saw tears brimming in her eyes. Was she regretting her decision?

'It's not too late to go back if you want to,' Meg said softly. 'I'll be fine here by myself, there's Leo and Sam and Rose for company. If you think you've made a mistake and want to spend Christmas with Dad, then do it.'

Sally shook her head. 'No, we're over. I feel sad about it, yes. I wanted a happy marriage, for us to grow old together, but it wasn't working, would never work, and I'd be lying to myself if I thought otherwise. I'm sad because our marriage has failed, not because I miss your dad and want to go back.'

'Don't you miss him even a little bit?' Meg asked.

'Of course I do. I miss the familiarity of our lives, our family, our home, but now I feel like I've got a future. That I can actually live my life instead of exist.' She paused. 'Does that sound selfish?'

Meg shook her head. 'No, but it's sad to think that you've felt like this for so long. I wish I'd known.'

'That doesn't matter. What matters is that I'll be starting the new year with hope in my heart and plans for the future. That's exciting.' She reached out and squeezed Meg's hand. 'I know it's different for you – you didn't want your marriage to end. I'm so sorry. But there's time for you to find someone else and, hopefully, have the family you want.'

I don't want to have a family with anyone else! As the words flashed across her mind, Meg knew that they were true. She didn't want anyone else, she wanted Oliver. And Oliver's children. Why couldn't Oliver see that they would be great parents, that he would be a good parent, better than his father? Why couldn't he love Meg enough to take the chance?

'Open your present, then. I'm dying to see if you like it.'

Meg put the mug down on the bedside table and picked up the cheerful Christmas bag. She took out the present, soft and squishy, wrapped in shiny silver paper and tied with a fine red ribbon and bow. It felt like a piece of clothing. A jumper perhaps, or a scarf. Slowly she unwrapped the paper to reveal an exquisite lemon cashmere jumper. She stroked it lovingly; it was so soft and just the right length to hover on the waistband of a skirt or pair of trousers. 'Thanks, Mum, it's gorgeous,' she said. 'It'll go perfectly with the new black pleated skirt I planned on wearing today.' She leant forward and gave her mum a hug. 'Now let me get your present.'

She scrambled out of bed and over to the chest of drawers, returning with a red rectangular box decorated with holly patterns. She hoped Mum liked the present. It was something she'd seen her look at it in one of the local shops the other day so had gone back to get it when they'd separated for an hour in order to buy each other's presents, and some personal things. It was a pretty scrapbook, with 'Live, Laugh, Dream' written on the cover in silver letters. There were pages for memories, for countries visited, hobbies, achievements. Meg had written inside, 'To Mum, may you build many precious memories and travel to exotic lands, love Meg.' She'd wondered afterwards whether she had done the right thing. Was it too early to give her mother a scrapbook to keep a record of her new life when her parents had only just split up? Then she'd reasoned that Mum could still use the book even if they got back together; she could keep a record of her new life with Dad, because she knew that her dad would have to make some major changes to get her mum back.

Sally carefully unwrapped the gift, her eyes widening with pleasure when she saw it. 'This is marvellous, darling. And I'm going to do just that – live, laugh and dream – and fill this book with wonderful memories. And I hope you'll do the same. I know both our lives have changed drastically but that isn't always a bad thing. This is the start of a new life, a new year for us, and we must make the most of it.'

She leant forward and embraced Meg in a hug. Meg swallowed the lump in her throat, the lump that was there whenever she thought about Oliver. Mum was right, she had to get on with making a new life for herself.

Her mum pulled away and wiped a tear from her eyes. 'Now how about we have breakfast then go for a stroll along the beach before we go to Rose's? It's only nine o'clock so we have plenty of time.'

'That sounds perfect,' Meg agreed. 'I'll give Dad a ring to wish him Merry Christmas, have a quick shower then I'll be ready.'

They'd just finished their breakfast – toast and marmalade – when there was a knock on the door.

'I'll get it.' Sally said. She returned with a very happy-looking Sam, who was holding up the bag of balloons Meg had given him for Christmas and a dinosaur balloon that he'd obviously just made.

'Thanks so much for this, it's cool,' he said with a big grin. He looked a very different lad to the surly one that she'd met a few days ago.

'You're very welcome – and that's a great dinosaur,' Meg told him.

Sam looked proud. 'Thanks. Mum said so too. She FaceTimed me and wished me a Merry Christmas,' he said. 'They've been out all evening and are going to bed now. It's early in the morning in the Caribbean,' he added.

'Isn't it great how the Internet connects everyone? Is your mum having a good time?' Meg asked, taking her empty cup and plate over to the sink. *What a daft question, Meg*, she scolded herself. *She's on her honeymoon in Jamaica, of course she's having a good time.*

'Yep, but she said she's missing me. I miss her too but it's okay here. I'm glad Dad's moved back here, by Gran and Uncle Rory, and that

I'm spending Christmas with him,' he said. Then added with a smile, 'And that you two are here as well.'

'Me too. We've all kept each other company, haven't we? Like our own little family,' Sally said warmly.

Sam nodded. 'Dad said to ask if you wanted a lift to Gran's?'

Sally looked questioningly at Meg, who nodded. 'That would be lovely.' She smiled at Sam. 'Are you having a nice Christmas?'

'Yes but Dad's stressed out 'cos Melanie's been on the phone for ages.' Sam rolled his eyes. 'I hope he doesn't get back with her.'

'Oh dear, don't you like her?' Meg asked sympathetically, remembering that Leo had told her he'd broken up with Melanie because she didn't want to spend Christmas with Sam.

Sam wrinkled his nose. 'No. She doesn't like me either, although she pretends she does when Dad's around. She's not cool, like you would be if you were his girlfriend.' He grinned at Meg. 'Dad said about one, okay?'

'Perfect,' Sally replied while Meg struggled to recover from the shock of realising that Sam hoped she and his dad would get together. Did Leo hope that too?

'He's just a child. Don't let his words worry you,' Sally said gently.

It was too late. Meg was worried. 'You don't think Leo is getting ideas though, do you?'

'We're just a group of friends spending Christmas together, Meg. Nothing more than that. I'm sure Leo thinks the same. We'll both be gone in a few days and probably never see them again.' Meg saw a glimpse of sadness in her mother's eyes. 'Now let's get changed and go for a walk. There's nothing like the sea air to blow the cobwebs away.'

Meg tried not to think of Oliver spending Christmas alone as she pulled on her parka and boots and set off for a walk along the beach with her mum. They were at the harbour when a message pinged in from Helen.

Happy Christmas, babe. And just in case you're beating yourself up thinking of leaving Oliver all alone at Christmas, we've just seen him in the Red Lion with his dad and they're both trashed already. So you have a good day and stop worrying about him. x

Meg read the message in surprise. Markus was the last person she'd expect Oliver to spend Christmas with. He must have turned up out of the blue, and finding Oliver home alone, he had persuaded him to go drinking with him. Well, at least as Helen said, she didn't have to feel guilty that Oliver was on his own. She messaged back:

Thanks for telling me. Merry Christmas. x

Now she felt freer to enjoy the day. Like Oliver was.

It was windy but not freezing, and they passed a few other people, all calling a cheerful 'Merry Christmas' to each other. Meg and her mum chatted away, recalling Christmas memories from her childhood and from her mum's childhood.

'Do you remember the time Dad wrapped up a gold ring you had wanted for Christmas, but to trick you he'd packed a big box with newspaper and hid the ring in that?' Sally asked.

'Gosh, yes! I was so upset. I thought I hadn't got a present after all and threw the paper in the bin, so Dad had to search all through it to find the ring,' recalled Meg.

'Thank goodness there was only paper from Christmas presents in the bin,' Mum said with a chuckle.

'And what about the time Dan and I made toffee for you and Dad for Christmas and it was so hard you couldn't eat it?' Meg laughed. 'Didn't Dad lose a filling?'

'That was me!' Mum told her. 'I had to go to the dentist as soon as it was open after Christmas. And you should have seen the state of the saucepan you made it in. I had to throw it away!' They both laughed at this.

If there's one good thing that's come out of this split, it's that I've got closer to Mum, Meg thought as they headed back. They'd been close when she was younger, but as she had got older, Mum had been busy working, and Meg had always been out with her friends, then dating Oliver, getting married, working. They saw each other regularly but hadn't chatted like this for a long time. Meg learnt things about her grandparents – they'd met at the local fair where Grandad worked on the rides, fallen in love and run off together, which had caused a big scandal at the time – and about how her mum had collected beetles as a child, keeping them in a box under her bed until they all escaped one day and Grandma had thought they had an infestation and sent for pest control. 'Can't stand the creatures now,' Mum said as they both chuckled.

The biggest surprises though were Mum's stories of Dad as a teenager. 'Your nan used to hate him going off on that bike. He'd go over the track at weekends and race some of the other bikers. I went with him sometimes, riding on the back of the bike, but if my mum had known, she'd have killed me!' She chuckled. 'That's what attracted me to Ted back then; he was so grown up and cool compared to other lads I knew.'

Meg listened to the tales in surprise. It was hard to imagine her staid dad riding a motorbike and being a bit of a 'wild teen'. She could see why her parents had grown apart though. Her mum was still young at heart, lively, up for an adventure, whereas her dad just wanted to stay at home.

Would she and Oliver have grown apart when they were older? Would their love have died too? She'd never know now.

Chapter Thirty-Four

Sally

Rory, to their amusement, greeted them dressed in a Santa outfit, complete with a wig and beard.

'You look like Santa, Uncle Rory,' Sam said, playfully pulling his beard.

'Maybe I could get myself a new part-time job?' Rory grinned. 'What do you think, Leo?'

'You do look really authentic,' Leo told him. 'You even have the belly!' He prodded Rory's tunic, which had obviously been padded with a cushion.

'Don't say that Rose is dressed as Mother Christmas,' Sally said with a chuckle as they walked into the lounge.

'I most certainly am not!' Rose shouted from the kitchen. 'I leave all the daft stuff to Rory.'

'And has he left all the cooking to you?' Sally asked, standing in the kitchen doorway and sniffing the delicious aroma of roast turkey mingled with other smells such as thyme – probably the stuffing – and cranberry – the sauce. 'Is there anything I can do?' she asked Rose, who was loading the dishwasher.

'Nothing at all. And Rory has done his share of the cooking; he loves it. Can't keep him out of the kitchen.' She closed the dishwasher door, wiped her hands on her apron, which was covering her long multi-coloured floaty dress, and walked over to give Sally a hug. 'How are you, my dear? I'm sure today is a difficult one for you.' She stepped back to admire Sally's black velvet flared trousers and red top. 'You look lovely, by the way.'

'Thank you. And so do you. I love those sandals,' she said, looking at the gold strappy sandals on Rose's feet. 'It is difficult, yes. I can't help thinking back to past Christmases – but I still think I've made the right decision.'

'No regrets, then?'

Sally sighed. 'Plenty. I wish it hadn't come to this. I wish we could have lasted the course, but for me it was the right thing to do. And Ted isn't exactly sitting at home moping on his own today.'

'Pushy Paula, eh?' Rose replied. Her eyes searched Sally's face. 'I know we don't know each other well enough for me to keep doling out advice. But if you still have feelings for Ted, it really isn't too late to do something about it.'

Sally had been telling herself the same thing. Last night she had kept thinking of Ted sitting at the table opposite Paula, tucking into her delicious home-cooked meal, drinking a glass of sherry, her hanging onto his every word, them maybe sharing a Christmas kiss under the mistletoe. Ted had clearly agreed to Paula's invite to get back at Sally, she was sure of that. To remind her that if she didn't want him, there would be plenty of women who did. Women like Paula. Did it bother her? It should do, and it did in a way, but it also made it easier for her to leave knowing that Ted wasn't sitting on his own moping at home.

'I still love and care for him, as a friend, but I'm not in love with him. Do you think that's daft, to want to be in love at my age? Ted's a kind man, a good husband even if he is a bit selfish and stuck in his ways. Am I wrong to rip apart our family and walk out on all the years we've had together?'

'Only you can make that decision, love; it's your marriage, your life,' Rose told her gently.

They both turned around as they heard a loud roar of laughter come from the other room. Rory.

'What's my brother up to now?' Rose said in mock-exasperation.

As Rose walked through the door into the lounge, Sally's phone, nestled in her handbag, pinged. She took it out and glanced at the screen. Ted. She hesitated then slid the screen to read the message.

Merry Christmas. I hope you enjoy our first Christmas apart since we met over 40 years ago.

She bit her lip. Ted was still bitter, then. Should she reply? She couldn't ignore him, not on Christmas Day. She typed back:

Merry Christmas, Ted. I'm glad you're not spending it on your own. Xx

Then she went into the lounge to join the others.

Rory was showing Sam some magic tricks, much to the youngster's delight, and Meg was perched on the arm of a chair, glass of mulled wine in her hand, talking to Leo. Sally watched them for a moment; Meg was smiling, her eyes sparkling, while Leo was waving his arm about animatedly, obviously recounting one of his tales. They seemed to be enjoying each other's company. At least Leo was taking Meg's mind off Oliver for a while.

Another message pinged onto her phone. It was from Dan.

Merry Christmas, Mum. I hope you and Dad sort this mess out for the new year xx

Typical Dan. She sent him a short Merry Christmas message back, promising to give him a ring later and speak to Tom. The little lad would be wondering why they weren't going to Nanny and Grandad's. Had Dan and Katya told him yet that his grandparents had split up? The thought of her darling little grandson running into the house expecting to see Nanny there brought the now familiar lump to her throat. It was all such a mess. *You'll sort it, and you'll get a home of your own and Tom can come and see you there*, she reminded herself.

As if sensing that she was behind him, Rory suddenly turned, his gaze resting on her briefly, his face breaking into that endearing smile. 'Come on, Sally. Let's see if you can guess this trick before Sam does.'

Sally smiled back as she walked over to them. 'Okay, but be warned, I have eagle eyes so it will take a lot to get past me.'

'Now there's a challenge!' Rory said, promptly picking up a pack of five cards and placing them fan-shaped on the table. 'Concentrate on one of the cards and memorise it.'

Sally stared at the ten of clubs and really concentrated on it.

'Now let me see if I can read your mind.' Rory picked the cards up, shuffled them and placed them face down on the table. Then he placed his hand on his forehead and closed his eyes as if he was really concentrating. To Sally's astonishment, he tapped one of the cards, turned it over… and it was the ten of clubs! Try as she could, Sally couldn't – to Rory's delight – see how he had done the trick.

'That's his party piece,' Rose said with a smile.

'Right, I'm off to get the parents now. Want to come, Sam?' Rory asked.

Sam's face broke out into a grin. 'Yes please! Are you going in your Santa outfit?'

'Of course I am. Your great gran and grandad will love it. Rory turned to Sally and Meg. 'Won't be long.'

'It'll be lovely to see your parents again, they were so kind to me and Ted,' Sally told Rose when Rory and Sam had left. 'I doubt if they will remember us though. So many people must have come to that café.'

'Dad's ninety-two and Mum almost ninety. They might remember you, though; they still have all their faculties, although they tire so easily now. They'll probably only stay a couple of hours, but it's lovely for us all to get together as a family.'

Rory and Sam returned about twenty minutes later with Bert and May. Despite the almost forty years since she had seen them Sally still recognised them, and when Rose had introduced her, May's eyes sparkled. 'I remember you and your husband, dear. Such a lovely young couple, so in love, just like me and my Bert.'

The old man squeezed May's hand and Sally felt tears prick her eyes. If only their love could have lasted, like Bert and May's had.

May looked around. 'Is your husband here?'

Sally hadn't got the heart to tell her that she and Ted had now split up. 'I'm afraid not, but I'll let him know I met you both again. You were both so kind to us on our honeymoon.'

As if sensing Sally's awkwardness, Rose clapped her hands. 'Right, everyone, dinner's ready. Take your seats, please.'

'At least let me help you dish up,' Sally offered.

Rory shook his head. 'You're a guest. Rose and I will do it together. You sit yourself down and relax.'

Well, I have to admit that it's nice to be waited on at Christmas, Sally thought as Rory pulled out a chair and indicated for her to sit down.

Usually she was the one cooking the dinner and waiting on everyone. Ted rarely did anything in the kitchen. No wonder he was happy to accept Paula's invitation to dinner – all he had to do was nip next door.

I'm not going to think about Ted and Paula having dinner together, she reminded herself. She was going to enjoy the day.

Sally found that she was sitting between Rose and Rory while Meg was seated opposite, next to Leo and Sam. Obviously, Rose was trying to ensure they all mingled rather than sitting her and Meg next to each other. It was something Sally would have done too.

'Bubbly, madam?' Rory picked up a bottle of cava.

'Yes, please.'

Rory poured everyone a glass of cava – fizzy apple juice for Sam, so he didn't feel left out, and for Leo, who was driving, and half a glass each for Meg and Bert – then went to help Rose bring the food in.

It was a wonderful meal. Roast turkey with all the trimmings, mashed and roast potatoes, a variety of vegetables, and lots of light conversation and laughter. Sally was pleased to see that Meg was enjoying herself – she threw back her head and laughed as she pulled a cracker with Sam, nearly falling off her chair as it tore apart, leaving her with the larger half that contained a bright red party hat and a motto. She placed it on her head, slightly askew, and Leo leant over and straightened it up. Meg laughed again. *She looks happy*, Sally thought, feeling glad that she'd talked Meg into coming down to Cornwall and spending Christmas with her rather than going to stay with a friend, or Ted. She didn't know what the new year would bring for either of them, but she would always be grateful that they'd had this special time together.

Chapter Thirty-Five

Meg

'Are any of you joining in the Boxing Day beach swim tomorrow?' Rory asked as they all tucked into home-made Christmas pudding and brandy sauce. He winked at Sally. 'I bet you're up for it.'

'Are you serious?' Meg asked. 'It's freezing.'

'I know, but it's a tradition on quite a lot of the beaches in Cornwall, usually for charity. Mum and Dad started it here years ago to support the RNLI – the lifeboats,' Rose said, dipping her spoon into her pudding.

Meg and Bert exchanged a smile. 'We raised a lot of money over the years,' Bert said.

'You certainly did,' Rose agreed. She turned back to Meg. 'It's only a pound to enter and it's great fun. Everyone gathers at the beach in front of the café – we allow wetsuits but a lot of places don't – and then we all take a dip into the sea. Some people come in fancy dress, others in really old-fashioned bathing costumes. We serve hot chocolate, toast and bacon butties afterwards, and all our profits go to the charity too.'

'Can we enter? Please, Dad!' Sam asked eagerly.

'Sure, I've got a wetsuit and bought one for you too, in case you wanted to take a dip.' He threw a challenging look at Meg. 'Are you up for it?'

'I haven't got a wetsuit or even a bathing costume with me,' she told him. Taking a dip in the sea hadn't even crossed her mind when she had packed. And she didn't really feel like paddling – never mind swimming – in the ice-cold Atlantic Ocean.

'Go in fancy dress then. I've got some costumes upstairs. I keep them in case any visitors want to join in the charity swim and don't have a costume with them.'

'I'll give it a go, if you don't mind me borrowing something to wear,' Sally said.

'Atta girl,' Rory said approvingly. 'I knew you would.'

'But only if Rory does too,' Sally added mischievously.

'I'm needed in the café to help Rose with the hot sandwiches and drinks,' Rory protested.

'Nonsense, I can get Maisie to cover for you while you have a swim,' Rose said, winking at Sally. 'No excuses!'

'Okay. I'm up for it. If Sally does it, I will too,' Rory announced.

'And you, Meg?' Sam said.

Well, she didn't really have much choice if Mum and Rory were doing it, did she? Besides, it sounded fun. She was always up for doing something different, and this Christmas was certainly different to any Christmas she had spent before. She nodded. 'Sure, I will, but only if Leo wears a fancy-dress costume instead of a wetsuit. It's only fair,' she added, seeing the mock-outraged look on Leo's face. 'Mum and I don't have wetsuits with us.'

'I think other than Sam, we should all wear fancy-dress costumes – you too, Rory,' Sally said.

'That's not fair. I want to dress up too!' Sam said.

'It's safer for you to wear a wetsuit, Sam. But how about you put a fancy-dress costume over it then take it off before you go into the sea?'

'Okay,' Sam agreed.

'Do you have enough for us all, Rose?' Sally asked. 'If not, Meg and I can sort something out, I'm sure.'

Rose's eyes twinkled. 'I definitely do. I'll bring the box down when we've finished our dinner and you can all rummage through and choose a costume.'

Rose had a huge box of costumes, ranging from pirate outfits to princess dresses, animal costumes and Victorian swimwear.

'I think you should wear this!' Sally told Rory, holding up a striped man's bathing suit from the 1920s.

'Only if you wear this,' Rory told her, pointing to a Victorian navy-blue two-piece swimsuit, complete with lace-trimmed bloomers.

Meg chuckled. She could imagine her mum wearing that!

After much laughter, all the costumes were chosen: a pirate outfit for Leo, Superman for Sam to wear over his wetsuit, and for Meg, a joker's costume consisting of a red-and-yellow tabard with matching leggings, complete with a hat with bells on it. They all took it in turns to try the costumes on in Rose's bedroom, agreeing not to show the others until they lined up for the swim.

It was only when she got home that night that Meg realised she'd hardly thought about Oliver all day. *I can get over him*, she thought. *I just need to keep myself busy.* And she wasn't going to wonder if, like her dad, Oliver had sought solace in another woman's company for Christmas. She couldn't bear to think about Oliver with someone else.

Chapter Thirty-Six

Boxing Day

Sally

'I can't believe we're doing this!' Meg said as she and Sally – clad in jeans and thick jumpers – went out to meet Leo and Sam, who they'd arranged to walk down to the beach with so none of them would feel so conspicuous. It was quite a mild day but there was a bite to the air.

'Me neither, but it will be fun,' Sally said, her cheeks red with the wind. 'Rose said that the Boxing Day swim even takes place if it snows so I guess we should be grateful it isn't any colder.'

Meg shivered. 'Well, I don't think I'd take part if it was snowing – although I reckon young Sam would probably try and talk us into it. Ah… here they are!' She waved as the front door opened and Leo and Sam came out.

Sam was practically bouncing up and down with excitement but Leo looked a bit more subdued. 'The things this one talks me into doing,' he said, jerking his thumb at Sam. 'Honestly, kids!'

'You love it! You have loads of fun with me, and you know it!' Sam retorted with a grin.

Leo grinned back and ruffled his young son's hair.

*

When they arrived at the beach there was already a crowd of people there, dressed in wetsuits and various fancy-dress costumes, and even one young woman in a bikini while her equally young partner wore a pair of Speedos.

'They make me feel cold just looking at them,' Meg said with a shiver.

Rose had told them that the council had given permission for the participants to use the beach huts to get changed, so Meg and Sally found an empty one and quickly undressed, folding up their clothes and placing them in the carrier bags they'd brought their costumes in.

'You look great,' Meg said admiringly. The Victorian swimming costume really suited her mum.

'So do you! Sam's going to love that costume,' Sally replied.

She was right: Sam's eyes widened as soon as he saw Meg. 'Dad, look at Meg! She looks amazing!' he shouted, pointing at her.

Leo – a very dashing pirate complete with a dark, curly wig and a moustache – turned around, his gaze sweeping over Meg from the tight one-red-leg and one-yellow-leg leggings to the short tunic and the jester hat. 'Fantastic!'

'Look at Rory!' Sally giggled as Rory strode towards them in the black-and-white bathing suit that came down to his elbows and knees, clinging to his rather fit and muscly body. No sign of a paunch, unlike Ted, Sally noticed.

Rory rubbed his hands together when he reached them. 'Okay, everyone. Five minutes until take-off so we all need to line up on the beach.'

Rose and a man and lady who Meg recognised from the Christmas Fayre – but whose name she couldn't remember – were collecting the one-pound entrance fee from everyone and writing their names down on a sheet of paper. Bert and May were sitting on deck chairs on the beach, a blanket over their knees, watching the action. Apart from the swimmers, there was a crowd of spectators and a reporter from the local paper. Lifeguards and first-aiders were also present. This was going to be quite an event.

'If you'd all take your places, please, I'll start the countdown.' Rose raised her voice to be heard above the commotion on the beach.

Everyone lined up on the beach, ready for the plunge into the icy ocean.

'Remember, you can swim or paddle, whichever you prefer. And don't get carried away and swim too far out. The sea is cold: you'll get hypothermia in no time,' Rose warned the waiting competitors. 'Now, I'm going to count down from five. Are you ready?'

'Yes!' came the chorus.

'Good. Here were go. Five, four, three, two... ONE!'

And they were off!

Rory raced across the sand like someone half his age; Sally guessed that working outdoors on his boat kept him fit. Leo was trying to keep up with him but failing. Meg sped past Leo, waving as she passed him, but he caught up again and they were neck and neck as they raced to the sea.

Meg lunged and jumped into the water just before Leo did. 'Aargh! It's cold!' she yelled.

'What do you expect in December?' Leo dived in and swam off a little way, Sam close behind him, then he turned back to keep an eye on his son.

Meg dived into the waves and Rory was already swimming off.

Sally hesitated; the water was cold but bracing too, tingling through her body, making her feel alive. What the hell, she was going to swim too. She dived into the water. *This is living!*

Suddenly a wave crashed over her, foamy white water gushed into her mouth, her eyes and she gasped for breath. She felt a hand grab her and lift her up, and she reached out for the solid body beside her, wondering who had rescued her from swallowing even more seawater.

It was Rory. 'It's okay. Take a breath,' he said, his arms around her, his face close to hers.

She took a deep breath. 'Thanks.'

'My pleasure.' His eyes were gazing into hers and she couldn't tear her eyes away.

'Well saved, Uncle Rory!' Sam's shout broke the spell and Rory released her, turning to his nephew. 'I used to be a lifeguard in my youth, you know.'

'Really? Wow!' Sam turned to his dad, who was swimming beside him. 'This is brilliant! It's the best Christmas I've ever had!' His face lit up with happiness.

'Mine too, son. Mine too,' Leo said, and he wrapped Sam in a hug.

Sally watched them both, her mind still in shock. What had happened then? She'd felt some kind of connection when Rory had gazed into her eyes like that. Had he felt it too?

After the swim, everyone got changed and headed back to the café for hot drinks and food. Rory settled Meg and Bert at a table in the corner, by the radiator, then went straight behind the counter to help Rose, despite her telling him to sit down as she had plenty of help, and Sally offered to help too. She wanted to keep busy; she didn't want to think about being in Rory's arms in the sea. She wondered if he felt awkward too, as he was suddenly busy talking to a group of people. *Is he avoiding me?*

It was a lively, friendly atmosphere with lots of jesting, and loud cheering when Rose announced the very generous amount they'd raised for the lifeboats. 'Thank you all for taking part,' she said. 'We're really grateful for your support.'

After a couple more drinks Sally glanced at her watch.

'Well, that was a fun way to work off the huge Christmas dinner we ate yesterday,' she said. 'What do you fancy doing now? Shall we go back home, have a shower then take a drive? We could go to Tintagel, see the castle and the village. Your dad and I had lunch in a lovely little inn with fantastic views of the cove. I wonder if it's still open.'

'That sounds fun,' Meg told her. 'I've always fancied going to Tintagel. I love all those stories about King Arthur and the Knights of the Round Table.'

'It's well worth a visit,' Rose told her. 'Mind, I don't know if you can go in the castle; they have been doing some repairs to it.'

'I don't mind. I'm happy to look around the village and see the castle from the outside. It'd be nice to do something today. I'm going back home tomorrow.'

'Are you, love? Well it's been lovely to meet you, and I hope everything works out for you,' Rose told her. 'Are you going too, Sally?'

'No, I'm here until next Friday. Then I'm not sure what I'm doing,' Sally told her. She was so glad that she'd decided to come down to Goolan Bay again, and had met these friendly people. She'd miss Meg, but she wouldn't be on her own when she left.

She was facing a future on her own though, wasn't she? A future without Ted. And yes, there was more than a tinge of sadness in that knowledge, but also an enormous sense of freedom.

Chapter Thirty-Seven

Oliver

Oliver groaned. His neck ached and his head was thudding – he'd fallen asleep in the armchair, he realised. He glanced at the clock on the lounge wall. Just gone eleven in the morning. Well, it was over. The first Christmas he'd spent without Meg since she'd walked into the garden he was helping redesign at her parents' house seven years ago. He'd fallen in love with her at first sight, and she'd told him afterwards that she'd felt the same. It wasn't long before they were inseparable, then living together, then married.

Now it was all gone.

How had he lost something so precious so quickly?

Oliver stood up and stretched, glancing over at his father, sprawled out on the sofa, snoring. How had his life got so crazy? If anyone had told him last year that he would split up with Meg and spend the next Christmas with his father, he would have laughed at them. God, he'd longed to spend Christmas with his father when he was a young boy. Yearned for him to turn up with a present, even if it was only a toy car. Now, the less he saw of him the better.

Christmas Day had been awful. They'd had a few drinks in the pub, where his dad had managed to integrate himself with a rowdy crowd who, on finding out that they didn't have a Christmas dinner to go home to, had invited Markus and Oliver back to join in theirs. They'd eaten with strangers – kind and jolly strangers but strangers nonetheless – who had plied them with food, drink and sympathy, and then they had staggered home, whereupon his father had immediately collapsed on the sofa in a drunken stupor and Oliver had poured himself another drink, then another, in an attempt to block out the misery of the Meg-free life he was facing.

He went into the kitchen to put the kettle on, stopping to look worriedly in the bunny pen, where Laurel and Hardy were lying list-lessly in the corner. They hadn't come to greet him as they usually did, standing on their hind legs against the mesh walls of the pen, begging to be let out. They hadn't rushed to greet him yesterday either. Or the day before. They were clearly missing Meg. He crouched down by the pen.

'Hey, guys, are you okay?'

Neither of the bunnies stirred.

Oliver got back up. *Rabbits like to sleep in the daytime*, he reminded himself. Later, they'd wake and he'd give them a bit of fuss. Right now he needed coffee and then a shower; he was still wearing yesterday's now-crumpled clothes.

Half an hour later, showered and dressed in clean clothes, he walked back into the lounge to see his father stirring.

'Any chance of a cuppa, son?' He yawned.

'Help yourself – the kettle's in the kitchen. I need to see to the bunnies.' Oliver made his way into the kitchen and opened the cage. Neither bunny moved. This was not good. No matter how sleepy they were, they always stirred when he opened the cage.

He grabbed some bunny treats and crouched down at the cage door. 'Hardy, Laurel, come and get some nibbles.' He held out his hand close to the bunnies so they could smell the treats. 'Here you are, guys.'

Hardy opened his eyes and made a funny groaning sound. Laurel carried on sleeping.

'I fed them earlier. I got up to go to the loo and they were making a lot of noise so I thought they were hungry.'

Oliver whirled around to look up at Markus, who had just come into the kitchen. 'What did you give them?'

'Some muesli. I couldn't find any rabbit food. They loved it. I gave it to them yesterday too. You should have seen how much they ate!'

'You shouldn't be giving them muesli! It's bad for them. And by the look of it you gave them far too much too.'

'Rubbish, they couldn't get enough of it. Besides, they'll only eat what they want; if they're not hungry, they'll leave it.'

'No, they won't. Especially Hardy. He's so greedy he'll carry on eating until he's sick.' He pulled his phone out of his pocket and did a quick google on the effects on rabbits of eating too much muesli. If only fed occasionally it wasn't drastic, thank goodness. They had probably gorged themselves and were sleeping it off. He'd leave the cage open so they could hear him walking about and they might come out in a while. He felt guilty that he hadn't given them much attention since Meg had left.

'Rabbits should be kept outside anyway,' Markus grumbled as he shuffled over to the kettle, shook it to check there was water in it then flicked it on. 'You could have made me one.'

'You were spark out.' Oliver watched in relief as Laurel suddenly stirred and looked at him.

'Hello, Laurel,' he said softly, crouching down near the door of the pen. 'How are you, girl?'

The bunny ambled over to him then scampered around his feet, softly grinding her teeth as she did when she was happy. Hardy raised his head then slowly got to his feet too. Good, they'd cheered up a bit. He'd let them run around for a while now; they'd been cooped up for long enough.

'It's been a good Christmas, hasn't it? How about we shack up together a bit longer?' Markus asked as he dropped a teabag into a mug. 'I could stay here until your missus comes back, then we can go rent a flat together.'

Oliver couldn't think of anything worse than having his dad as a flatmate. 'I told you last night, I'm moving to Cheshire. I've been offered a job there,' he said. 'And I'm actually going early tomorrow so I could really do with you out so I can sort the house out and pack my things. Sorry.'

'You're turfing me out?' Markus looked aghast then surprised. 'Why the hell do you want to go and live in Cheshire?'

'Because it's a fantastic job and I need to get away, Dad. I need to make a fresh start.' Laurel was licking his ankles now, and Oliver bent down and stroked her. 'I'm sorry but I can't put you up any longer. Haven't you got a friend you can stay with?'

Markus scowled. 'I can't believe you're doing this to your old man.'

'Dad, I'm in a difficult situation and I don't owe you anything. You walked out on me when I was a kid.'

'And you're never going to let me forget it, are you?' A sullen look crossed Markus's face. 'I've got a mate I can stay with but I can't leave today; there's no trains and hardly any buses and I don't have any money for taxi fare.'

Oliver was at the stage where he just wanted his dad to go, so he took his wallet out of his pocket and handed him fifty pounds. 'There, that should be enough for a taxi. I need you to leave this afternoon.'

'Can't wait to get rid of me, can you? Charming, that is.' Markus grabbed the notes and shoved them in his pocket. 'I don't suppose you can give me a bit more for food?'

Oliver hesitated. His father had seemed to have plenty of money on him yesterday when he'd been buying rounds of drinks. He took another twenty out of his wallet. 'Sorry, that's all I have.'

'That'll have to do then. Thanks, son. I'll go and freshen up and be on my way.'

Markus disappeared up to the bathroom just as Oliver's phone rang. It was his mother. She had tried to phone him on Christmas Day when he and his dad had been out. Oliver had sent her a quick 'Merry Christmas' text and promised to phone back later. With all the partying, he'd never got round to it.

'Miriam told me that she saw you with your dad in the pub yesterday,' she said before he could even say, 'Hi, Mum.'

Miriam? He searched his mind for someone he knew called Miriam, but his mum was still talking. 'She said you were both drunk. I guess that's why you didn't call me back. What's going on, Olly?'

Okay, so Miriam was one of the locals. His mum seemed to know someone wherever he went.

'Meg's walked out and then Dad turned up on my doorstep saying he had nowhere to go so I let him stay for Christmas,' he said flatly. 'He's leaving in a few minutes. I've called him a taxi.'

'What?' It was almost a squeak. 'Why did Meg walk out? When? Have you been playing away?' He could hear the suspicion in her voice. Nice that she assumed it was all his fault.

'Nearly two weeks ago. And no I haven't. She wants kids and I don't—'

'Why on earth not?' his mum interrupted.

God, this is nothing to do with anyone except for me and Meg. 'I don't want to talk about this, Mum.'

'Did you even talk about it to Meg? She's a lovely girl, Olly, and you're mad about her. You know you are. So where has this come from?'

'We want different things, Mum. Nothing I can do about that,' he replied. 'Anyway, I was going to call you today to let you know I'm moving away tomorrow. I've got a job in Cheshire.'

'What!' This time it was a yell. 'What are you playing at, Oliver? You can't move away, you need to sort things out with Meg.'

He took a deep breath. Why did mothers always think they knew best? And honestly, with her track record, his mum had no right to give him relationship advice. 'It's sorted, Mum. Meg is moving back into the house until it's sold. I'll give you my new address as soon as I've moved in.'

Silence. *Well, that's unusual for Mum.*

'Oliver, please don't be like your father and run away as soon as you hit a problem. Please sort this out.'

'I didn't run away, Mum. Meg did. And it's because I don't want to be like my father that I'm not going to have any kids. I don't want them to have the life I… we had,' he corrected himself.

'That's no reason to not have a family. You don't have to be like your dad, and you won't be. You'll be better than him because you're kind and caring. And you'll be better than me too.' He could hear the emotion in her voice. 'Because I know I haven't been the best of mums, and yes, we've struggled, but I have *never* regretted having you, Oliver. You are the best thing that has ever happened to me. You have added so much to my life. Please don't deny yourself the happiness of having a child because of the mistakes we made.'

Oliver was too stunned to reply. First, his self-centred father had told him that he had never regretted having him, and now his mother, who had always struggled to support him, was saying the same. All his life he had felt a burden to them yet they both said that they were glad to be parents.

'Oliver…' His mother's voice broke through his thoughts. 'I love you, Oliver. And your father loves you too in his own way. Please talk to Meg.'

Chapter Thirty-Eight

Ted

Well, that was Christmas over, but what happened now? If truth be told, Ted had expected Sally to come to her senses and come home for Christmas. Actually, he'd thought she might be back as soon as she knew he was going to Paula's for dinner, which was one of the reasons he'd accepted the invitation and had deliberately not mentioned that Paula's dad would be there too. Sally hadn't returned though. In fact, she hadn't seemed at all bothered. Probably realised that there was nothing to worry about on that score. Paula was a very nice woman but she was a neighbour, that was all. There was nothing between them. Sal was the only woman for him. They knew each other, were used to each other, and even though things weren't always ideal between them, they chugged along okay. He wanted his wife back and life to return to normal. He hated change. Routine, familiarity – that's how Ted liked to live his life.

But what could he do? He'd tried to compromise, told her that he'd go on holiday with her once a year, have the occasional night out. What more did she want? He'd heard of women going a bit funny when they were going through the menopause; maybe that's when it had all started with Sal. She had suddenly realised she was growing old and wanted to grab at life while she could. Well, he wouldn't stop her and would try not to sulk when she went out or away in future. He didn't have to join in though, did he? He was happy with his life – or he had been until Sally had walked out. There must be some way they could fix this. He'd give her a ring, see if they could talk things through.

'Yoo-hoo! Ted!' The back door opened and Paula came into the kitchen carrying a plate with a tea towel over it. 'I've cooked you a lovely steak and kidney pie for your tea and some cherry cake, your favourite,' she said, putting it down on the table then striding over to the sink. 'I'll put the kettle on, shall I? Dad's having a nap so he won't miss me for a while. I'm sure you'd love a bit of company.'

It was very kind of her, and he did fancy a cuppa and a piece of cake. He didn't know what he'd have done without Paula the last few days; she always checked on him when Sal was away too. She was a kind woman. She was lonely, he guessed. It wasn't nice living on your own. He'd hated it when Sal was away but he'd filled the days, knowing she'd be back. Now the days stretched out in front of him: long, empty days without Sal. He had to get her back.

Paula chatted away while she made the tea, asking Ted's advice about the garden – she was having a problem with her cabbages – sitting down beside him and hanging onto his every word. Sal never did that; she always half-listened as if she couldn't wait to get away.

'Fancy another cuppa?' Paula asked. 'There's enough cake for another slice each.'

'That's very kind of you,' Ted said, draining his cup and handing it to her. He'd phone Sal later; it was nice to be talking to someone who enjoyed his company and asked his advice. Sal never asked his advice about anything, she thought she always knew the answers herself. Anyway, she wasn't interested in gardening. Or anything else Ted wanted to do.

They had just finished their second slice of cake when there was a knock at the front door. 'You sit and finish your cake, Ted. I'll get it.' Paula was up and halfway down the hall before he could protest.

'What are *you* doing here? Where's Dad?'

It was Dan. Ted rose to his feet just as Dan burst through the kitchen door, followed by Katya and Tom. 'Hello, Dan. You didn't say you were coming.'

'I was worried that you'd be moping here on your own without Mum, but you seem to have found her replacement already.' Dan looked furious.

'Dan…' Katya protested.

Paula gave Dan an icy look. 'I'll ignore that as I know you're upset.' She patted Ted on the shoulder. 'I think I'd better go, Ted, leave you both to talk. I'll see you tomorrow.' With a curt nod at Dan and Katya she was off.

'Where's Nanny?' Tom asked, looking around. 'Want Nanny.'

'She's gone out, poppet.' Katya picked up the little boy then gave the two men a stern stare. 'I don't want you two shouting at each other and frightening Tom so I'm going to take him out into the garden for a few minutes and leave you to talk. And keep your voices down.'

Dan pursed his lips but waited until his wife and child had gone out into the garden before demanding, 'What the hell are you playing at, Dad?'

'It was just a cup of tea, don't make a drama out of it.' Ted folded his arms stubbornly. Dan had no right storming in here and making ridiculous accusations.

'And you went to hers for Christmas dinner yesterday. Anyone would think you don't want Mum back.'

'It's your mother you should be talking to. She's the one who's swanned off down to Cornwall. What do you expect me to do? Sit around moping?'

'Go after her.' Dan paced around the kitchen agitatedly. 'Tell her you want her back. Book a holiday somewhere so you can get away and talk things over properly, get your marriage back on track.' He turned around and the desperate expression on his face shocked Ted. Dan was really upset about this, he realised.

'I did go down there – and it was clear that she was enjoying herself and didn't want me there,' Ted pointed out crossly. He softened his voice. 'I'm going to call her later and try to sort things out. I don't want our marriage to end either, son. I want your mother back and things to be exactly how they were.'

'That's the trouble, Dad. Mum doesn't want things to be how they were. I've spoken to Meg and she said that Mum's been really unhappy for ages. She wants things to change.'

'And it looks like it's me who's got to do the changing.'

'Just try to sort it, Dad. Please. Tom wants his nanny and grandad back together.'

'So do I, son. So do I. But compromise works two ways.'

When Dan had gone and he was finally alone again, Ted sat down and put the TV on. He was exhausted. And he'd eaten so much he felt uncomfortable. He loosened his shirt collar, put his feet up and closed his eyes. He'd phone Sally tomorrow.

Chapter Thirty-Nine

Meg

'It's breathtaking!' Meg exclaimed as she gazed at the majestic ruins of the famous Tintagel Castle, remembering how she had been fascinated by the stories she'd read in her teens of the young King Arthur being swept away to sea and waking up half-conscious in a sea cave, to be greeted by the old magician, Merlin, who promised he would be king one day. Of how Arthur rose to be king, formed the Knights of the Round Table and fell in love with Guinevere only to be betrayed by Lancelot. Tales of magic, sorcery, bravery and love. Looking at the ruins of this ancient castle, set on the clifftop high above the dramatic Cornish coastline, she could believe them all. She wished that Oliver was here with her to see it. He would love it – and would definitely want to make the perilous-looking climb up the steps to visit the castle.

'Amazing, isn't it? Your father and I had a tour of the castle when we were here. We were younger then and could manage the steps, and it wasn't as windy as today,' Sally said.

'It's so wild and magical.' The wind blew Meg's hair over her face as she gazed around her. 'I can imagine how it was hundreds of years ago.'

They made their way back across the rugged coastal path, linking arms as they walked. Meg's mind was full of the old romantic Arthurian legends she'd heard, Arthur, Guinevere and Lancelot, Tristan and Yseult, tales of great and forbidden love, of lovers who never gave up despite the obstacles. Not like she had done. She'd given up on Oliver and their love for each other as soon as a major obstacle had come their way.

That poignant last line of Oliver's new song went round and round in her head.

But sometimes love isn't enough.

Maybe it was enough, though, she suddenly realised. Oliver had always been enough for her. It was Oliver she had fallen in love with, Oliver who held her heart, brightened her life. He was right: it had started with just the two of them, and if it remained just the two of them for the rest of her life, then that would be enough. She would rather have a life with Oliver and no children than a life without Oliver. Why hadn't she realised that before?

Because you were angry and hurt that he hadn't told you earlier, she reminded herself.

And she had a right to be, but she had to get over that. She couldn't throw away their future because of it.

They were now back in the historic village of Tintagel, with its mixture of old and new houses and shops, decorated with a festive assortment of Christmas lights.

'Let's stop for a cream tea,' Mum said as they passed a quaint little café, a bright red star shining out from the middle of its leaded windows.

Meg was happy to agree; her feet ached and she could do with a snack.

As she spread her scone with cream, Meg thought about tomorrow, when she would go back home and Oliver would be gone, miles away to his new life in Cheshire. Unless she did something about it quickly. Or was it too late? Had Oliver decided their marriage was over?

'I'm going home in the morning. I want to catch Oliver before he leaves. I need to talk to him.' Meg almost blurted the words out. 'I can't let him go, Mum. I don't care if we don't have a child – well, I do, but I want Oliver more than a child. I wish I'd realised that before.'

'Then why wait until tomorrow? Phone him now. Or go home tonight,' Sally urged her. 'We can be back at the cottage within the hour and you can travel up then.' She leant forward and squeezed Meg's hand. 'Don't wait, Meg. Oliver might decide to leave earlier.'

'Thanks, Mum.' Meg sniffed then pulled away a little. 'What about you and Dad?'

'I'm going to have to go back too and sort things out, I know that, but I'm not ready. I need more time. I feel so guilty, Meg, and I'm worried that I'll be guilt-tripped into going back. Then I'll be stuck for the rest of my life.' Sally bit her lip. 'I know that sounds horrible, as if your dad is an awful man, which of course he isn't. But I don't want to stay married to him. I really don't.'

Meg's eyes softened. 'You do what's best for you, Mum. Dad will be okay. You can't stay with him out of guilt. You deserve better than that and so does he.'

'Thank you.' They embraced again. 'Now, let's finish this snack and get home so you can pack and get off.'

Back at the cottage, Meg quickly packed her case. She couldn't wait to be back home and see Oliver again. She gave her mum a hug. 'Thanks for inviting me down here, Mum. It's been so nice to spend this time with you. You take care of yourself.' She felt that she and her mum had grown closer, formed a tighter bond. It had been a precious time, a small interlude that they would probably never have again but that she would always treasure.

'I'll be back myself in a few days,' Mum said. 'Now you drive carefully and let me know how it goes, when you can.'

'I will,' Meg promised. 'I'll just pop and say goodbye to Leo and Sam before I go.'

As she turned to leave, her phone rang. It was Dan. *Just what I need!* 'Here we go,' she said to Mum. 'He'll have something to say when he knows I'm going home but you're not.'

'Meg!' She froze as she heard the panic in Dan's voice. 'Meg, is Mum with you? Dad's been rushed to hospital. He's had a stroke!'

Chapter Forty

Sally

Sally packed in a panic. Heart thudding, her mind whirled with terrible thoughts of Ted dying or being paralysed for life. And it was all her fault for leaving him, for putting him under stress.

Oh God, how will I ever forgive myself if anything happens to him?

'Shall I drive? Leave your car here and we can collect it another day?' suggested Meg, obviously worried that Sally was too upset to drive safely.

Sally shook her head. 'No, I'll need it to visit Ted in hospital. I'll drive carefully – and you make sure you do too.' She could see that Meg was distressed and no wonder.

Oh Ted, what have I done?

They both went to say goodbye to Leo and Sam, explaining what had happened, and giving them the keys to the cottage to pass on to the owner.

'I'm so sorry. I hope your husband is okay,' Leo said, looking very concerned. 'Let me know, won't you?'

'I'm keeping in touch with your mum so I'm sure she'll tell you,' Sally told him.

'I'm going to try and sort things out with Oliver. I was about to head back when we had the phone call about Dad,' Meg said.

Leo nodded. 'I'm pleased. It's obvious you still care deeply about him.' He kissed her on the cheek. 'I hope everything works out for you. Take care.'

'You too. And thank you both for your company over Christmas. It's been lovely to meet you,' Meg told him.

'I'll miss you.' Sam ran to Meg and gave her a hug too. 'Wait a minute,' he said and ran back into the house. He came back out with a lop-sided balloon poodle. 'I made one for you to say thank you,' he said.

Meg hugged him. 'It's lovely. Thank you, Sam.'

Leo gave them both a goodbye hug too then Sally and Meg made their way to their cars for the drive home.

She tried to keep calm and focused, reminding herself that strokes weren't always fatal and didn't always do much damage if caught in time. Had Dan caught Ted in time? There had been no time to question Dan; he'd told her what hospital Ted was in and that he was going in the ambulance with him – so he had obviously been with him at the time, thank goodness – and then he was gone.

Oh God, please let Ted be okay.

Luckily there was hardly any traffic on the road and they made it to the hospital in just over an hour, parked beside each other, then dashed into the hospital together. Dan was already in there, pacing around. He marched over as soon as he spotted them, his face ashen.

'How is he?' Sally asked, her voice quivering.

'I don't know yet. He's got a doctor with him.'

'What happened?' This was from Meg.

Dan led them over to some vacant chairs in the waiting area and told them about the afternoon's events, how angry he'd been to see

Paula making herself so cosy. 'We had an argument and I marched out. But Tom had left Bluey behind and couldn't sleep so I went back for it.' Bluey was Tom's cuddly dolphin toy; he adored it. Dan paused, looking visibly upset. 'Dad looked odd when he came to the door, and his words were all slurred, as if he was drunk. He said he felt dizzy and had to sit down. Then I noticed his smile was a bit droopy and I remembered that ad on the TV about the signs of a stroke so I phoned the ambulance.' He buried his head in his hands. 'It's my fault. I should never have had a go at him like that.'

Sally put her arms around him. 'Stop blaming yourself. If anyone is to blame, it's me for leaving your dad and causing him all this stress.'

'Mrs Carter?'

Sally turned around. The white coat and stethoscope on the woman standing behind them told Sally that she was a doctor. 'That's me. Is Ted… my husband… okay?'

'He's had a mini-stroke, but fortunately his son's actions' – she nodded at Dan – 'prevented it from being anything more serious. We're keeping him in for observation tonight, but apart from a slight weakness in his right leg, he seems to be absolutely fine.' She smiled at Dan now. 'Well done, sir, for acting so promptly.'

Sally felt so relieved she couldn't stop the tears falling. 'So he will make a complete recovery? There are no permanent side effects, are there?' she asked, her voice shaking.

'Not that we can see. The numbness in his leg should go eventually. He does have high blood pressure, which could have caused the stroke, so we're putting him on medication to lower that. Has he been under any stress lately?'

Dan shot Sally an accusing glance. She swallowed. 'We broke up recently…'

'Ah, I see. Well, that would be stressful – for you both. But please don't blame yourself,' the doctor said kindly. 'A TIA – a transient ischemic attack, or mini-stroke as it's commonly called – can happen any time, especially at your husband's age, and with him being a little overweight and having high blood pressure.'

'So he is completely okay? Are you sure it's safe for him to come out tomorrow?' Meg asked.

'We'll keep a close eye on him today, but if he continues the way he is, then yes, he can go home tomorrow,' the doctor assured her. 'Now you can see him if you wish, but no more than two at a time please.'

Her bleeper went off and she excused herself and hurried away to attend the emergency she'd been called to.

'You two go in first,' Sally told them. 'I'll see your dad afterwards.' She wanted time to compose herself, to think about what she was going to say. There was no way she could leave Ted now; it was the stress of her actions that had caused this mini-stroke. She would never have forgiven herself if he had died.

How selfish and stupid to want to be free at my age, she scolded herself. Ted was right, she should settle for what she had: a lovely home and a husband she could rely upon and was very fond of even if he wasn't exactly how she wanted him to be. She was too old to be chasing dreams. Look at the damage she'd caused to Ted.

Meg came out first, looking troubled.

Sally rose to her feet. 'How is he?'

'He's fine. A bit pale and shaken up but nothing serious. It's you I'm worried about.' She reached out and touched her mother's arm. 'You can't blame yourself for this, Mum. And you can't go back to him because of it if you don't want to. It's not fair on either of you.'

Sally bit her lip, fighting back the tears. 'It is my fault that he was under so much stress. Of course I'm going back home. Your dad will need someone to look after him for a while and make sure he takes it easy.'

'Then I'll stay with you tonight. I don't want you to go home to an empty house,' Meg told her. 'I'll go home first thing in the morning and catch Oliver before he leaves.'

Although Sally wanted to protest that she would be fine, she had to admit that she would be glad of Meg's presence tonight. Ted's TIA had really shaken her up. She knew how fatal it could have been if it had been a full-blown stroke.

'Thank you, but at least message or phone Oliver and let him know you'll be coming home early so you can talk to him,' she told Meg.

'I will,' Meg promised.

A few minutes later, Dan came out. 'Dad wants to see you,' he said to Sally.

For a moment panic overwhelmed her at the thought of seeing the husband she'd walked out on almost two weeks ago lying in a hospital bed – because of her.

'Do you want me to come in with you?' Meg was looking at her worriedly.

Sally took a breath and held her chin up. 'No, thank you, love, I need to do this alone.' She pushed open the door and walked into the private ward, her eyes going straight to Ted, propped up in the bed, looking pale and weak, with various wires and equipment attached to him.

'Hello, Sal,' he said.

'Hello, Ted.' She walked hesitantly over to the bed, expecting him to have a go at her any minute, tell her how this was all down to her. She kissed him on the forehead and sat down on the chair beside his bed. 'How are you?'

'Not bad. Not bad.'

His eyes were still holding hers and she wanted to cry for the hurt she had caused. She reached out and held his hand and Ted clasped hers.

'Thanks for coming to see me.'

A lump formed in her throat. 'I'm coming home, Ted. I'm so sorry for causing you all this stress. I'm moving back in tonight and I'll be there waiting for you when you come home tomorrow.'

She wondered how it would feel to walk back into the house, her home for over thirty years, where her family had been raised, which held so many happy memories, and which she had walked out of so readily.

It was the same, yet it wasn't.

She had thought that perhaps she would feel at home again, as if she had been on holiday and come back, relieved maybe, wondering what had possessed her to walk out in the first place. Instead she felt like an intruder, as if she shouldn't be there. Inside she had made the break, planned a new life for herself, and now it was all gone.

You should be happy that Ted has made a good recovery; it could have been so much worse, she told herself. And she was happy. She loved Ted, even though she wasn't in love with him, and certainly didn't want anything to happen to him, but now she really did feel trapped. How could she leave Ted when it was the act of her leaving him that had made him have a stroke? The new life she had planned for herself had just been a silly dream. Her place was here, always had been, always would be, and she had to accept that.

She was glad that Meg was with her, even though they were both so exhausted when they got back that they had a hot drink and went straight to bed.

I hope she makes up with Oliver, Sally thought as she lay in the double bed she and Ted used to share. If only one of them could have a happy ever after. She let the tears flow, tears for Ted and the knowledge that she could have lost him, tears for the life she could no longer walk away from and the dreams she had to give up, tears for Meg and the heartbreaking decision she had to make of never having a family if she chose Oliver. Finally, she fell into a restless sleep, her pillow still wet with tears when she woke up the next morning.

Chapter Forty-One

Saturday, 27 December

Meg

Meg waited until her mum had phoned up the hospital and made sure Dad was well enough to come home, then set off home herself. It was well before ten so she should have time to talk to Oliver before he left. What should she say? Ask him not to accept the job, or offer to go with him? That had been the big question that had stopped her phoning Oliver last night, as her mum had suggested. Some things were better face to face.

She parked her car out the front. There was no sign of Oliver's hatchback – he'd probably left it out the back, with their van. Their garage was full of Oliver's gardening equipment and their Party MO stuff so there was never room to park any of the cars. Meg sat there for a few moments, looking at the house, remembering how happy she and Oliver had been living there. And could be again if she could persuade him that she had changed her mind, that she loved him enough to let go of her dream of having a family. She took a deep breath to calm herself down and got out of the car, leaving her case in the boot.

She walked down the path, keys jangling in her hand, and opened the door. Immediately she felt an overwhelming sense of relief: she was home. Where she belonged.

The house was silent. 'Oliver!' she called, wondering if he was in the shower.

At the sound of her voice Laurel and Hardy started making little soft squeaky noises. They had heard her and were happy that she was back. How she had missed those bunnies! She ran into the kitchen, calling their names, and they both did a happy flip then scrambled over to the pen door. As soon as Meg opened it, they trotted out, dancing around her ankles, full of happiness.

'Oh, you little darlings, I've missed you so much,' she said, sitting down on the floor, legs outstretched in front of them, letting them scramble all over her, licking her happily.

She was home. But where was Oliver?

It was then that she saw the white envelope with her name scrawled across it, propped against the kettle. Her heart thudding, her mouth dry, she gently scooped the bunnies off her and got up, walked slowly over and picked up the note with shaking fingers. There was only one reason Oliver would leave her a note. To say goodbye. He had already left.

Tears sprang to her eyes as she opened the note then spilled down her cheeks as she read it.

Dear Meg,

I decided to leave early this morning; no point staying around any longer. I'm sorry things didn't work out between us, that I can't give you the family you want and deserve. I hope you can forgive me for not telling you sooner, but I truly didn't know how strongly

I felt about it until it was time to make a decision. I hope you find
someone else who will make you happy and who wants a family too.

    The place I'm moving to is called Meadow Manor and is in Little
Ofton. I'll be in touch soon, so we can sort out the divorce. Be happy.

    Love,

    Oliver xx

He'd gone. She'd missed him. If only she had phoned him last night, as her mum had suggested.

Meg didn't know how long she'd sat there crying, both bunnies curled up on her lap. Oliver had gone. He was heading for a new life miles away and suddenly her future felt empty. She'd tried to hide from her heartbreak when she was away, to keep herself busy. Spending time with her mum, Leo, Sam, Rose and Rory had kept her mind occupied, helped her to not dwell on a future without Oliver, but now she was back, in the home they had made together, and the memories and loss were flooding in. Her and Oliver cuddled up on the sofa together watching Netflix, sitting at the kitchen table talking animatedly as they ate breakfast, lunch, dinner. They'd always had so much to say to each other, to share.

Yet he hadn't told her about this job offer. Had he been about to when they had argued? Had he decided not to take it but then couldn't face living here without her, as she couldn't without him?

Hardy had scrambled off her lap and was happily tucking into a carrot now, so Meg gently eased Laurel off her and walked along the hall and up the stairs to their bedroom. The door was open and the bed was made. Oliver had tidied up before he'd left. She crossed the room to the wardrobe and saw that most of Oliver's clothes had gone; only a couple of shirts still hung there. She walked over to the bed and noticed a cream jumper on the chair beside it, the chair Oliver had always dumped his clothes on when he couldn't decide whether to wash them or wear them again. She picked up the jumper and pressed it to her lips. It was soft and there was a tang of the fresh, spicy deodorant Oliver used. She held the jumper close, remembering the last time she'd seen Oliver wearing it. They'd gone for a walk. They often did that – they loved the fresh air and walking was so relaxing, they walked miles, talking as they walked.

They talked about everything. Why hadn't they talked about the important things, what mattered to them, talked properly about having a family? Why hadn't she asked Oliver why he didn't want children instead of running away like that? Or questioned earlier why he kept fobbing her off when she mentioned having a baby?

If only she had come home earlier, had a chance to talk to him. If only she had realised sooner that she wanted a life with Oliver more than she wanted a baby without Oliver. She didn't want any man's child; she wanted Oliver's child. She wanted *their* family. And if she couldn't have that, then she would settle for having Oliver in her life. He was enough for her. Why hadn't she told him that?

She could message and ask him to come back, tell him that she wanted to talk to him.

Or she could go after him.

She shook her head. What was the point of driving all that way only to be hurt all over again? If Oliver had loved her as much as she loved him, he wouldn't have gone early, would he? He knew she was coming home today; he would have waited, wanted to see her, to try and talk things over. The truth was that he had made up his mind and was wiping Meg out of his life, happy to make a fresh start hundreds of miles away.

She held the jumper to her and sobbed for the love they had once had, and the future she had lost.

Chapter Forty-Two

Meg

Finally, Meg's tears dried up and she pulled herself together. It was no good wallowing in self-pity like this; she had to face that her marriage was over. Somehow she had to find the strength to get on with her life.

Settling the bunnies back in their cage so they could sleep, Meg set about doing her washing. Once the machine was whirring away she checked the Party MO calendar to remind herself what parties had been booked. The next one was on 3 January, a party for a six-year-old. She couldn't let them down at such short notice; she would have to do it herself. It would be so hard without Oliver. Everything was hard without Oliver. The memories of him were everywhere. She would survive though. She had to.

A sudden thought struck her. Oliver had booked the van in for a service over the Christmas holiday. She would have to see to that – and decide if she wanted to carry on with Party MO. Maybe Oliver had left details of the appointment in the glove box, along with the other papers. She went out to the garage, where the yellow van was parked outside, as usual. Seeing the empty space beside it, where Oliver's hatchback was always parked, brought a lump to her throat. She would never see it there again.

She walked slowly over to the van, looking up at the big, rainbow-coloured letters spelling out 'Party MO' across the side of it. She reached up and traced the letters with her fingers, sadness engulfing her. How proud they had both been when they'd bought the van, had it spray-painted to announce their own little business. They had such plans to expand, to organise parties for adults too, and themed events.

What did she do now? Did she keep up Party MO by herself? Or give it up, and her freelance promotions work, sell the van and take a full-time job? Her half of the money from the sale of the house would only be enough for a deposit for a small flat, she was sure, and she would need a regular wage to get a mortgage. Or she could try and buy Oliver's share of the house and stay here.

She found the details of the appointment for the service – Monday morning – and luckily it was a local garage. Then she went back into the house, determined to work out her finances. She could probably just about scrape together Oliver's half if she got a lodger, as her mum had suggested, and if he was prepared to accept the deposit money back in instalments – and he might do that seeing as accommodation was included in his new job.

But did she want to stay here? Wouldn't it be better to make a fresh start? New year, new life.

A life without Oliver.

She blinked back the tears. She was not going to cry. She was going to get on with her life, make a success of it. She didn't need Oliver. She didn't need anyone.

She wondered how her mum was doing. She'd had a brief text from her saying that she was on her way to pick Dad up from the hospital. Dad's mini-stroke had given them all a shock and Mum was determined to save their marriage now. Meg was sure that Dad would be pleased about that, and a big part of her, a selfish part, was pleased too – no one wants to see their parents split up, no matter how old they are. She felt a bit sad though when she remembered how happy her mother had been down in Cornwall, how much she had wanted her freedom. Meg knew the sacrifice her mum was making and hoped that she wouldn't have to compromise too much. Meg wanted her to be happy. She deserved to be. But then so did Dad.

What about her and Oliver? Didn't they deserve to be happy too? Should she give up on their marriage so easily? She should phone him, explain how she was going to come back early because she'd had a change of mind, but her dad had been taken to hospital. She picked up her phone to make the call then stopped herself. It was a long way to Cheshire; Oliver could still be driving and the call could distract him. She'd wait until she was sure he had got there.

The washing had finished now. She walked into the kitchen, took out the wet clothes and put them in the tumble dryer. She'd have to think about making something to eat. She didn't feel hungry at all but she'd had nothing since breakfast this morning.

Her mind was full of thoughts and regrets, remembering how Oliver was here alone over Christmas. Except he hadn't been alone, had he? Helen had said that his father had shown up, and they'd both been out drinking all day. But she wondered why Markus had turned up on Christmas Day – probably skint again. He was always having a 'cash flow' problem and sometimes messaged Oliver for a loan. He was a selfish man, loud, brash and he talked about himself a lot. Never asked Oliver how he was. Oliver said he'd hardly seen his dad when he was growing up, but that he'd turned up when he was older so he could borrow money off him. *It must be awful to have a parent like that.*

She stilled, turning her head, catching her breath as she heard a key in the lock and the front door open. Only one other person had a key! Oliver had come back. Had he forgotten something? Did he think she wouldn't be here yet? She almost ran out into the hall then stopped, her eyes rooted to him as he stood inside the front door, gazing at her. His brown, soulful eyes met hers, held them, and she felt that familiar heady tug at her heart. Time seemed to stand still, it was as if nothing existed except her and Oliver.

'Did you forget something?' she asked, her voice sounding high and squeaky even to her ears as she tried so hard to stop herself from running over, flinging her arms around him and telling him that she was sorry and she loved him.

He paused. Then he put his bag down and walked slowly towards her, arms outstretched. 'You,' he said softly. 'I forgot you.'

She stared at him, stunned, unable to move, as he walked closer and closer.

'I love you, Meg. I don't want to lose you. If having a child is what it takes to keep you, then let's do it.'

Finally, she found her voice. 'I love you too. And you're enough for me. It doesn't matter about having a family.' Her voice broke. 'I would rather be with you than have a family with someone else. I'm so sorry that I didn't realise that sooner. I came back early to tell you that but you had gone.'

Then they were in each other's arms, kissing, caressing, holding each other tight as if they would never let each other go again.

'It's not that I don't want a family, Meg. It's that I'm scared of being a father. I should have talked to you about it more, tried to explain it to you,' he said between kisses.

'And I should have asked you why. I should have known you had your reasons. I was just so hurt. I thought you had lied to me, led me on.'

'I didn't mean to. I genuinely kept thinking I would feel different in a year or two but the longer we left it the more scared I became.' He paused. 'You said you came back early to tell me you wanted to be with me?'

She raised her hand and touched his cheek with the tips of her fingers. 'I was coming back home last night, but Dan phoned to say that Dad had a mini-stroke.' Seeing the panic on Oliver's face, she added, 'He's okay. But I had to go to the hospital instead.'

'Oh, Meg, that's awful. I'm so sorry. You must have been so worried! Why didn't you phone and tell me? I would have come to the hospital too.'

'It was all such a panic. All I could think of was seeing Dad, hoping he wouldn't die. Then when we got to the hospital, the doctor said he was fine, no lasting damage, Dan had got him to hospital in time. So, I thought I'd tell you when I saw you today but you'd gone.'

Oliver held her in a big hug and she rested her head on his shoulder, taking in the familiar scent of him, the comfort, the love. 'How's your mum? She must have been distraught.'

'She was. And blaming herself too. She's decided to go back to Dad. She thinks it's the stress of leaving him that caused the mini-stroke.'

'And he's definitely all right?'

She nodded. 'Definitely.' She wound her arms around Oliver's neck and kissed him, slowly. He responded immediately, his hand going to the back of her head, gently easing it towards him. Gently, she pulled away, his arms still around her, wanting to talk, to explain before they acted on the desires they were obviously both feeling. 'I'm so glad you came back. I was going to phone you later, tell you that I'd changed my mind and ask you if we could talk.'

'You were?' He locked eyes with her and she knew without any doubt that he loved her and that was enough for her. 'Let's talk now. Let's sit down and let me try to explain why I didn't want children.'

Didn't? Does the use of the past tense mean that he has changed his mind? Don't overthink, Meg. Just listen.

Hand in hand they walked over to the sofa and sat down, still holding hands.

'Take your time,' Meg said gently.

Holding her hand tight, gazing ahead as if recalling things from long ago, Oliver slowly explained about his childhood. 'My mum did her best but she was young, fragile. I realise now that she was probably suffering from depression. She had no one. Her parents split up when she was a child and she was put in care. She told me she was desperate to have a family of her own, a proper home,' he said softly. 'When she met my dad she fell for him straight away – he can be a bit of a charmer when he wants to – and he was crazy about her too. They moved in together, then my mum got pregnant and they got married. That's when things went wrong: Mum struggled to cope with me and my dad was no help.' His eyes met Meg's and she could see how much this was hurting him. 'Dad got fed up of being second best – he told me that himself at Christmas – so he walked out, leaving Mum on her own with me. She tried hard, took so many dead-end jobs, cleaning, waitressing, which destroyed her confidence. She'd been at college, doing a secretarial course, when she fell pregnant with me. I always felt that I'd ruined her life.'

Meg's heart ached at the pain she saw in his eyes. 'Of course you didn't. You were an innocent child.'

'I realise that, but I knew that if she hadn't had me, Mum would have had a good career, friends, a social life. Instead she was tied to me, struggling to feed us both.' His voice cracked a little and he swallowed before continuing. 'I tried to help her, did as much as I could myself. As soon as I was old enough I got a paper round, cleaned cars, got a Saturday job, helped to keep the house clean and put food on the table. Dad popped in now and again – usually to doss on the sofa for the night or to borrow money – then popped back out again. Mum had a few boyfriends. I didn't blame her. She was lonely. And most of the time her boyfriends were really nice to me.'

Most of the time. The words sent a chill down Meg's spine. She wanted to weep for the poor little boy that Oliver had been, feeling a burden to his mum, trying to lighten her load, keeping out of the way if one of her boyfriends hadn't been nice to him. God, what a childhood. No wonder he wasn't close to either of his parents, although he clearly had a lot of love for his mother. No wonder he didn't want children himself. Who could blame him?

'So, you see, Meg, I have no idea how to be a father. I never had the role models you had, the stable home, the family holidays, the love and security. Mum loved me, I always knew that, and she did her best, but I always felt a burden. And Dad simply didn't care. He only turns up now when he wants something. I don't want to do that to a child.'

She pulled him tightly against her, trying to hug away the unhappy memories. 'If you thought you'd be a good dad, would you want a child?' she asked gently.

'Yes, of course. I love kids. I'd love a family, but Meg…' He looked into her eyes, where she could see the fear. 'I was so scared I'd mess up. I didn't want to take the risk.' He rubbed a hand across his eyes as if wiping away the memories. 'Children are so vulnerable, Meg. They can't do anything about their lives; they just have to put up with whatever their parents do until they are old enough to get out. I felt like my parents both wished they hadn't had me, and I didn't want to do that to a child of mine.'

Poor Oliver. She had been so lucky that both her parents had always adored both her and Dan, and that they'd grown up feeling secure and loved. Why hadn't she talked about this with him instead of storming off? She should have known there would be a good reason. How could she have been so stubborn and selfish?

Oliver was smiling at her now. 'Then, over Christmas I spoke to my parents and they both said – even my dad, can you believe it? – that they love me and have never regretted having me. I was shocked but I really believe they meant it.'

'Of course they did.' How could anyone regret having a child? Especially someone like Oliver.

'And they also both said that just because they had messed up didn't mean I shouldn't have a family myself. That I should make sure I'm not like them, that I do better.'

Meg caught her breath. *Is he saying…?*

'And they're right. I think you and I could do better, Meg. I'm going to make sure I do. I'm going to make sure I'm the best dad ever, that I'm there for my… our child. That is if you still want a family with me?'

Did she ever? Meg reached for his chin and gently turned it to face her. 'Yes! Yes, I do. You will be the best dad ever. You'd never walk out on your child, like your dad did. Even if we split up, you would be there for them. You know you would.'

And she knew he would too. Like Leo was for Sam. The future was never guaranteed but if she and Oliver had a child together, she knew for certain that both of them would put that child first, no matter what, that Oliver would always be a hands-on dad even if he and Meg parted. They wouldn't part, though, she was sure of that; their love for each other was too strong. Even through this their love had brought them back together.

'I wish you had told me all this before, but I understand why you didn't. And I should have asked you what your reasons were. I was just so hurt. I'm sorry I walked out without talking to you properly.' She wrapped her arms around his neck. 'I love you, Oliver. All I want is you.'

'And all I want is you. I'm sorry that I let you go. But I'm never going to let you go again.'

They were in each other's arms, kissing, caressing, tugging at each other's clothes, then somehow they were naked on the floor and Oliver was on top of her and they were both writhing with passion. She was home.

It was much later before Meg remembered that Oliver was supposed to be starting a new job in a few days. 'What about your job?' she asked as they lay in each other's arms. They'd scrambled back up on the sofa now, their desire sated, and pulled a throw over them.

He smiled down at her, her head resting on his chest. 'I'll call them and tell them I've changed my mind and won't be able to come after all.'

She raised her head and smiled up at him. 'Or we could both go.'

Where did that come from? The words had popped out before she'd even known she was going to say them, but she realised that was what she wanted. To make a fresh start with Oliver.

She saw the surprise register on his face. 'Are you serious?'

'Yes. Think about it. I can work anywhere. And I've heard that Cheshire is lovely. We could put this house up for sale and live in the cottage.'

'That sounds perfect – are you really sure? What about your family and friends?'

Meg hugged him. 'They'll still be there – it's not like we're going to the other side of the world. Besides, you're my family.'

There was a loud squeak from the kitchen, as if the two sleeping bunnies had woken up and heard her words. Meg and Oliver both burst out laughing. 'And Laurel and Hardy too, of course.'

'Oh, Meg, I'm so glad I changed my mind and came back. I never want to lose you.'

'Me neither,' Meg told him and then they were in each other's arms, kissing again.

Chapter Forty-Three

Sunday, 28 December

Meg and Oliver

'We haven't done Christmas together yet. Let's celebrate it today,' Oliver suggested as they cuddled up together in bed after a day and night of making love, dozing then making love again.

Meg sighed contentedly. She was happy to be back home with Oliver and equally happy to do nothing but lie here all morning. Oliver was right though: both their presents were still wrapped under the Christmas tree and she for one would like to see what hers were. It would also make up a little for the sadness of being apart on Christmas Day. 'That sounds good to me, as long as you don't want us to cook a turkey dinner. I definitely don't fancy cooking.'

Oliver kissed the tip of her nose. 'No cooking,' he promised. 'But we still have our Christmas presents to open, and so do the bunnies. Let's go and open them now, then we can go out for dinner later and celebrate us getting back together. And my new job and our new life. You do still want to go to Cheshire, don't you? I can turn it down if you prefer. I honestly don't mind.'

She smiled up at him. 'Yes, I do want to go. It'll be a great opportunity for you, a fresh start for us both. And a lovely place to bring up a family.' She paused. 'If you're sure that's what you want?'

He looked into her eyes and held her gaze. 'Absolutely positive.' His lips lowered to meet hers and they kissed, slowly, deeply, sensuously.

Suddenly Meg remembered their party booking. 'What about the party next Saturday?' she asked, easing herself out of Oliver's arms. 'We can't let them down. And we have to take the van in for a service tomorrow.'

'Gosh, I'd forgotten about that.' Oliver rubbed the stubble on his cheek. 'I can ask Hugh if I can start the job a week later, explain that I have a few things to tie up first. I'm sure he won't mind.'

'That sounds perfect. It gives me time to make sure Dad is okay and for us to say goodbye to our friends,' Meg said with a smile. 'Now, shall we open our presents downstairs? I want to give Laurel and Hardy their stockings too.'

Oliver nodded, throwing back the duvet. 'I'll go and make a cuppa.'

'I'll have a quick shower then I'll be down,' Meg told him.

A few minutes later, clad in a warm jumper and jeans, she stepped out of the bedroom to the smell of fresh coffee wafting up the stairs. *Mmm.* She'd missed home. She hurried down the stairs and into the kitchen as their Amazon Echo started to play 'The Power of Love'. Their song. Oliver was standing by the coffee machine, one mug of coffee on the worktop, the other filling up with the aromatic liquid. He turned towards her and held out his arms.

How could she resist when he looked so temptingly beddable with his jeans slung low on his waist, toned bare chest, tousled hair. God, she'd missed him. She moved into his arms and they started to dance the steps they had done on their wedding day.

When the song had finished, Meg rested her head on Oliver's shoulder, enjoying the warmth and closeness of his body. 'I never want us to split up again,' she said softly.

'We won't,' he said, kissing her on her forehead. 'We're for keeps.'

A shrill squeaking noise alerted them to Laurel, running around, flicking her long ears about, trying to get their attention. Meg and Oliver both laughed.

'Laurel wants some of the fuss but Hardy's too busy tucking into his Christmas carrot to bother; food always comes first with him,' Oliver said with a chuckle as Meg scooped up Laurel and held her close. It was so good to be back home.

After a breakfast of fresh coffee and hot, buttered toast, they sat on the sofa and 'helped' the bunnies open their presents – a willow ball to nibble, a maze to keep them occupied when Oliver and Meg were out and a big plastic ball with a bell inside it – and a stocking each of bunny treats. They both laughed as the bunnies sniffed their presents then played happily with the wrapping paper.

Meg told Oliver to open his presents first. She had chosen them so carefully: a new tablet, a smartphone projector, a guitar case and music stand – he loved them all. Then Meg opened hers: a gold necklace with two hearts entwined – which brought tears to her eyes at the thought that they had almost split up for good, the pale blue leather jacket she'd tried on a few weeks ago in an upmarket boutique in town but they hadn't got her size, some of her favourite bath stuff, and the thing that really brought a smile to her face because she had always wanted one, a 'name the star' certificate. She hugged it to her. 'Thank you, they're all perfect.' She waved the star certificate. 'I'm going to call it OllyMeg, after us.'

'I thought you might want to keep it until we have a child and name it after them,' Oliver said.

She smiled happily but shook her head. 'No, the first star has to be named after us, because it all begins with us. We can get another star for our baby.'

Oliver reached for her and they kissed and hugged as if they would never let each other go.

Oliver phoned Hugh to explain about Meg's dad having a mini-stroke, and him and Meg getting back together, and ask if he could start the new job a little later. Hugh was very sympathetic and told Oliver to take until the end of January – which was plenty of time for Meg to make sure her dad was better, for them to complete their bookings for Party MO, to decide what to do about their house and to sort out what they were going to take with them to their new home. Then, after phoning her mum to check that she and her dad were okay – all fine, Dad was sitting in the lounge watching TV – Meg and Oliver went out to lunch.

They walked into their local pub, hand in hand, and were greeted by a loud cheer from a group of their friends sitting over in the corner.

'Come and join us,' Josh called, waving to them.

Oliver glanced questioningly at Meg. They had been planning on having a romantic couple's lunch, but it was nice to see their friends again, she thought, nodding at him.

'Thank goodness you two are back together,' Helen said as they pulled out chairs to join them. 'I was beginning to lose all faith in love.'

'We've got some news though…' Meg looked at Oliver; it was his announcement to make.

He wrapped his arms around Meg's shoulders. 'I've been offered a job in Cheshire so we're moving away at the end of January,' he announced proudly.

'Wow, really? Well, we're going to miss you guys,' Helen replied.

'Big time. But good on you, mate,' Josh said.

The discussion then turned to Oliver's new job, where they were going to live, what Meg was going to do and – most importantly – whether they were having a goodbye party.

'There's no time, we've got masses to do before we go,' Oliver told them. 'We can all go for a farewell meal though.'

Everyone agreed that was a good idea.

'We'll be back for visits, and you're all welcome to visit us once we're settled in,' Meg added.

Josh raised a glass. 'Well, here's to your new home. We all hope you'll both be really happy there.'

As everyone raised their glasses, Oliver reached for Meg's hand underneath the table and squeezed it tight. 'We will be.'

Chapter Forty-Four

New Year's Day

Sally and Ted

It was back. That familiar feeling of being trapped, of being on the outside looking in, of being on autopilot as she went through the motions, but not really living her life. Sally had tried so hard since she'd come home but the last few days had seemed an eternity. She and Ted were polite, friendly even, to each other but there was nothing between them. Ted had taken it easy for a few days, given himself the chance to recover, pottering in the shed rather than gardening. Sally was sure the mini-stroke had scared him even more than it had scared her. The evenings were spent quietly, sitting side by side on the sofa, watching TV in silence apart from the odd, 'Do you want a cup of tea?' They kept to their own sides of the bed, both of them careful not to touch each other. She wasn't even sure if Ted was pleased she was back. He had never said.

The other morning, Paula had called to Sally over the garden fence to ask how Ted was, and Sally had told her that he was on the mend and that she was back home to stay. They hadn't exchanged any words since, although yesterday she had seen Ted and Paula chatting over the fence when he'd gone out to check on his vegetables.

How she wished that she were back down Cornwall with Rose and Rory, Leo and Sam. Rose had messaged her a couple of times, asking how Ted was and telling her that Leo had given her the cottage keys and that she would hand them in tomorrow, 2 January, the date Sally had booked the cottage until. In her last message Rose had written:

Do keep in touch and let me know how you are. I've come to value your friendship in this short time we've known each other.

Sally felt the same; she and Rose had clicked instantly and she missed her warm, no-nonsense manner. She missed Rory too, with his big reaching-his-eyes smile, calmness and daft humour. She'd known them both less than two weeks but she realised that she felt more at ease with them than with Frances, Sylvia or any of her other friends. Frances was back from the cruise now, wanting to know all the gossip, having heard through the grapevine about their break-up, and Ted's mini-stroke. Sally had fobbed her off, saying she was busy and would talk later.

I wish I was still in Cornwall, Sally thought miserably. Then she immediately got annoyed with herself. She had to pull herself together. She had a lot to be thankful for. Ted could have died. And Meg and Oliver were back together, thank goodness, and moving to a new home in Cheshire later this month. Meg had phoned her to tell her that they had talked things through and agreed to start planning a family once they were settled in their new home. She had sounded so happy.

'I'm so pleased that you two have worked things out,' Sally had told her.

'Me too. How about you, Mum?' Meg had sounded concerned. 'Is everything okay?'

Sally had assured her that she was fine, and she wanted to be back home with Ted. Which she did. Well, she wanted to want to, and was trying very hard to be upbeat and supportive.

The family were coming this afternoon for a New Year's celebration, the first time that they had all been together since before Christmas. A sort of celebration that both Sally and Ted, and Meg and Oliver were back together. And to congratulate Meg and Oliver on Oliver's new job and their new home.

I'll miss seeing Meg, Sally thought as she started laying the kitchen table. They'd grown so much closer over the past couple of weeks. Though she was pleased Meg was happy again and that she and Oliver were making a fresh start, Cheshire was a good four hours' drive away, so she doubted if she would be seeing a lot of them once they moved.

Sally had made a large fruit cake, which she now placed in the centre of the table, and a variety of sandwiches – ham, cheese and salmon – all neatly arranged on a plate with a clear plate cover over them. The trifle was setting in the fridge. She'd been busy, needed to keep herself occupied. Ted was out in his shed. He was keeping out of her way, like she was keeping out of his. She guessed this was how it would be from now on.

She opened some crisps and mixed nuts, putting them into bowls, trying not to think about the strain of keeping up a façade in front of the family this afternoon. Strange how difficult it was to do since she'd been away, yet she had managed it successfully for years.

It's because you had your freedom and have now lost it again, she told herself.

If coming back home had shown her one thing, it was how unhappy she was here, how empty her life felt.

There's more to life than happiness, she reminded herself as she laid out some serviettes. She stood back and surveyed the table. It looked good. She glanced at her watch. Almost four. She'd asked everyone to be over for half four, so they had plenty of time to chat. She was looking forward to seeing little Tom again – she had missed him so much – and to seeing the smile back on Meg's face.

She turned around as Ted came in from the garden. He looked so tired, and not quite himself. But then he would, wouldn't he? It could have all been such a lot worse. 'I hope you're not doing too much,' she said. 'Sit down and let me make you a cuppa.'

'Can you leave that a minute, Sal? I'd like to talk to you. Can we go into the lounge?'

That sounded serious. What had she done now?

'Of course.' She followed Ted into the lounge, feeling rather anxious. Ted wasn't one for talking. Had he had some bad news about his health, something he hadn't told her yet?

'Is everything okay, Ted? Aren't you feeling well?' she asked when, to her surprise, he sat down on the sofa – Ted always sat in his favourite armchair. She hesitated then sat down beside him.

His eyes met hers, which again surprised her; they rarely looked at each other in the face when they talked. In fact they seemed to avoid eye contact at all costs.

She waited anxiously for Ted to tell her what was on his mind.

He coughed to clear his throat, his eyes still on her face. 'That mini-stroke gave me quite a shock. I could have died if Dan hadn't been here and called an ambulance for me.'

Here we go, he's going to tell me how my selfish behaviour nearly killed him. She'd been waiting all week for that particular accusation. She dropped her gaze to her hands, fidgeted with her fingers, twisted her wedding band around. 'I know. I'm sorry I wasn't here.'

'The thing is, Sal, it made me think. You're right: life's short, we've got to seize it with both hands, live it. All those clichés you kept saying to me are right.'

Sally raised her eyes back to his face in astonishment. He looked thoughtful, as if he was carefully considering the words he was saying. Was he going to tell her that he wanted to go away with her after all, to get out more? If he did, she appreciated the effort, but she knew that it was more than that which had driven them apart. They no longer loved each other and had nothing in common apart from their children. And she didn't see how they could ever get that love back. They had to be content with being polite to each other.

'So, that's what I intend to do. I could have died that evening and there are so many things I haven't done, places I haven't seen. Lying in that hospital bed I realised that, and I've been thinking about it ever since.' He coughed again, awkwardly, and she knew he was feeling embarrassed. Ted wasn't one to talk about serious stuff. 'The thing is, I want to live my life now and I want you to live yours.' He looked away, staring at the wall as if he could find the words he wanted to say written there. 'I appreciate you coming back to look after me, but I don't want you to sacrifice your life for me. I want you to live it how you want to live it. Go and travel, see the world.' He swallowed and turned his gaze back to her. 'I'm setting you free, Sally.'

'What do you mean?' She stared at him uncomprehendingly. Was he saying he wouldn't stop her from going away? Wouldn't sulk about it when she came back? Well, he didn't have to worry about that; she had no intention of going anywhere. She wasn't going to leave him now – what if he had another stroke? 'I don't want to go away, Ted,' she told him. 'I'm going to stay right here and look after you.'

'Don't you see? I don't want you to.' He raised his voice now, red spots appearing on his cheeks. 'You're unhappy, Sal, I can see that. And I'm not happy either. We're not good together any more, haven't been for a while. You were right all along but I was too pig-headed to admit it. I didn't want things to change – I was scared of them changing – but now I am starting to see that change is a good thing.'

'You mean that you want us to split up?' She couldn't believe it.

'Yes, because that's what's best for both of us. I want us to divorce while we're both still young enough to make new lives for ourselves, and while we can still be friends, can still bear to be in the same room together. You were right, we've just been going through the motions for years, and I don't want us to do that any longer. Life's too precious to waste like that.'

He was saying what she had been trying to tell him when she'd left before Christmas. Did he really mean it or was he telling her what he knew she wanted to hear? 'Are you sure, Ted? What if you have another TIA?'

'Positive. I've been thinking about it ever since I had the TIA. The doctor said there was no lasting damage, and as long as I take care of myself, there's no reason why I should have another one. It's no more risk than you having one,' he pointed out. 'We can't let the thought of one of us being ill bind us together. Accidents and ill health can happen any time. We've got to live our lives while we can.'

He was serious! She felt a huge burden lift from her and wanted to hug him, which seemed terribly inappropriate when he'd just agreed to them splitting up. 'What will you do? And what about the house?'

He rubbed his head. 'I'm not sure yet. We'll sell the house, of course – it's too big for me and, like you, I want a fresh start. I feel like I've been given a second chance at life and I want to make it count. For now, how about you take half from the savings to pay for rent on a place, and for anything else you want to do. We'll sort out all the rest of the stuff later.' He leant forward and placed his hand on hers. 'Be happy, Sally. Go and do all the things you've dreamt of. And thank you for all the years you've given me and for being willing to put your dreams on hold to come back and take care of me.'

'Are you sure, Ted?' she asked, her heart fluttering in her chest, hardly daring that it was going to be set free. 'Are you really sure?'

'I'm positive,' he said and he held out his arms. 'Happy New Year, Sal. Let's start it in a good way. Friends but apart.'

'Oh, Ted!' She flung herself into his arms, sobbing silently, and for the first time for years they really hugged. When she pulled herself away, Sally saw tears in Ted's eyes too.

'Happy New Year to you too. And thank you, Ted,' she whispered, her voice breaking. 'I want you to know that I will always care about you, and I'll always be there if you need me.'

'I know, Sal,' he stammered, taking his hankie out of his pocket and wiping his eyes. 'And me for you.'

Chapter Forty-Five

Meg

'Nanny!'

Meg smiled as Tom raced down the hall towards her mother, his face beaming, his arms outstretched.

'Tom-Tom!' Sally called, using her pet name for little Tom. She bent down and held her arms out, swooping her grandson into a big hug. 'Tom, darling. I've missed you so much!'

'He's missed you too. He was looking for you at Christmas,' Katya told her. 'It's good to see you back, Sally. Happy New Year!'

'It certainly is,' Dan agreed. He and Katya had come in just ahead of Meg and Oliver. They'd all arrived within minutes of each other and had stood outside chatting for a while, with Dan and Katya saying how pleased they were that Meg and Oliver were back together again, and that their parents were too.

'And it's so good to see you all. Happy New Year, everyone!' Sally said with a big smile.

Meg studied her mum's face worriedly for signs of strain. Sally had been so happy down in Cornwall, and while she understood – and was pleased in a way – that her mum had decided to go back to her dad, she was concerned about what effect that would have on her.

She looked tired, Meg thought, and so did Dad, but she was relieved to see that there didn't seem to be any awkwardness between them. On the contrary, Dad was smiling as Mum hugged Tom, asking him what presents he'd had for Christmas and listening attentively as Tom listed them all. It seemed as if her parents had come to some kind of understanding.

Mum put Tom down and turned towards Meg and Oliver, her face breaking into a huge grin as she encircled them in a double hug before releasing them and saying, 'I can't tell you how happy I am that you two have sorted it out. And your move sounds so exciting. Cheshire is a beautiful part of the country. What a wonderful way to start the new year.'

'Oliver's boss has sent us some photos of the manor, and the cottage we'll be living in,' Meg told her. 'It's gorgeous. I can't wait.' She smiled at Oliver. 'We're still going to be running Party MO there and I'll continue with my promo and social media work too, of course.'

'You must all come up and visit when we're settled in,' Oliver said.

'We'd love to.' This was from Ted. 'Now come and sit down, all of you. Your mum's done quite a spread, as usual. The raspberries in the trifle were from my garden last summer,' he added proudly. 'We've got a couple of bags of them in the freezer.'

They all gathered around the table, pulling out chairs, sitting down – Tom in between Sally and Katya because he wanted to chatter to his nanny – grabbing plates, and helping themselves to the food, talking to each other and over one another as they did so. Dan told them all about the patio he was planning on laying in the back garden, then Katya relayed Tom's latest achievements, and then the conversation moved on to Oliver and Meg's new home and how exciting it all was. The conversation flowed, crackers were pulled, cava was poured for those who weren't driving – Dan and Meg – and non-alcoholic beverages for those who were. Then Sally suggested they all open their Christmas gifts, which were still piled under the Christmas tree.

It's strange to all be here like this, as if the Christmas break-ups never happened, Meg thought as she watched everyone open their presents with exclamations of 'oooh, that's lovely!' and 'just what I wanted', and a burst of laughter from Ted when he unwrapped Oliver's jokey present – a mug and coaster with the message 'Gardeners never grow old, they just go to pot' written on it.

It had been a heartbreaking time for her and Oliver but they had come through stronger because of it. They had loved each other enough to work it out. What about Mum and Dad though? Mum had come back because she was worried about Dad and felt guilty, not because she missed him and wanted to be with him. Although they did seem to be getting on, and there wasn't any obvious antagonism between them, so maybe Dad's health scare had made them both realise that they wanted to be together after all.

When the gifts had been unwrapped and everyone had eaten as much as they wanted, Ted stood up, a glass in his hand, and Dan gave a mock-groan. 'Make it a short speech, Dad,' he teased. Everyone laughed – Ted's speeches were notoriously short and to the point.

Ted nodded at him. 'Actually, Dan, I think this will be the longest speech I've ever made.'

More mock-groans.

Ted paused, as if gathering his thoughts. 'First of all, I want to wish you all a very happy New Year!' He held up his glass and they all followed suit, chorusing, 'Happy New Year!'

'Next, I want to propose a toast to Meg and Oliver, to say how pleased I am that you've sorted things out, and to congratulate you on your exciting move.' He turned and raised his glass to Meg and Oliver.

Everyone raised their glasses. 'To Meg and Oliver.'

'And I would like to thank Dan for acting so quickly when I was taken ill. His actions probably saved my life.'

Dan flushed but looked pleased as they all raised their glasses and chorused, 'To Dan.'

Then Ted turned towards Sally. 'Lastly, I would like to thank Sally for rushing back to look after me even though we had split up.' He turned back, his gaze resting on everyone sitting at the table.

Meg whispered to Oliver, 'He looks serious. What's he going to say?'

'The mini-stroke really shook me up, as I'm sure it did all of you. And it made me realise a few things too.' He took a slow sip from his glass as if trying to find the words. 'It made me realise how short life is, and that I don't want to waste any of it. And that Sally was right, we have grown apart and we are holding each other back from living the lives we want to live.' He reached down for Sally's hand. She took it and stood up by him. 'So, I want to tell you all that we've agreed to part – but there is no acrimony between us. We've had many happy years together and will now have many happy years apart.'

'What!' Dan gasped but Katya put her fingers to her lips, warning him to shush.

Meg was astonished too; this was the last thing she had expected. She could see the tears in her dad's eyes, and in her mum's eyes too, and she felt a lump in her throat. This hadn't been an easy decision for him to make but she was pleased he had made it and that her parents were both at peace with the decision and with each other.

It was Sally's turn to speak now. 'We know you might be disappointed by this, but it really is the right decision for us.' She looked around, her gaze resting on Dan, Meg then little Tom. 'And it doesn't stop us being a family. We can still all get together at times like this and will both always be there for you all.'

'And we're both going to have a great life apart,' Ted added. He raised his glass one more time. 'To the future.'

'To the future,' they all chorused.

Chapter Forty-Six

A few weeks later

Meg and Oliver

Meg followed Oliver in the yellow van down the long leafy lane, hoping they didn't have to travel much longer. They'd been on the road for over four hours, although they had taken a couple of coffee breaks. Now they were finally in Little Ofton, the village where Meadow Manor was situated. She was tired but excited to see their new home. She would have preferred them to travel together, so they could chat on the way, but they could fit more of their possessions in the van so it made sense for Oliver to drive that and for Meg to follow in her car, with the rabbits in their carriers on the back seat. They both planned on going back next weekend to get more possessions and pick up Oliver's car. And to make sure Dad was okay now Mum had gone back to Cornwall. For the time being, Meg and Oliver were going to rent out their house and make sure they settled in Cheshire and that Oliver liked his new job before selling it. It made sense not to burn their bridges just yet.

She saw the van lights come on and realised that they were nearing the end of the lane now. In front of them were two imposing iron gates, a pair of majestic white stone lion heads adorning the pillars at each side. Oliver pulled up and got out of the van. *This must be it!* Meg got out of her car and ran over to him. He pointed to the decorated nameplate tile on the left pillar: Meadow Manor. 'We're here.'

Meg peered through the gates. A long path, flanked by conifer trees that lined immaculate lawns and flowerbeds, ran up to a set of steps leading to a courtyard. She could make out a fountain and a couple of large statues. Running across the back of the courtyard was a huge, sprawling house that looked like it had been standing there for hundreds of years. She and Oliver had done a bit of research on it and knew that it had been built in the 1700s and had eight bedrooms and four bathrooms as well as a basement and an attic. The two-bedroom cottage they were going to live in was at the back of the house. Meadow Manor had looked fabulous in the pictures they had seen on the Internet but was even better in real life; there was a kind of majestic splendour about it.

'Hugh told me to phone him and let him know I'm here rather than ring the bell on the gate,' Oliver said, taking his mobile out of his jacket pocket.

A quick call to Hugh and the gates opened, allowing Oliver and Meg to drive in. Hugh had told them to park at the back so they drove around the house to the large paved drive. As they both pulled up, a man dressed in a tweed jacket and dark brown corduroy trousers strode down the steps to greet them.

'Pleased to meet you, Oliver,' he said, shaking Oliver's hand. 'And you must be Meg.' He shook Meg's hand warmly. 'I'm Hugh. Welcome to Meadow Manor.'

He gave them a quick tour of the house and the grounds, then showed them the lovely thatched black-and-white cottage that would be their home. It was picture-postcard perfect. Meg immediately took a photo to send to her mum later, then followed Hugh and Oliver inside. Thankfully the cottage had been modernised, with a gas range and a gas fire, despite the high beams and the historic feel of it.

'We can't change the windows, we're afraid, as the cottage – and the house – are listed buildings, but we've had radiators fitted and it gets very cosy in the winter,' Hugh told them. 'You're welcome to live here, rent-free, as long as you want. It comes with the job.'

Hugh left them to settle in, telling Oliver he would see him Monday morning, the date they had both agreed he would start work.

Hand in hand, Oliver and Meg walked around the cosy cottage then out into the garden. It was twice the size of their previous garden, and a bit wild, but Oliver would soon sort that. Meg was delighted to see a pretty fountain, an apple tree and several rose bushes.

'We can put a pen for Laurel and Hardy over there.' She pointed to a large grassy area at the back of the garden.

'And make a swing to hang from the apple tree,' Oliver added. 'There's plenty of room for a sandpit and a paddling pool too.' He reached out and took Meg in his arms. 'What do you think of our new home?'

Meg snuggled into him. 'It's perfect.'

His lips found hers and they were kissing, caressing, gently at first then more urgently, and Oliver whispered in her ear, 'How about we continue this inside? I think a baby would make our new home complete, don't you?' and Meg thought she would explode with happiness.

Chapter Forty-Seven

March

Sally

'Well, that's all sorted then. We've got the bed and breakfast rooms booked for our route through France. When we've had enough there, we can move on to Spain and then the rest of Europe.' Rose closed the laptop lid. 'I can't believe I'm really doing this. I've been planning it for years but never actually thought the day would come.' She smiled at Sally. 'I'm so pleased that you're coming with me. Good company is always better than travelling alone.'

'I'm delighted that you asked me,' Sally replied. She could hardly believe that she'd only met Rose a few months ago; it was as if she had known her all her life. Sally had returned to Cornwall after leaving Ted and luckily Smuggler's Haunt had been available for another couple of weeks. She had spent a lot of time with Rose and Rory, feeling so comfortable with them both, that when Rose had invited her to travel around Europe with her, and to stay in her spare room until then, pointing out that it was silly to pay holiday rental prices for a couple of months, Sally had gratefully taken up the offer on the condition that she pay Rose rent. They all got on so well, she, Rose and Rory, and the house was big enough for them to not have to live in each other's pockets.

She was so looking forward to travelling around Europe with Rose. They were leaving in a couple of weeks, planning on spending six months touring, and sharing the driving of Rose's trusty hatchback, leaving Sally's car parked in Rose's garage until they returned. Although Sally had never driven on the right-hand side of the road before, she was sure she could manage it.

Things were finally working out. Meg and Oliver were happy together, and Ted was making a life for himself. He had put the house up for sale and was seeing a lot of Paula, but Sally honestly didn't mind. She just wanted him to be happy. Like she was.

'It's freezing out there.' Rory came in, rubbing his hands. He glanced over at the paperwork spread all over the table. 'Have you two finished planning your big trip then?'

'We have. We leave on the fifteenth of March for six months,' Rose told him. She got up and picked up her bag. 'I'm popping out to the corner shop now to grab some milk. I'll leave you to tell him all the details about the trip, Sally.'

Sally knew that Rose was being discreet, giving them both a chance to talk; she'd done this a few times over the weeks. It was probably as obvious to her as it was to Sally and Rory that there was a connection growing between the two of them, a closeness that Sally was trying to fight against. She enjoyed being with Rory – he was funny, kind and caring, and yes, she was going to miss him and the long walks they sometimes went on together – but she didn't want to get attached to him. She didn't want to get attached to anyone. She wanted to be free, to live her life how she chose. She didn't want to be trapped ever again. She had her future planned out and didn't want to have to compromise those plans.

She would really miss Rory though. He had been her rock over the last couple of months, always ready with a silly joke, a kind word, a bit of home-spun advice or an interested ear as she had struggled with the complexities of splitting up with Ted and sorting out her own life.

Rory stood in front of the fire now, warming himself. 'And what are your plans when you return from your big trip?' he asked. 'Are you coming back to Cornwall?'

That's the question she'd been asking herself. She loved this village, and had made friends here, so yes, she would like to come back. She doubted if she would have enough money to buy a house herself, even when the divorce settlement came through, but she could rent one. Much as she loved living with Rose and Rory, she needed her own space, to make a home for herself.

'I'd like to, if I can find somewhere to rent,' she told him.

'I'm pleased to hear it. We'll miss you. Do you want me to look out for you, let you know if something comes up?' he asked. 'Long-term rentals aren't easy to find here so soon get snapped up.'

Pleased to hear it. His words thrilled and scared her. Scared her so much that she wondered if she should come back. She could see something in Rory's eyes, the same feeling she was fighting against. Maybe she should make a clean break and start off fresh somewhere else?

She didn't want to though. Rose was a good friend. And Sally didn't like the thought of never seeing her or – she had to admit – Rory again.

'Please. A little cottage would be ideal, not far from the beach, like Smuggler's Haunt,' she said with a smile. Then she got up. 'I'm making a cup of tea. Do you fancy one? It might warm you up a bit.'

'I'll do it,' Rory told her, stepping forward just as Sally did and almost colliding into her. 'Sorry.' He put out a hand to steady her and she jumped back, her nerves tingling at his touch.

'It's fine.' She quickly pulled herself together, averting her gaze. Damn, now she was acting like a stupid teenager. That's how Rory made her feel, like a teenager falling in love for the first time. She had an idea that he felt the same way too. It was a good job she was leaving soon; she could do with putting a bit of distance between them before things got complicated.

'Sally.'

Her eyes flitted to his face. He looked serious and was standing much too close. She stepped back a little and fixed a smile on her face. 'Yes?'

'I just want to say… Look, I'm not good at this. There hasn't been a woman in my life since Gloria, and I've been happy to keep it that way, but you… you're different. I like you, Sally. A lot. And I think you like me too.'

She stared at him, unable to speak. This was the very conversation she had been trying to avoid. She thought about denying her feelings, but how could she, the way he was looking at her? Besides, she was pretty sure that they were written all over her face. So, she nodded wordlessly and waited for him to continue, wondering if he was going to ask her not to go travelling with Rose. She tried to scramble the words in her mind to let him down gently. Nothing was going to stop her doing that; she had waited too long.

'Don't look so worried,' he said gently. 'That doesn't mean that I want to tie you down or stop you going off for six months. It means that if you feel the same way, I'd like us to keep in touch, and maybe when you come back and have your own place, we can see each other, go out now and again.'

Really? He was happy to wait for her? Relief flooded through her. She smiled. 'I'd like that.'

His face broke into a grin. 'No commitment now. You've got your life and I've got mine. I can see that you need to be free and that's what

I want too.' His eyes, kind and tender, met hers. 'If you meet someone while you're travelling, then that's fine, just let me know.'

'I will,' she whispered, although she doubted if she would meet anyone else like Rory.

'Now enjoy your trip. You deserve it.' He held out his arms. 'How about a hug goodbye?'

She stepped into his embrace, leaning her head against his shoulder, trying to ignore the desire to kiss him that was building in her. She lifted her head and looked up to see him smiling down at her, then his lips found hers and they were kissing and it felt right even though she hadn't kissed anyone like this since Ted – and that had been a long time ago, when their marriage had still been young and fresh.

'At last! I thought you two would never get it together.'

They both turned to see Rose standing in the doorway, a big grin on her face. 'Do you want me to go back out for an hour or so?'

Sally flushed, knowing what Rose was implying. That wasn't a step she was ready to take yet, but maybe soon. 'I'm still going around Europe with you,' she said.

'Of course you are. Rory isn't one to clip anyone's wings. He likes his own freedom too much. Maybe you can fly over to join us for the odd weekend though, Rory?' she suggested.

Rory looked questioningly at Sally. 'Please do. I'd like that,' she told him.

'So would I,' he agreed.

'That's settled then. Now who's for something to eat? I've got a cottage pie in the fridge that needs eating up.' Rose headed off into the kitchen, leaving Sally and Rory to continue their embrace.

Chapter Forty-Eight

June

Meg

It was positive.

Meg stared at the test strip in a mixture of disbelief, elation and anxiety. Positive. She was pregnant. She was having a baby, a little Oliver or Meg. It seemed incredible that a new life was already forming in her tummy. As the months had passed by she'd worried a little, wondering if they had left it too late. Oliver had tried to reassure her, told her that it would happen in time, and although she hadn't asked him, she had wondered if he was glad it hadn't happened yet, if he still had doubts about having a child.

She sat down, still holding the stick, thrilled but nervous. What would Oliver's reaction be when the reality that he was about to be a father hit him? Would he be thrilled too or would the old worries resurface? What if he'd only agreed to have a baby to make her happy and still didn't feel ready for the responsibility?

She bit her lip. When she'd realised her period was late, she had wondered if she was pregnant, hoped desperately that she was, but she hadn't mentioned it to Oliver, thinking it might be a false alarm. But it wasn't, and now she had to tell him.

Clutching the pregnancy test in her hand, she made her way down the stairs and into the garden where Oliver was standing on a stepladder, hammering in the asphalt on the roof of the shed he'd just assembled. It was a perfect June day, sunny and warm. Laurel and Hardy were out in their pen enjoying the fresh air. She imagined their child sitting on a blanket spread out on the grass, playing with their toys. Maybe a little playhouse too.

Oliver half-turned towards her. 'Nearly finished now. What do you think?' Then he frowned. 'What's up?'

This was not a good time to tell him, not when he was standing on a stepladder.

As if sensing her hesitation, Oliver got down from the ladder, wiped his hands on his jeans and walked over to her. He placed his hands around her waist. 'Tell me.'

She met his eyes, searching them for a reaction as she whispered, 'I'm pregnant.'

His eyes lit up as his face broke into a huge grin, and then his arms were around her and he was swinging her up into the air. 'That's fantastic!'

She wanted to cry with relief. 'Really? You really are pleased?'

He set her back down again, tilted her chin gently with his finger and smiled into her eyes. 'Of course I'm pleased. We planned this. It's what we both want.' He kissed her, slowly, deeply, and feeling his lips on hers, his arms around her, her doubts faded away.

He gently released her. 'Well, if we have a baby on the way, I'd better get this garden sorted, hadn't I? We'll be wanting an area for a swing and a slide soon.'

Meg placed her hand over her still-flat tummy. A baby. It still seemed so incredible. When she thought about the new life growing inside her, the responsibility of being a parent, she got the collywobbles herself. Oliver had been right to worry – what if she wasn't a good mother? Why had she never thought of that before?

'Hey.'

Oliver's voice broke through her thoughts. She blinked and raised her eyes to his face, which was covered with a big smile.

'I recognise that worried look. Remember what you told me. We don't have to be perfect parents. We simply have to love our baby and do the best for him or her.'

He was right, she had said that. Who would have thought that when she finally got pregnant, Oliver would take it so calmly and she would be the one to panic?

Meg put her hand over her tummy again, still hardly believing that she was going to be a mother. 'I know it's early days so we don't want to spread the word yet, but do you mind if I tell Mum?'

'Go ahead. She'll be delighted. If anything will make her come back from her travels, it'll be the news that we're having a baby. I guess I'd better start getting the spare room ready as a nursery.'

Meg walked into the lounge and sat down on the sofa, her legs curled up beneath her, to make the call. It had been tough for her mum to leave her dad, but she was now so happy travelling around Europe with Rose, and her dad seemed happy too. He'd spruced himself up a bit and was spending a lot of time with Paula.

Their Christmas in Cornwall together had brought Meg and her mum even closer, and a week didn't go by without them having a long chat, no matter where in the world her mother was. Right now, it was Italy.

'Hello, darling, how lovely to hear from you. How are you? How are you getting on with Party MO? Has Oliver sorted out your garden yet?'

At the sound of her mother's cheery voice, Meg felt herself relax. 'I've got lots of bookings for Party MO, Mum. And Oliver is putting up a shed in the garden as we speak.'

'That's wonderful. I'm so glad everything's coming together.'

'How's Italy?'

'Beautiful. We're in Rome at the moment. We went to the Sistine Chapel yesterday – it was awe-inspiring. I can't tell you how much I'm enjoying this trip, Meg. And Rose is marvellous company – a young lad tried to pick her pocket yesterday and you should have seen how she chased after him; she gave him a whack across the ear too.'

Meg chuckled at the thought of the no-nonsense Rose chasing after the lad and giving him a clip across the ear. It was good to hear her mother so happy. 'I've got some news, Mum…' She paused. 'I'm pregnant!'

'Oh, darling, that's wonderful news. When is the baby due?'

'I've only just found out so I think about March.'

'Maybe on my birthday then. What a marvellous present that would be.'

They chatted some more, with Sally promising that she would come over for a weekend visit soon. 'I can't wait to see you both and your new home.'

Later in the week Meg and Oliver went to visit her father and tell him. She was surprised to see a motorhome parked outside the house, the side door open and Dad and Paula inside, titivating some cushions.

Dad waved when he saw them and popped his head outside the door. 'Do you like it?' he asked proudly. 'Paula and I are going to take off for a few days every now and then, see a bit of the UK.'

'That's great, Dad,' Meg said, pleased to see him looking so cheerful. Mum had been right: she and Dad had both been trapped in a loveless marriage, both holding each other back from what they wanted to do. Look at them both now: even Dad was spreading his wings a bit and looked a lot happier. To be honest, initially she hadn't really liked Paula; she'd felt that she'd been too ready to step into her mum's shoes, almost as if she'd been waiting in the wings for them to split up. But Dad liked her, and Paula seemed to care a lot about him, so Meg felt herself warming towards her.

'I came to tell you that you're going to be a grandfather again,' she announced. She smiled at the incredulous look on her father's face.

'Oh, that's wonderful news, pet, wonderful.' He stepped out and hugged her proudly then patted Oliver on the back.

Paula followed him, a big smile on her face. 'That's marvellous, Meg. Congratulations to you both.'

'Come into the house, both of you. Let me put the kettle on and you can tell me all about it.' Dad shut the door of the motorhome, locked it then set off down the garden path.

The house had a different air about it now, almost as if her mother had never lived there. It had been tidied up for the sale – 'minimalised' as Paula called it. She wondered what Dad would do when it was sold, but as she watched Paula fussing around putting the kettle on, taking a home-made cake out of a tin and slicing it up, she had an idea he wouldn't be moving very far away.

Epilogue

The next summer

'She's beautiful,' Oliver said, gazing down at their four-month-old daughter, Katie, lying in Meg's arms, dressed in the cream lace christening gown that both Dan and Meg had worn, and Sally too, and her mother before her.

Meg watched him gently stroking the baby's cheek with his finger, her heart bursting with love and pride. Oliver doted on Katie, and despite his previous fears, he was a wonderful, hands-on father, always ready to take his turn with the night feeds and nappy changing. She was so glad they had sorted out their differences.

They heard a shout and turned around to see Sally walking towards them, waving cheerily. She looked tanned and happy, her face wreathed in smiles. Beside her, looking remarkably at ease in his smart jacket and trousers, was Rory. Meg blinked. She'd only ever seen Rory in jeans and jumper, and his beard had been trimmed too. She smiled to herself; she guessed this was for her mum's benefit. She waved back and walked over to them, Oliver beside her, his arm around Meg's shoulder, cradling their baby daughter carefully.

'I'm so glad you could make it, Mum,' Meg said as she kissed her mother on the cheek.

'As if I would miss such an important occasion.' Sally's eyes were full of love as she gazed at her little granddaughter. 'She's grown so much the last couple of months.' Sally had driven up from Cornwall for a weekend visit as soon as Katie had been born.

'She looks like you,' Rory said, his gaze going from Katie to Sally.

'I thought that too,' Meg said.

'Well, let's hope she isn't as stubborn as me or you'll have your work cut out!' Sally replied.

Laughing, they all walked down the garden to the rows of chairs Meg and Oliver had laid out around the fountain. They'd only invited immediate family and best friends to Katie's naming ceremony and had decided to have it in their garden because it was more personal. Helen, Miles, Josh, Natasha and Alex were already gathered there, as were her dad, Paula, Dan, Katya and Tom. Oliver's father wasn't there, but his mother, Faye, was, looking radiant with a smartly dressed man by her side. She'd introduced him as Adrian, and Oliver had told Meg in surprise, and delight, that this was the man she'd met in Portugal and they'd been together a few years now.

Alison, the naming celebrant, led the service, welcoming everyone to such a special day, and lighting a candle each side of the fountain. Then Oliver and Meg took it in turns to read out the poems they had chosen, and their pledges to Katie.

Oliver said the words of his pledge first: 'I promise to love and protect you, Katie, to be the best father I can be, and to do everything in my power to provide you with all that you need.'

Meg knew that he meant every word he said. She took her turn too, promising to love and guide Katie, to teach her to be strong and independent.

Everyone clapped. Oliver and Meg sat down and it was their parents' turn to say something Faye stood up and said how proud she was of Oliver and the man he had become, and how pleased she was to have such a lovely granddaughter who she intended to spoil as much as she could.

Sally spoke next, promising to love and cherish Katie, to always be there with a listening ear and a kind word. Then Ted gave a short speech about how delighted he was to have such a gorgeous little granddaughter.

Alison asked Meg to put Katie in her basket on the grass and for everyone to form a circle around it. She joined everyone's hands with a yellow ribbon as they stood around Katie, announcing that she was uniting them all in their vows to love and protect the child. Then she cut the ribbon so that everyone was wearing a ribbon bracelet. Meg fingered her ribbon, thinking that it made a lovely memento of the day. It was a beautiful ceremony.

To Meg's astonishment when the ribbon ceremony was over, Oliver went to the shed and took out his guitar. 'I've kept this a surprise, even from Meg, but I've written a song for Katie, which I want to sing to you all.'

He walked to the front and started strumming the strings of the guitar. Meg held her breath as she cuddled Katie; she remembered this tune. Oliver gazed at Meg and Katie as he started to sing.

> *Love makes you walk over mountains,*
> *Through roaring flames and raging seas.*
> *Love makes you strong enough to fight,*
> *Gives you strength to give and to please.*

Love is why you try to do what's right.
And I promise you, my little Katie,
My love for you will always guide me.

Meg had tears in her eyes as he came to the end, and so did the other guests. Oliver had changed the words of the song he had written just before they'd split up that Christmas, about love not being enough, and had turned it into a testament to the power of love instead.

As Meg looked around at her family – her mum and Rory, her dad and Paula, Dan, Katya and Tom, Faye and Adrian – she knew that even though her family had been fractured, it hadn't been broken. The spirt of love was still there, bringing them all together to celebrate this precious day. And that no matter what happened in the future, she and Oliver had enough love to see them through and do the best for their little girl. Love was definitely enough.

A Letter from Karen

To my lovely readers,

I want to say a huge thank you for reading my book. I really appreciate your support and I hope you enjoyed reading Meg and Sally's story as much as I enjoyed writing it. If you would like to keep up-to-date with all my latest releases, just sign up at the following link. Your email address will never be shared and you can unsubscribe at any time.

www.bookouture.com/karen-king

The seeds of this story were sown when I read an article about the number of older women who felt trapped because they were no longer in love with their husbands, that they were living their lives on autopilot, going through the motions, doing what was expected of them but not what they wanted to do, how they were screaming inside to be free but that they didn't have a good enough reason to leave because their husbands hadn't really done anything wrong. It was this, and the many women's comments supporting and identifying with the piece, that inspired the character of Sally. Meg and Oliver's story was inspired by a piece I read about a man who had never felt loved as a child so was scared to be a father himself, and he had chosen to have a vasectomy to make sure he never had children.

If you've read any of my other books, you will know that Cornwall is one of my favourite places, having lived there for many years myself, so I couldn't resist setting the story down there again. Cornwall is such a beautiful place, whatever the season.

If you did enjoy reading my book, I wonder if you could spare the time to write a review for me. I'd love to hear what you think. It doesn't have to be a long one, and I'd be very grateful as reviews make such a difference helping new readers to discover my books for the first time.

I love hearing from my readers too, so do get in touch on my Facebook page, through Twitter, Goodreads or my website. I always answer every message I receive.

Thank you again for choosing my book to read.

Love,
Karen xx

KarenKingRomanceAuthor

karen_king

www.karenking.net

Acknowledgements

There are several people who have made writing this book possible. First, my husband Dave, who always believes in me even when I don't believe in myself and understands that I completely lose track of time – and everything else – when I'm in my writing world. My four daughters, Julie, Michelle, Lucie and Naomi (who has two house bunnies and patiently answered my many questions about them) for being supportive of my work and providing me with lots of inspiration.

I will be eternally grateful to my fabulous editor Isobel Akenhead, for asking me to join the Bookouture team, for seeing the gems in the rough drafts I send her, and for helping me make my stories shine, to DeAndra Lupu for her excellent copy-editing, and Alexandra Holmes, Becca Allen and all the Bookouture team. Also to the dynamic marketing duo that is Kim Nash and Noelle Holten, for the wonderful support and promotion they do for us authors and for making the Bookouture Author Facebook page such a fun place to hang out.

Thank you to my fantastic Facebook author friends, in particular the members of the Romantic Novelists' Association, for their advice, support, laughs and assurance that I'm no crazier than any other author. And special thanks to Lyn Fegan for giving me advice on naming ceremonies and checking the final scene for me.

A special mention to Helen Bushell who entered a raffle to raise funds for Acorns Children's Hospice, and won the prize for her name to be used as one of the characters in this book. Obviously, this character is completely fictional.

Finally, as always, a massive thank you to my readers for buying my books, taking the time to message me, write reviews and spur me on to write more stories. And to the many reviewers and bloggers who are kind enough to give me space on their blogs, take part in my blog tours and help promote my books. Much love to you all. Xx